"You are a stranger to me," Soren said softly. "One I do not wish to know."

Perhaps she could blame the sword's Call to the power in her blood on her attraction to this man who obviously despised her. Or perhaps not. The years that had passed didn't prevent her from remembering the way she'd felt about him when she was a girl. He'd been boyishly handsome then and princely to her Cinderella.

Now he was hardened and scarred and angry.

And, still, she yearned.

Her eyelids opened. She couldn't hide from this meeting by closing her eyes. His gaze locked on hers and she was caught by the swirl of emotions behind the golden brown.

If there was only anger and distrust left between them, why did she want to touch his frowning face?

Barbara J. Hancock lives in the foothills of the Blue Ridge Mountains, where her daily walk takes her to the edge of the wilderness and back again. When Barbara isn't writing modern gothic romance that embraces the shadows with a unique blend of heat and heart, she can be found wrangling twin boys and spoiling her pets.

Also by Barbara J. Hancock

Harlequin Nocturne

Brimstone Seduction
Brimstone Bride
Brimstone Prince

Legendary Warriors

Legendary Shifter
Legendary Wolf

Harlequin E Shivers

Darkening Around Me
Silent Is the House
The Girl in Blue

LEGENDARY WOLF

———

BARBARA J. HANCOCK

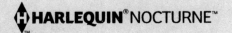

Recycling programs
for this product may
not exist in your area.

ISBN-13: 978-1-335-62963-0

Legendary Wolf

Copyright © 2018 by Barbara J. Hancock

Printed in U.S.A.

Dear Reader,

I've always been fascinated with legendary couples and timeless fairy tales, so it's been a wonderful adventure to bring them together for Harlequin Nocturne. Because the Legendary Warriors series spans centuries, I've been able to explore love, fate and what eternal devotion really means.

What kind of hero would love forever? What kind of heroine would inspire his devotion?

Oh, my, what a big heart Soren Romanov has. It goes along with his big bite. Anna, the Light *Volkhvy* princess, has weathered so many years with her beloved's heart just out of reach. I enjoyed going along for the ride as she determined she was worthy of happily-ever-after, even though her "ever after" took some unexpectedly long detours.

I love writing survivors. Anna and Soren never gave up. Not on life or on each other! They are my legendary lovers. Hang on tight while they come together in a fiery modern-day reunion with a *Little Red Riding Hood* twist.

Sincerely,

Barbara J. Hancock

For the believers. And for those that want to believe.
Hang on—you've got this.

Chapter 1

The thick evergreen wood was nearly impenetrable save for the hollowed-out paths that wound through the snarled low-hanging branches and twisted tree trunks. Wild animals had made the paths—the deer headed for clearings where grass and water could be found, and the predators, who naturally followed in the deer's footsteps, hungry for hot blood.

Anna was neither predator nor prey, although she was on the hunt.

It was dawn and a cool, damp mist rose around her and the gnarled spruce trunks as the sunrise heated the mountain air. The white fog curling down the same pathways she tried to traverse contributed to the forest's shadows. It would disperse eventually. It was autumn and the temperature would rise high enough to dry the air, even in the Carpathian Mountains of Romania, where the chill of winter settled in earlier than elsewhere.

But it wasn't warm yet.

Her breath, quickened by the uncertainty of low visibility, came from her parted lips in visible puffs. The hood of her scarlet cloak protected her hair from the damp, but the cool misty air still managed to brush her face and encroach with fingerlike tendrils on her neck and chest. Her hands were encased in long black leather gloves. They kept her fingers warm…although that was merely a side benefit.

She might be forced to take them off.

She dreaded taking them off here, of all places, but she would if she had to.

There were wolves in these woods. Natural ones that posed a certain amount of danger and the deadly unnatural ones she sought. Those were the ones that made her dread taking off her gloves while possibly making their removal necessary all at the same time.

She clenched her hands into fists at the thought of using her newfound *Volkhvy* abilities at all, but against one legendary wolf in particular.

The forest was silent around her.

No birds called. No breeze stirred the evergreen needles. Only the silent mist swirled and eddied as if it was caught in the maze created by massive trees and winding pathways. Anna felt trapped, too, but it was a familiar feeling. One she was well used to accepting and persisting through. She'd been trapped in a cursed castle for centuries. This ancient wood was nothing in comparison.

Or, at least, it would be nothing in comparison, if she weren't here to find Soren Romanov.

Her connection to the Romanov wolves—and the red Romanov wolf in particular—was a decidedly tortuous entrapment. She'd wanted to avoid Soren for the rest of her life after they'd discovered that her mother was the

Light *Volkhvy* queen, Vasilisa, who had cursed the Romanovs for centuries.

The *Volkhvy* were a race of witches that drew their power from the Ether, an invisible plane that surrounded the earth with energy. But the Ether was like a black hole. Its vacuum expelled energy and, at the same time, it took. Light witches managed this hunger carefully, most of the time. Dark witches…didn't. And sometimes even a Light *Volkhvy* could be consumed by the Ether's Darkness.

Her mother was a powerful witch who had made Dark decisions and her actions had cost Anna and the Romanovs tremendous pain and sacrifice. Elena Pavlova and Ivan Romanov's love had defied the Light *Volkhvy* queen's rage. They had broken Vasilisa's curse six months ago.

But all was not forgiven.

Soren's rejection of Anna following the revelation of her blood when the curse was broken would haunt her forever—and witches, like legendary wolves, lived a very long time.

She had embraced her new name and accepted her position as the Light *Volkhvy* princess because this was her life now. There was no place for her with the Romanovs.

If she could stay far away from the red wolf who had once been her most loyal companion, she might be able to recover. She might be able to come to grips with the power in her blood and maybe even learn to control it. She might forget Soren…eventually.

But the emerald sword had other ideas.

Even now, with her chest rising and falling too quickly in almost-panicked respiration, the sword's Call couldn't be ignored.

Her mother had created the legendary Romanov shifters as champions of the Light *Volkhvy*. With her magic, she had crafted three enchanted swords for the warrior women who would eventually become the enchanted shifters' wives. The sapphire sword had Called Soren's brother's mate from across impossible time and distance to fight by his side. Elena was a human, but she had risked her life to find Bronwal and the legendary black wolf so he could help her defeat an evil witchblood prince who stalked her. She and Ivan had then worked together to break Vasilisa's curse.

It was cruel irony that the red wolf's sword would decide to Call the one woman who would prefer to stay as far away from the Romanovs as possible.

Her.

They had been her friends and companions. The red wolf had helped her survive a curse that had trapped her at Bronwal. The curse had threatened her life and her sanity for hundreds of years. Waiting to see Soren Romanov's human face again had helped her endure.

Only to have him turn away from her in his wolf form and desert her once the curse was broken—because as the curse broke, it was revealed that Vasilisa was her mother.

Anna was a witch.

She'd had to deal with the red wolf's desertion, and at the same time she'd nearly been overcome by the horror of her true parentage. He had run. But, she'd had nowhere to run from the horrible truth and no one to run away with.

Anna had come to a place in the forest where the path widened because it intersected with several other paths. Those trails led off in different directions, then disappeared as if the thick woods they tried to penetrate swallowed them.

She flexed her leather-encased fingers. The gloves on her hands helped to focus and contain the fledgling powers she was only beginning to understand. She hadn't had the luxury of rejecting who and what she truly was.

Her *Volkhvy* heritage was in her blood. Once she knew, it couldn't be ignored.

She'd thought herself an orphan for too long.

Soren's father, Vladimir Romanov, had kidnapped her and kept her as insurance against the queen he planned to overthrow. Anna had grown up alongside his children as a foundling they called "Bell." She'd been ignorant of her witch heritage. When her mother had learned of Vladimir's part in destroying the village where her baby daughter had been hidden from the threat of the Dark *Volkhvy*, she had cursed Bronwal to punish Vladimir for "killing" her daughter. Anna had been caught up in the curse, as well.

The knowledge that she was loved so much that her mother would weave a horrible curse as punishment for her supposed murder was a hot knot in her chest that was composed as much out of relief as it was of guilt.

But she was also filled with fear. She wasn't just any witch; she was the daughter of the most powerful witch in existence. How could she trust herself to use the power her own mother had abused?

She forced the tingling in her fingers to ease off. She willed away the energy she inadvertently tried to channel because of her nerves. Before she'd discovered her identity, her powers had been dormant. Once her mother had begun her training, the power was always there, just beneath the surface of her skin, waiting to be released. It was entirely up to her to keep the energy she could channel in check. As she focused on control, the silence in the forest screamed a warning that roared deep in her ears along with the pounding of her heart.

There were wolves in the quiet wood.

She carefully picked her way down the path, heeding the warning that flared at the edges of her perceptions. She wasn't alone. Ivan was busy at Bronwal. He and his new wife, Elena, were helping all the people who had survived the curse reclaim a modern life. She'd been there first and witnessed the construction, education and modernization that Vasilisa herself was helping to bring about as she tried to make amends.

That left Anna alone in the woods with Ivan's brothers, the red wolf…and the white.

Coming back here was a mistake.

Her pounding heart most dreaded seeing Soren again, but her head knew that Lev—the white wolf—posed the greatest danger. He was feral. Completely out of touch with the man he'd once been. If it wasn't for Soren, she would already have her gloves off and her hands would be free in case the white wolf decided to go from stalking to attack.

She could feel hungry eyes on her back. She'd tried to dismiss the feeling as imagination, but it persisted. Goose-flesh rose on the back of her neck, and it wasn't the damp air that made her shiver. While she hunted for Soren, she was being stalked herself. Something was definitely out there, hiding in the trees and shadows. It might be the white wolf. Watching and waiting for the perfect moment to attack.

At the castle, they had told her that Soren was out looking for Lev. That he spent every waking moment trying to catch his wild twin brother and bring him back home. Coming into the woods after Soren Romanov had felt like a risk she had to take, but now she wasn't so sure.

Suddenly, a long ululating cry broke the silence.

The howl came from far away, rising and falling in a weak, thready tone that she immediately pegged as coming from a natural wolf's throat. She'd heard the Romanov wolves howl. Their shift from human form to wolf could shake the earth. Their vocalizations were much more powerful than this one. The weak howl fell away to nothing, and silence reigned once more.

Mist swirled. Shadows lurked. Her ears strained to pick up the slightest sound.

Every instinct she possessed screamed that she wasn't alone, even as the hush deepened around her.

The sudden howl had caused her to freeze. Adrenaline rushed to her extremities and, in spite of her cloak, she shivered again against its cool, familiar flow beneath her skin. Her fear had helped her survive Bronwal during the curse. Now it caused her to stand motionless for only a moment before she reached to remove a glove. She couldn't afford to be frozen by fear. She had to be fueled by it.

The long shafts of her leather gloves reached almost to her elbows. She pushed the left glove down to her wrist, but then another noise interrupted its removal.

A step sounded behind her.

A twig snapped.

She registered the quality of the sound before she whirled to face her stalker.

The snap had been caused by the tread of a boot, not a paw.

Her fingers fell away from the loosened glove. She hadn't fully removed it. It was abandoned in a bunch around her wrist. She forgot her intention to free her magic as her hands dropped to her sides. They fisted in response to a strange yet hauntingly familiar face as a man materialized from the shadowy path behind her.

She should be glad it wasn't Lev.

She should be relieved she wasn't facing the feral white wolf.

As her chest tightened until she could hardly breathe, it wasn't relief that claimed her. The large man who stepped toward her seemed as feral as the wolf she'd expected, and his altered appearance stabbed through her with a jolt of shocked recognition that pinned her in place.

She'd last seen Soren as her beloved companion, the red wolf. Before that, she remembered him as the handsome teenager who had been her loyal friend. They'd grown up together at Bronwal before the curse fell. She'd been an orphan. He'd been one of the legendary Romanov wolves, practically royal but somehow also *hers*.

The man who stalked her now had a heavy thundercloud brow and a mane of wild red hair around his bearded face. He was well over six feet tall with a muscular build and broad shoulders. He was Soren, but he wasn't *her* Soren. He was changed. She backed up several paces until her spine came up against a tree. Its old, solid trunk wouldn't allow her to retreat any farther.

This man was different, but as he approached she could see the giant wolf she'd known so well in his coloring and his movements. He was large but graceful. He was furious, but his fury was contained. She'd seen the red wolf stand against the Dark *Volkhvy* in just this way hundreds of times before. She had gloried in this moment, again and again. She had seen him confront and drive off countless marauders intent on stealing his brother's enchanted blade.

The difference was that she had been by his side then and not the object of his fury.

"You aren't welcome here, *Volkhvy*. Why have you come back?" Soren asked.

His voice. His human voice. When she'd heard it last, the world had been so much younger. There hadn't been airplanes or automobiles. There hadn't been blue jeans or cell phones. She had believed in loyalty and friendship. They had survived the passage of centuries together until his reaction to the truth had torn them apart. And now he sounded like an angry stranger. His voice was hard and rough. He spoke as if he'd howled alone at the moon far too many times.

"I had to come. There's something you need to know," Anna said. Her voice didn't waver. Her whole body trembled from the shock of seeing him as her adversary, but her voice was as firm as it had to be. So much had changed, and she wasn't sure if she would ever be comfortable with the power in her blood, but she had faced down a curse without cowering. She wouldn't be timid now when she most needed to stand.

"There's nothing you have to say that I need to hear," Soren said. Shock had stabbed her, but it was his sharp words that penetrated the tightness in her chest. With every harsh syllable, he found the tenderness she hid, and the arrows kept coming. Her heart was pierced a thousand times, but she didn't sink to the ground. In fact, she straightened away from the trunk she'd used as support longer than she should have. She stood, straight and tall. He didn't need to see her distress at his transformation. She didn't need to show him her fear or her pain.

Because it was pain that burgeoned outward from her heart like spreading blood from a seeping wound.

His rejection wasn't new, but seeing it up close was almost more than she could bear.

"There's something you have to hear. Whether either of us wants to talk to each other or not," Anna said.

He'd stalked closer and closer to her as she spoke. She refused to step back again. Besides, there was nowhere left to go. She'd left his rejection behind. She'd left to go to her mother's royal seat on an island off the coast of Scotland, but the sword's Call had found her. She wouldn't retreat anymore. There was no point. She couldn't run away from this or him. She had to face it.

Anna forced air in and out of her lungs. She firmed

her resolve and lowered her eyes to her gloves. Carefully, as if she hadn't a care in the world, she straightened the shaft of the one she had begun to pull off. She smoothed the black leather back up her forearm and into place. As she smoothed, she tamped down the power she'd been prepared to summon from the Ether if she'd had to. Her control felt too tenuous. Her fear burgeoned as she wondered if she was already becoming too like her mother. Her hood had fallen back. The rising mist moistened the dark brown curls around her face.

She'd worn Soren's cap once. She'd worn it for a long time. She'd saved it for him, but now his head was bare.

He was a full-grown man who hadn't needed her to save a boy's cap after all.

Soren had stopped several feet away from her. Close enough so that she had to raise her chin when she was finally in control enough to look into his eyes. His face was shadowed in the dark forest and by the unbound waves of his red hair, but she could see the amber of his irises. His gaze narrowed when she boldly met it and searched it for the person she had known.

To no avail.

This Soren Romanov was not her friend or her loyal wolf companion. He was recognizable to her only because she would know him in any form, anywhere. Her soul knew his. Every cell in her body was attuned to every cell in his. The connection that had once saved her was cruel now.

They were enemies.

His pause was more obviously tense than hers. His whole body was stiff and still. He towered over her and held himself in place with an iron will, but he wasn't calm. He seemed seconds away from the howl that roughened his voice.

"I have no time for you or for talking. My brother hasn't come home since the curse was lifted. I was as close as I've come to luring him home when you came into the woods this morning," Soren said. "No one at Bronwal wants to see you. Least of all my brothers or me. Especially Lev. You know he's gone feral. He won't suffer a witch in our midst. He will see you as the enemy."

No other arrows were required; her heart was destroyed. There was nothing of that soft organ left. Only its weak ghost kept her alive with shallow beats, only her hardened core of determination kept her on her feet, as it always had. She was a woman honed by a curse. It didn't matter if he didn't trust her. It didn't matter if she barely trusted herself. She still had her feet planted firmly on the ground.

And she had a job to do.

Soren might be her enemy, but she had other friends and loved ones at Bronwal. People who needed her to do the right thing, even if it hurt, to try to protect them and make up for the mistakes her mother had made.

"If the Dark *Volkhvy* are allowed to keep the emerald sword, peace won't be possible at Bronwal. A Dark witch might manage to tap into the sword's ability to enhance and channel the Ether's energy even more powerfully than a witch can channel the Ether itself. With the sword, a Dark leader might take control of all *Volkhvy*. Hate me if you must, but know there is a much worse threat at your door. At your brothers' doors," Anna said. "Your emerald sword has been taken, and it must be retrieved."

She had some pride and a healthy bit of self-preservation. She didn't tell him that the sword's Call had come for her. She didn't tell him that by rejecting her, he'd rejected his destined mate. Destiny or not, she disagreed with the sword. There was no way a witch could be the mate of a Romanov wolf. Not after all that had happened. And there was no safe way for her to wield a Romanov sword as a witch. She couldn't deny her heritage, but that didn't mean she was going to trust her fledgling power to join with an enchanted object that held that much sway over Soren Romanov's fate.

The truth was her *Volkhvy* blood was too powerful to be trusted with the sword's enchantment. She was already struggling to learn how to control her abilities. Connecting with the sword would only make her more powerful. The possibility that she would become like her mother, leaning toward Dark uses of her powers, was a constant worry. As if the *Volkhvy* part of her blood carried a chill throughout her body with every beat of her heart. She'd spent her entire life fearing witches. Now she lived more closely with that fear than ever before.

She stood, flayed inside, as she offered him her help, not as an old friend, but as a Light *Volkhvy* witch with no choice. She couldn't repair what her mother had done. She could only control her abilities with an iron will and continue to fight against Dark witches who might do worse than her mother had ever imagined if one managed to connect with the enchanted blade.

"Your mother's evil enchantments are no longer my concern. I left the sword hidden in a deep ravine on a battlefield long ago when I abandoned my human form during the curse," Soren said. "But if you haven't noticed, I'm a man, not a wolf now, and your mother is no longer my queen."

His voice was a threatening growl, low and angry. He looked ready to tear the forest apart rather than finish their conversation.

"I see you," Anna said. This time her reply came out as a whisper. She couldn't help it. She'd waited to see his human face for so long. It was torturous to see it now that she knew *Volkhvy* blood coursed through her veins. Soren didn't trust witches. He certainly wouldn't trust the daughter of Vasilisa. How could she blame him when she didn't yet trust herself?

Her eyes tracked hungrily over his features. She couldn't stop the perusal. Yes, she was a witch who, as yet, had no idea what that might mean for her future. Yes, he was angry and wild, a man with an enchanted wolf barely beneath the surface of his skin. But he was also beloved to her memories. She couldn't help the desire to compare and contrast and seek whatever familiarity she could find.

His damp, dark lashes blinked beneath her appraisal as if he was startled by her penetrating stare. His eyes glowed golden as a stray sunbeam managed to find its way through the forest canopy over their heads. In spite of his anger and his bitter words, she wanted to brush his unkempt hair back from his angular face. She wanted to smooth his beard and mustache to reveal the sculpted lips she could barely see.

Her carefully controlled hands didn't betray her desire with any movement whatsoever.

He was Soren, but he wasn't her Soren. The reminder hurt, but not as much as forgetting would hurt. He wouldn't want her touch. He wouldn't lean into her glove-covered fingers. She should be glad of that. How could she trust herself to touch him, knowing the potential for power that pulsed beneath her skin? Because that potential for power also came with the potential for its abuse. She'd seen what her mother had done. She'd barely lived through it.

"You come here dressed like a *Volkhvy* princess. I well remember your mother's preference for red silk before she turned to the mourning color of purple," Soren said.

"Should I keep wearing mismatched rags like I wore before? I am a *Volkhvy* princess. I am a witch. I am Vasilisa's daughter. There's no point in denying the truth. Just as there's no point in refusing my offer to help you retrieve the sword," Anna replied. It hurt to say it out loud. That she was no longer human. That she'd never been human. How long would it take for her to get used to being a witch? His rejection hurt all the more because she couldn't walk away from herself. She was stuck with what she'd become, come what may. Her mother had danced with the Darkness when she'd thought she'd lost her child. Who was to say that Anna would do better if she was ever challenged in the same way?

"The emerald sword was forged by an evil queen for her champions. I'm no longer her champion, therefore, I don't give a damn about the sword," Soren said. "Let them have it."

He edged closer as he spoke, and Anna's pulse sped up, giving lie to the idea that her heart was ruined and unable to pound. Her back came up against the tree trunk again, even though she hadn't meant to move.

She watched his eyes widen slightly. Either he was surprised by her sudden retreat or he was taking in the change of perspective. When he was in his wolf form, he was much larger than a natural wolf. The red wolf had come to her chest in height so she leaned over him to speak and he pointed his nose to the sky in order to meet her eyes.

As a man, he dwarfed her in height and breadth.

The difference was stunning.

He loomed large and intimidating, but also…something more. Her reaction wasn't entirely one of shock. There was a more pleasurable thrill pulsing beneath her skin, as well.

Attraction.

Her retreat had been spurred in part because she wanted to step forward to meet his advance and she knew she shouldn't. He wouldn't welcome her. And she had to maintain control of the powers she didn't trust. The nearer she came to him, the less control she had…in all things.

He was so close now. Only inches away. When she inhaled, a woodsy scent rose from his skin warmed by his body heat into something more human and masculine than spruce, fresh air and autumn leaves. She'd been angry at the red wolf's rejection. In part because she had no way to reject herself. Her reaction to his human form was much more complicated.

She reached to hold the tree at her back, one hand on either side of her hips.

Her mother had begun the process of teaching her how to channel and control the power that *Volkhvy* drew from the atmosphere of the invisible Ether that surrounded them all. She was a novice. Her mother had already been a queen when she'd lost control and fomented a curse that plagued the Romanovs and, inadvertently, her own daughter for centuries.

The tightness in Anna's chest was magnified as Soren paused and his amber gaze tracked over her features. He had tilted his head closely over hers and his hair fell on either side of her face, a russet curtain against the darker surroundings. She held her breath rather than trying to force air into her stubborn lungs.

And, heaven help her, she closed her eyes.

Even curse tempered, her bravery had its limits.

"You are a stranger to me," Soren said softly. "One I do not wish to know."

Perhaps she could blame the sword's Call to the power in her blood for her attraction to this man who obviously despised her. Or perhaps not. The years that had passed didn't prevent her from remembering the way she'd felt about him when she'd been a girl. He'd been boyishly handsome then and princely to her Cinderella.

Now he was hardened and scarred and angry.

And, still, she *yearned*.

Her eyelids opened. She couldn't hide from this meeting by closing her eyes. His gaze locked onto hers and she was caught by the swirl of emotions behind the golden brown.

If there was only anger and distrust left between them, why did she want to touch his frowning face?

"If you care about your family, then you have to care about the sword. The Dark *Volkhvy* will use it against Bronwal if they have it long enough for one of them to discover how to connect with its power. Ivan and Elena and all the Romanov people will be endangered by a Dark witch connected to the emerald sword," Anna said. Her lips moved to persuade him of desperate practicalities, but she held the rest of herself still beneath his harsh stare. It was far worse than she'd expected to stand nearly toe-to-toe with him. He despised *Volkhvy*. She didn't trust her own blood or the connection the sword tried to forge between them. And yet, her desire to reach out to him wasn't quelled.

"Why do you care? About any of us?" Soren asked. "Bell is gone. She died with the breaking of the curse and you've been reborn as someone we hate." The growl was still in his voice, but it was accompanied by a new emotion he'd hidden until now. She recognized grief. He mourned for who she had been as if she'd died. As if Bell and Anna weren't the same person.

The idea that she was dead to him was worse than rejection. She felt more abandoned to her *Volkhvy* blood and adrift in its power than before. For the first time since he'd stepped out of the woods, an ember of anger rekindled beneath her breast.

"My blood doesn't negate who I was before," Anna said. Although she wondered. She'd wondered from the moment her parentage had been revealed. "Of course I care…about Bronwal and all the people in it." Not about him in particular. Not anymore. It wasn't wise and it wasn't safe. It wasn't *controlled*, and she wouldn't allow it.

"Witches only care for themselves. Your mother manipulated our genes with magic before we were born. She made us monsters and then she cursed us when our father proved too monstrous for her to handle. You can't expect me to trust her daughter," Soren said.

He whirled away as if he couldn't stand the sight of her. He paced several steps in the direction from which they'd come, but then he stopped in the middle of the path. His hair fell down his back in tangled waves. It created a halo around his head where the sunbeams fell. His clothes were still the mismatched, poorly mended type of garments that denizens of Bronwal had pieced together during the curse. He wore scuffed leather breeches and a long woolen cloak. His boots had seen better days.

There was something about his manly size and shape paired with the poor quality of his clothing that made her tight chest ache. His castle was on the mend, but he, himself, was still in the midst of the curse. It had been broken. But it didn't matter. Lev was still a feral wolf. She was the daughter of his worst enemy. Soren's nightmare wasn't over.

"You don't have to trust me. I'm not here to gain your trust," Anna said. She couldn't protect her secret and help him at the same time. Self-preservation and pride gave way, because her pain mattered less than keeping the people of Bronwal safe. "I'm here because the emerald sword Calls to me, Soren. Vasilisa sent me to help you find it."

Soren's entire body stiffened. It was as if his spine turned to steel as she watched him harden from his head to his shoes. She waited as he slowly turned back around. It seemed to take an eternity. Her breath caught in her throat as she both dreaded and anticipated seeing his face again.

No. No. No. No. No.

"No," he said. His eyes met hers, and his amber irises no longer needed the sunbeam. They blazed with his emotion alone. "No."

His words still sliced through her, even though they only echoed her own rejection of the sword's Call.

"There's nothing I can do to change it. I tried to ignore its Call. The enchantment is too strong. It can't be ignored. My destiny and yours were forged into its blade and burned into the heart of the emerald in its hilt," Anna said. "The two of us have to work together to prevent the Dark *Volkhvy* from using the emerald sword's power to hurt the people of Bronwal. Only we can stop them. We have to prevent the emergence of a new Dark prince."

"Or princess," Soren added.

Her cheeks were heated. She could feel the flush flaming there against the cool morning mist. She hadn't wanted to tell him, but she saw no other way to convince him that he needed her. He couldn't ignore the enchantment without exposing his family and his people to further harm.

"I won't be manipulated by Vasilisa's enchantments," Soren continued. "Never again. There is no chance I will accept that you are…that Vasilisa's daughter…is destined to be my mate. And there's no way I'll work with you to retrieve the sword."

Anna thought she'd experienced shock before, but she'd been wrong. He would turn his back on his responsibilities in order to turn his back on her. He hated her that much. Soren's face had become pale marble behind his russet beard. His pupils were so large that his eyes looked black. The tightness in her chest suddenly released. She was hollowed out and empty. The hollowness seemed to be reflected in those bottomless pits as they stared at her.

The idea of her as his wife was repugnant to him.

Of course it was.

That should come as no surprise.

But he refused to hear her reasonable arguments because of her blood as well, and his stubborn refusal shocked her to her core.

She couldn't reject her blood. She couldn't reject the mother she'd found after centuries of having none. She might never trust her blood or her mother, but she couldn't change them. She could only endure his opinion of her the same way she'd endured the curse. One foot in front of the other, for years and years and years.

She was a *Volkhvy*.

Soren Romanov despised *Volkhvy*.

And yet, the sword had chosen her, so it was only a Light *Volkhvy* princess who could lead him to the sword.

"I don't want the sword or the connection between us. I only want to stop the Dark *Volkhvy* from using its power to do more harm. I'm not here to claim the sword. Or you," Anna said.

The Call of the emerald sword echoed in the shell of her body as all she'd once felt for Soren Romanov evaporated like mountain mist in the rising sun.

Chapter 2

I'm not here to claim the sword. Or you.

Her words echoed in his ears long after the silence of the forest had descended around their standoff once more. His feet were planted on firm ground. His muscles responded when he tightened his fists. His chest rose and fell. His heart beat. But none of those things negated the feeling that he stood on a jagged, dangerous precipice waiting for the suck of gravity to take him down, down, down to the floor of the canyon somewhere far below.

Bell was gone. But she was also mere feet away from where he stood waiting to fall to his death. The fall never came, of course. That would have been an escape, and there was no escape from this. The feeling of being on the edge of a cliff was only the emptiness her presence caused deep in his gut.

Because she wasn't really here.

This wasn't the girl he'd known. She wasn't even the

woman the girl had become as they'd endured the curse together, side by side. He'd been Bell's protector. Her constant companion for more years than he could count. He'd been in his wolf form, but he remembered every second, every one-sided conversation, every wistful sigh and every battle. Those intimate memories scalded his already raw emotions.

The beautiful witch who faced him with wide green eyes and damp curly hair was a stranger, an enemy who was interfering with the hunt for his brother right when he was as close as he'd ever been to luring Lev home.

Soren had no time for *Anna*. He had to make the distinction between the girl he had known and the witch she had become clear in his heart. He had to save his brother before it was too late. Talk of swords and witches only prolonged the inevitable moment when he would have to see her leave again. Even if she only left once he had driven her away.

The howl that sounded around them was so different from the natural wolf's howl she'd heard before that Anna jumped away from the tree. She'd have time later to mourn what she might have had with Soren Romanov if she'd actually been the foundling he loved.

For now, she swallowed her fear and chose to survive.

She had her left glove off before her feet hit the ground, and as she landed with her boots planted wide apart, the other glove fell beside its partner. Beneath her scarlet cloak—her *princess* garb—she wore deep green insulated leggings and a matching microfiber jacket that would have seemed at home on a cross-country skier's body.

She'd grown used to eclectic dress as the orphaned waif of Bronwal. She saw no reason to change now. She was still Bell, even as she found her way as Anna, whether Soren understood that or not.

The veins in her hands glowed a pale green beneath her porcelain skin in the forest shadows as her cloak fell back from her shoulders to hang in a long flow of scarlet down her back.

"Don't scare him. It's taken me months to get him this close to the castle," Soren ordered gruffly.

"Don't scare *him*? Okay. Right. Makes perfect sense," Anna replied. But the veins in her hands dimmed in response to Soren's concern. She saw herself through his eyes, witchy and strange.

Another ferocious howl followed the first without pause. It was accompanied by a chorus of weaker howls that sounded from all directions around them. They stood in the center of the path. Her leap had instinctively taken her to a defensive position beside Soren. The weaker howls indicated a pack of natural wolves were following the white wolf's lead.

"Scaring them away might be our best chance to survive," Anna warned.

"Not an option," Soren growled. He moved to place his back up against hers as he spoke. His rough voice vibrated against her. She ignored the pleasant thrill the vibration caused deep in her stomach. Her physical reaction to him was a distraction and his sharp words and even sharper rejection of who and what she'd become flustered her in harsher ways. She focused on the approaching howls instead.

The wolves were hunting.

And they wouldn't be hunting one of their own.

They were coming for her, not Soren.

"They'll tear me apart if I don't defend myself," Anna said. "And maybe even if I do."

"That's not going to happen," Soren said.

This time she wasn't able to ignore the thrill in response

to his proclamation. These words were more like the Soren she'd known for so long. He might hate her now. He might want her to go away. But this was Soren Romanov, and he wasn't going to throw her to the wolves—even if one of the wolves was his brother.

"I'll take that as a promise," Anna replied.

They were surrounded by the haze of morning mist that slowly rode the unseen drafts in the air around them. The mist's movement made it nearly impossible to note whether or not the shadows in the undergrowth moved, as well. Anna strained her eyes to try to penetrate the mist and the shadows. A hulking canine shape detached itself from the trunk of a tree only to melt into nothingness again when she thought she'd finally focused on the shape of a wolf. It happened again and again until she finally knew there were dozens of wolves among the trees. They were in constant motion, but none of them stepped forward onto the path.

"Damn it, Lev. You don't belong in the forest. Let this pack go and come home to Bronwal," Soren said.

Even in his human form, Soren's eyes were better than her own. He saw and spoke to his brother before the massive shape of the white wolf materialized out of the mist. Anna couldn't help it—she gasped when Lev came out of the trees. He was as familiar to her as Soren, but he'd always kept his distance. For centuries he'd been a savage but ghostly presence on the periphery of her existence. She'd always known to be leery of him. She'd avoided him just as she'd avoided the other denizens of Bronwal who were Ether addled.

But his appearance now startled her so badly that her hands flared without her giving them permission. *Volkhvy* power was incredibly hard to harness and control. It came from the Ether itself, and many a Dark witch had been consumed while trying to tap into a greater share of the energy than they should. Light *Volkhvy* were careful, thoughtful and almost reverent with their abilities...most of the time.

Anna swallowed against her fear—both of Lev and of herself. She tamped down her desperate desire to bring more energy to life in her hands. She could contain and control. She had to.

"That's new," Soren said.

For a second she thought he was talking about Lev's crazy fur, matted with mud and dried blood, or the ferocious snarl aimed in their direction.

"You're glowing," he continued.

Of course he would be talking about her powers and the obvious flares and flickerings that said she wasn't exactly an expert at harnessing their strength.

"That's what *Volkhvy* do," Anna said. "Especially when we're threatened."

She didn't tell him the emerald sword's Call might be enhancing abilities she hadn't learned to completely control.

The white wolf growled, and the pack of natural wolves he led was emboldened to come forward and ring the two people in the center of the path.

"He won't hurt you," Soren said.

He sounded so certain. Even though they were no longer friends, his confidence in his brother caused her chest to tighten again. Soren wouldn't give up on the white wolf. Ever. He never had in all the years they'd lived with the curse. He'd even followed Lev into wolf form in order to better keep watch over his feral brother. But Soren was wrong. It was obvious that Lev would hurt her. It was obvious from the bloodstains on his muzzle and the dried blood caked in his fur that he'd been in on many kills since he'd run away from the castle. There was no way of knowing how far he'd ranged or if he'd been feeding on man or beast.

"You're wrong. He wants to kill me," Anna said.

This time she didn't dim the power in her hands. She was only beginning to control her abilities and she needed to be careful, but she had no intention of being stupid. Or naive. The anger Soren had toward her was nothing compared to the fury that came off his savage brother. It hit her in waves of heat that weren't soothed by the cool misty air.

"She's going to leave, Lev. I promise. And she won't be coming back," Soren said.

Anna was too busy watching the white wolf approach to feel greater loss at Soren's proclamation. If he wouldn't act to stop the wolves, then she had to defend herself. She held herself back until Lev was only a leap away. She waited as long as she could, but Soren didn't shift. He carried no weapon that she could see. He continued to speak to his brother in calming tones that seemed to have no effect.

When she decided to tap into the Ether to send the natural wolves away in the hope that Lev would be more reachable without them at his back, the air crackled with electricity. The morning mist instantly disappeared as all the moisture droplets suspended in the air were sucked into the nothingness that had swallowed Bronwal and all the people in it on a perpetual cycle during the curse.

Light *Volkhvy* were usually careful and reasonable… until they weren't. Her mother, Vasilisa, had almost gone completely Dark when she thought Vladimir Romanov had murdered her daughter. The curse had been the darkest use of *Volkhvy* magic anyone had seen in an age, and it had been worked by the Light *Volkhvy* queen.

For love and loss.

Vasilisa had mourned for centuries even as she'd perpetuated the curse.

Anna guarded against the hollow ache in her chest and the supreme pain of losing her red wolf when she channeled the power she needed with her hands. The better to keep from unleashing too much, too soon, too harshly. She was learning. The flare she radiated outward toward the pack all around them was too powerful. The impact of green energy when it hit the trees shook the whole dark wood and rebounded back to her hands, sending her to her knees.

Her ears rang with the implosion of power as she desperately sent it back into the Ether.

Chapter 3

When the ringing faded away, she was left in utter silence.

The wolves were gone.

All the wolves were gone.

Anna opened her clenched eyelids. She'd landed hard. The pain had brought tears to her eyes. She blinked the stinging moisture from her lashes as she looked around the empty clearing.

The white wolf was nowhere to be seen.

"What have you done?" Soren asked accusingly. He was still on his feet only because he was incredibly strong. His muscular legs were planted and dug into the packed earth of the pathway where the impact of her energy had sent him backward several feet. "Lev!" he shouted. "Lev!"

There was no reply.

"I didn't mean to send him away, too. I was aiming for the pack," Anna said. She looked around and reached for her gloves. She shakily pulled them onto her hands as she rose to her feet on wobbly knees. "I still have a lot to learn."

"You went with her. You willingly became her pupil. After all she's done," Soren ground out between gritted teeth. "And now you're using the Ether. You're using power you can't control."

Once again, he looked at her as if she was a stranger. His face was tight. His eyes glared. His fists were held at his sides and pressed into his hips as if he needed to contain them.

"I can't change my parentage any more than you can, Soren. She was wrong to curse us. She's sorry." At his harsh bark of laughter, she fisted her hands, too. "I know that's not enough. She can't take it back. What's done is done. But I can't deny my blood just because we're scarred by the memories of what we endured. I always wondered… Who were my parents? Who was *I*?" Anna said. "You can't ask me to turn away from the answer."

"You were Bell. You were our friend," Soren said. "You were my…"

"It was a lie. Your father kidnapped me from the human foster parents my mother had used to hide me. He said I was an orphan. I was your father's captive until he was gone and then I was a wanderer, a survivor. We were never truly friends if you can turn your back on me now," Anna said.

Her chest expanded fully for the first time since Soren had appeared on the path. Hot anger rushed in to fill the hollow of where her heart used to be. It supplanted the sword's Call. She gladly accepted its warmth in place of the feelings she'd had before. Anger had sustained her for weeks on her mother's island, Krajina, after the curse was broken. It was a relief to feel it again.

"I never belonged in Bronwal. Even after I knew its

cavernous rooms and twisted hallways like the back of my hand. It was our jail, but it was never my home," Anna continued. "I'm still trying to find my way back to a place I can call my own. Part of that journey is learning about my *Volkhvy* abilities." She didn't tell him that she had her own doubts. That she was afraid. Once upon a time, the red wolf had been her confidant. That time was past.

And part of her journey would be learning to let her red wolf go. No. Not hers. Never hers. *The* red wolf. She had to let her silly childish dreams concerning Soren Romanov go.

"You scared Lev away right when I'd almost reached him," Soren said.

He was lying to himself. The white wolf had been wilder than the wildest beast. He hadn't been a creature who looked anywhere near ready to be civilized again. But she didn't argue. Soren wouldn't hear reason. Not from her.

Anna straightened her back and firmed her smarting knees. She took another deep breath and faced the man in front of her. She composed her face one taut nerve at a time. She wouldn't apologize for protecting herself, although she hadn't meant to send Lev away. She needed to accept that she was no longer someone that Soren would care for and protect. His priorities had changed. Hers needed to change, too. She would learn to control her powers and she would use her anger to survive her time with Soren Romanov until the sword was found.

Soren blinked in the face of her sudden icy calm. He raised his hands and opened his fists to push his fingers up into his hair. He held the tangled mass back from his face on either side as if to better see the witch she'd become.

Her forced calm was shaken when he seemed to harden again right before her eyes. He lowered his hands. He lifted his chin. Even beneath the beard, she could see the sharp angles of his chiseled face as his jaw tightened. He stepped toward her and she had to brace herself to keep from retreating.

She held her ground until he was only a foot away. Only then did he speak again, and this time his voice was pitched seriously low. For her ears alone. As if he didn't even want the forest to be privy to their complicated relationship.

"You came back because you heard the emerald sword's Call?" he asked.

She inclined her head in response, because her mouth had gone too dry for her to speak. She was braced, but she was also nervous. Her anger threatened to drain away, and in its place was an ache that said her heart was still there and the worst was yet to come.

"Good. You can lead me to where it's being held," Soren said. "*So I can destroy it.* Then you'll be free to go back to your queen and I'll be free to save my brother."

She thought she'd experienced the ultimate rejection, but now she knew better. She hid her emotions. She forced her jaw to relax and her eyes to meet his. His were trained on her face as if he wanted to memorize her reaction. Her skin was cold. Every drop of blood had drained from her cheeks, but she forced herself to lick her stiff lips and speak.

"Anything to silence the Call that won't leave me in peace," she said.

He blinked and looked away, as if her words had shocked him. Only her anger kept her from reaching up to bring his gaze back to hers. He wouldn't want her gloved fingers on his face. He wouldn't want her touch.

It was better this way.

The sooner the sword was destroyed, the sooner she could control her powers and forget the red wolf, who had savaged her without baring a single tooth or claw.

* * *

Lev had disappeared without a trace. It was too much like the old nightmare that had plagued him during the curse. Soren had always materialized to face the fear that he might have lost his brother for good. He'd never known—would this Cycle be his brother's last? Or this one?

Bell had been his constant. His anchor. Even when he'd chosen to retreat into his wolf form to make it more possible to watch over Lev, he'd depended on Bell to always be there—human, rational, determined to survive.

And then he'd lost her.

He'd died a little that day after the curse was broken, but he'd buried himself in his vow to save his brother. He'd pushed himself mercilessly on two wobbly human legs that he had to relearn how to use again, but the push had kept him from mourning for Bell. He'd grown stronger and stronger as he'd lived in the woods tracking the white wolf. He hadn't allowed himself to shift, because it would have been too easy to lose himself and follow his brother into the wilderness, never to return.

He couldn't allow himself that luxury.

Instead, he'd become a wild man, driven by loss and determination, living at the edge of civilization even as he tried to urge his brother back into the fold.

He felt the wild now, closer than it had ever been. It howled in his heart. He kept it at bay the only way he knew how—by subsuming his heart and his desires in his devotion to saving his brother.

He searched the entire forest for Lev before he admitted defeat. The whole wood was devoid of life. With her witchery, Anna had frightened every creature away. Only the leaves stirred in the trees as he passed by.

Anna wasn't Bell. The glowing veins in her hands and

forearms proved it. Her face and form were all too familiar, and his human form reacted to her in startling and unacceptable ways. As a man, he was plagued with a better perspective of her eyes, and from them he thought he saw neither a witch nor the woman he'd known gazing back at him. She looked frightened. He'd seen her scared many times when they'd been trapped in the curse and fighting for their sanity and their lives. This was different. Back then she'd always been bold. She'd always seemed confident that she could handle whatever came around the next bend in the maze of the castle's hallways.

How often had she taken a stand at his side against Ether-addled madmen or intruding *Volkhvy*? So often that he could close his eyes in the shadowy forest and remember her standing as a young girl and again and again on up until she was a young woman still standing, still fighting for him, for survival and for Bronwal.

She didn't look confident anymore.

He opened his eyes beneath the trees, and yet he could see her as she'd been moments before. She looked afraid. Her uncertainty shook him to his core. As the red wolf, he would have leaped up to defend her from whatever threatened. But that was then and this was now. He was no longer her protector. His responsibility was to his beleaguered brother. He couldn't protect Anna anymore. She was lost to the blood in her veins.

She was a witch.

He continued deeper into the woods, and the hunt for Lev helped distance him from Anna until he could trust himself to keep that thought in mind. She had driven his brother away. It had been such a relief to see the white wolf again. To know that he hadn't vanished into the Ether. But his relief had been short-lived. Anna's sudden use of her power had made sure of that. Now Lev was gone again and Soren could only go after him.

He no longer had Bell to protect. What he did have was an obligation to save his brother and a frightened and unpredictable witch claiming the Call of the emerald sword Vasilisa had forged for his mate.

Soren had never been a natural wolf. He'd also never gone feral like Lev. Even in the form of the red Romanov wolf, he'd had a human's understanding. He'd watched over Bell as she grew—older, wiser and stronger. He'd cared for her deeply, as a wolf, but in his current form he was buffeted by sensations and emotions he wasn't prepared to handle.

His body still hummed a secret song from her nearness. His heart still raced and his mouth went dry because his breath came too quickly between lips half-parted to utter words he could never allow himself to say.

He should only feel betrayed. His only concern should be finding his brother and saving him from the wild that Vasilisa had crafted into their hearts with her magical tampering.

But every step that took him farther away from the woman he'd left in the clearing seemed a lie.

How could you mourn someone who had never existed? How could you long to touch a witch you should despise?

She'd frightened Lev away, but when she'd said the emerald sword had Called her, Soren's first feeling had been one of triumph, as if every cell in his body wanted to claim the connection.

No.

Bell was dead to him, and Anna was a dangerous stranger. Her acceptance of her heritage had changed her from friend to foe. The flare from her hands had been brighter than any use of *Volkhvy* magic he'd ever seen.

For all he knew, she might have sent Lev into the Ether. As the daughter of Vasilisa, she couldn't be trusted. She threatened his family. She had proved it by getting in his way as he'd tried to help his brother. He was no longer the Light *Volkhvy* champion, but he'd been standing against evil for too long to stop now. After all he'd endured, how could he see any *Volkhvy* as anything but evil? Even one that he'd once…

He tamped down whatever attraction he had for the green-eyed witch. He hardened his heart and his soul against any of the former softness he'd felt for the woman who must now be his enemy. She'd looked for that softness in his eyes when they'd stood face-to-face. He'd done his best to kill it right in front of her searching gaze.

He would forget the weakness that had threatened to claim him when her eyes had widened and moistened with pain and fear. He would forget the familiar righteous anger that had flamed to life in his chest when she'd been threatened.

The only way he'd survive the loss of Bell would be to send Anna back to her mother as soon as possible. Bell was gone and Anna would soon be out of his life, as well. He wouldn't allow her to accept the sword's Call. There had been a girl the Call had been meant for, but she was gone. He might be a man, but he was also a monster created by a *Volkhvy* queen, and the only woman who had ever made him long to walk on two legs again was gone.

By the time Soren returned to Anna's side, every bit of softness in his heart was gone, as well.

Chapter 4

It was evening before Soren came back to the castle. She'd wondered if he would come back at all. If she'd had the ability to shift into a wolf, she might have chosen that option rather than face him again.

As the daughter of Vasilisa, she had to dress for dinner when she was summoned by the master and mistress of Bronwal. Ivan and Elena were trying to treat her as a guest rather than an enemy. The least she could do was meet their efforts halfway…even if it meant exposing herself to more of Soren's scathing reception.

She'd packed light, but she'd also been conscious of the fact that she would be visiting a castle and its recently reinstated king with his newly wedded queen. Ivan Romanov had been every inch a royal even before the curse had been lifted. He'd ruled Bronwal far longer than his father, continuing as its master after all hope of surviving the curse was lost.

Bell had been one of his subjects.

He'd tried to help her survive, never knowing that she was the daughter of the witch who had cursed them all because of Vladimir Romanov's betrayal.

The least she could do was pull the carefully rolled evening dress from her backpack and shake out its white silken folds. She'd chosen the color carefully as a gesture of truce. She was fairly certain her mother had it put in her closet for a night like tonight. Anna would be Vasilisa's envoy in a place where the Light *Volkhvy* queen herself would probably never be welcome.

No pressure.

The dress slid liquidly over her skin and settled into place as a simple shift, although the shimmer of the exquisite material gave lie to simplicity when she moved to slip on her shoes. The satin slippers would have been ruined in minutes in the old Bronwal, but now the floors were clean and covered in finely woven carpeting.

It was strange to dress in a bedchamber that was clean and modernized in a castle that had been more haunted than functional for centuries. In addition to the cleanliness and the carpeting, running water and sweet-scented toiletries startled her. She felt far removed from the desperate waif she'd been as she tamed and styled her curls on top of her head. Tendrils of gleaming chestnut were the only ornaments around her face.

But she couldn't resist bright ruby lips and lush mascara. To those dashes of color she also added contours of blush on her cheeks. She had been as pale as death since she'd encountered Soren in the woods. The cosmetics might help to disguise her continued reaction to his transformation as well as her own. Her preparations didn't soothe her. She felt alien when a servant she'd never known came to escort her to a sitting room, where her hosts waited.

Elena Romanov wore a stunning dress crafted of pale peach layers in crepe and chiffon. As always, no matter what she wore, she looked as if she might still pirouette rather than step from room to room. Every movement from her smile to the turning of her head was graceful and artistic.

But the former dancer was no delicate swan.

She had been as hard as she had to be to accept the sapphire blade's Call. Tonight, she wore glittering sapphires in her ears and around her neck in honor of the blade she'd left elsewhere. Thankfully, she also wore a genuinely warm smile for Anna. They had become friends before her parentage was revealed, and it seemed that Elena had chosen to continue that friendship.

Of course, she was new to Bronwal. Vasilisa had only been her enemy for a short time, and the curse had actually brought her and Ivan together.

"Soren is back," Elena said. She approached on light steps and Anna allowed her to grasp both of her gloved hands without flinching. It was only dinner. There was no reason to fear that her power might flare. Elena didn't mention her elbow-length gloves, even though they didn't exactly match her evening apparel. She only squeezed her fingers and met her nervous gaze. "He hasn't been back for months. I hoped you might have some positive influence."

"According to Soren, she frightened Lev away. He searched the entire wood and the white wolf was nowhere to be seen," Ivan Romanov interjected as he entered the room.

Anna pulled her hands from Elena's and turned to face the alpha wolf in his human form. Unlike Lev, he had resisted shifting for centuries until the savagery of the black wolf gleamed from his dark eyes and his wild, wavy hair. Although the curse had been broken, he still looked barely civilized. Maybe because he was free to shift at will now with his warrior mate by his side.

He wasn't smiling.

As he approached, his expression was guarded and his brows were heavy. He'd always looked as if the entire weight of Bronwal rested on his broad shoulders. That hadn't altered, unless you could call the addition of more weight and more responsibilities a change. He now had a wife and a rematerialized people to stand for.

Not to mention a former charge turned witch.

"It was an accident. I didn't want to be eaten. Lots of things have changed, but that remains the same," Anna said.

"I understand," Elena said. The feral white wolf had also threatened her when she'd first come to Bronwal. Maybe her understanding would remind Ivan of that fact.

"Soren says they're leaving in the morning," Ivan continued, as if Elena hadn't spoken. But he did pause by her side and place a large hand gently on her petite shoulder. Anna was hypnotized by the giant man's soft touch against his wife's arm. His face was lit by concern for his brothers and a wariness for Vasilisa's daughter, but it was softened by his love for Elena.

Anna suddenly realized that she might not have been welcomed at Bronwal if not for the tiny dancer turned fierce warrior. The sapphire blade was nowhere to be seen, but Elena had its glow in her eyes when she faced her powerful husband. She was his equal as well as his lover. And her friendship with Anna would be respected as much as the king could allow.

No matter his personal trust issues about the waif turned witch in their midst.

He had been the only liege Anna had known for centuries. She hadn't been close to Ivan Romanov. No one had.

He'd been a lone wolf even when he'd chosen to only walk on two legs. But even cursed, he had been the legendary champion of the Light *Volkhvy* and master of Bronwal in all of its dark, labyrinthine glory.

He saw her as the enemy now. That hurt. It also shook how she saw herself.

"He won't give up on Lev, but there's something we have to do," Anna said. She hoped no one, least of all Soren, would mention the emerald blade to Ivan Romanov. His distrust might erupt into fury, and the tingling her hands told her that her reaction, even in self-defense, might be irredeemable.

Ivan was dressed in a black suit that matched his queued hair. His eyes glittered in the soft light of candles. The castle was being modernized, but even with Vasilisa's magical help, updates took time. There were numerous silver candelabra that had been brought in to supply light to Elena's sitting room. The doorway glowed in a soft, wavering spotlight created by fire. In the spotlight, Soren appeared out of the shadowed corridor.

He was not in a suit.

The tangle of his red hair was still in a wild mane around his face and shoulders.

His full russet beard still covered half his angular face. Above it, his amber eyes reflected a thousand flickering flames.

He didn't need a suit to be striking. He was breathtaking in a homespun tunic, open at the neck, and leather leggings. Mainly because the clothing rode his muscular legs, arms and chest without covering up his masculine power.

If you haven't noticed, I'm a man, not a wolf.

A woman would have to be dead not to notice, and Anna's breathless reaction proved that, in spite of everything, she was very much alive.

He stalked into the room, and Elena gasped. Maybe because she still wasn't used to seeing him in his human form. Maybe because he looked as if he should be out hunting for dinner rather than preparing to sit down and eat at a table with them.

Anna glanced at her friend and saw the queen's eyes widen and her cheeks flush. She saw Elena reach for her husband's arm and squeeze as if she was making an unspoken request.

"The witch is our dinner guest, brother," Ivan said. His voice was calm, and Anna's heartbeat sped up because she recognized it as similar to the voice Soren had used to try to reach Lev in the forest. Was Soren so wild that the king felt it his responsibility to soothe him?

The tingling in her fingers increased to an almost-painful gathering of electricity. Her breath caught. Every hair on her body stood to attention. Only Soren noticed. Elena and Ivan were completely focused on him. But he was looking at Anna. He stopped several feet away. His eyes met hers. She felt her eyes widen, and she fisted her hands. His gaze left hers to sweep from her head to her feet and then back again.

He stayed frozen except for the working of his throat as he swallowed.

"Shall we eat?" Elena said into the sudden stillness.

The electricity in Anna's fingers faded as Soren held himself back. She wasn't under attack. He wasn't going to pounce. Not to harm her…or for any other possibility that suggested itself in the echoes of tingles that flowed along her veins for reasons other than magic.

And suddenly, as their gazes met again, his amber to her green, she realized he wasn't going to throw her to the alpha wolf, either. He didn't mention the emerald sword or its Call.

Her secret was safe for now.

* * *

He had charged into Elena's parlor with concern for Lev fueling his every stride. He'd seen no sign of the white wolf, although he'd searched all day. Then he'd come back to Bronwal for the first time in months, only to be confronted by its obvious signs of healing. People *bustled*. People *laughed*. There was hot running water in a dressing room that had been converted to a bath off his bedchamber.

He eschewed it all.

Every guffaw. Every clean, sparkling corner. Every damned piece of perfect clothing tailored with modern cloth.

Lev was lost while Bronwal and everyone in it recovered.

And Bell was lost, as well. Long gone somewhere he could never follow.

Ivan had come to his room while he threw off the torn and soiled rags he'd worn for weeks in the forest. While he'd bathed and changed into his usual homespun shirt and leather pants, he'd told his brother about Anna's use of magic and Lev's disappearance.

He hadn't mentioned the sword.

He hadn't known why until he saw the petite witch standing beside the alpha wolf with panicked eyes and fisted hands.

And then he'd looked at Anna, daughter of Vasilisa, the Light *Volkhvy* queen—really looked from her beautiful chestnut curls to her figure-hugging silk gown—and his ability to reason had flown out the nearest window.

He didn't know why she was frightened.

Maybe anyone in their right mind would fear the alpha wolf, the Romanov king, the once and present champion of the Light *Volkhvy*. Ivan was the largest wolf. The black alpha. The last one left standing on two legs when he and Lev had failed. Did it really matter that Soren's failure had been on purpose to take care of his brother, the white wolf? That by sacrificing his human form, he'd given up the only years of living by Bell's side as a man he might have had?

Ivan Romanov would be even angrier over the emerald sword than he was himself. Ivan's truce with Vasilisa was uneasy at best. Nearly hostile at its worst. He needed her help as Bronwal recovered from the damage she had caused with her curse, but Ivan didn't fully trust the queen. He probably never would.

Or was Anna afraid of the power she might unleash if Ivan Romanov shifted to protect them all from her claim on one of the Romanov blades?

Soren chose not to find out.

He swallowed his wolf. He controlled his concern for Lev. It helped that Anna's appearance left him with barely enough energy to walk into the next room, where a small, intimate dinner had been set up on a long table he could remember as being covered in dust and debris.

It had been washed and sanded and polished. Candles filled the room on every surface. Elena must have commandeered every candelabrum in the castle and some from the towns in the valley below.

"Elena informs me eating at a fine table is like riding a bike. Although, as you know, I've never ridden a bicycle in all my long life," Ivan said. He walked to the head of the table and pulled out the queen's chair as if he hadn't lived as a recluse in a cursed castle for more years than she'd been alive. Elena smiled at him, and Soren forgot how to breathe for long seconds as the love his brother had found punched him in the gut with the knowledge of the love he'd lost.

"Don't worry. This is a family meal. No more. No less. No prying eyes as we learn how to do this again," Ivan continued. He sat in a chair beside his wife at the head of the table. But the two other place settings were beside them in an intimate configuration that would be brutal for him as long as it lasted.

"Soren doesn't consider me family. Not anymore. I'm an unwelcome guest at best. I'll excuse myself. Perhaps I should have asked for some bread and cheese in my room," Anna said. How often had he watched her nibble on a crust of stale bread? How often had he helped her forage for food or whatever else they needed?

Not her.

Bell.

He wouldn't feel sympathetic for a witch who didn't feel welcome.

"Sit. Eat. We are free to enjoy an actual meal at a table and we will enjoy it, by God," Ivan said. But Soren's spine stiffened, because he heard the alpha wolf's command in the order. His brother, the king, wouldn't be denied.

Nor should he.

If Soren's main responsibility was restoring the white wolf to life and limb, Ivan's main responsibility was restoring Bronwal and all the people in it to normalcy, or the closest thing to normalcy that people out of time and no longer cursed could have. He hadn't worn the suit Elena had provided for him. But he would eat with his brother and his wife, even if they insisted that a witch princess sit at the same table, too.

Had she hoped a dress and some lipstick would soothe the savage beast?

Anna was angrier with herself than with the stubborn man who sat across the table from her. He tore into his chicken and potatoes with gusto, and she nearly did the same, pausing only to wash down large mouthfuls with sweet red wine. The sooner they finished, the sooner she could escape back to her room.

If one meal together felt like the end of the world, how would she survive the coming days...and nights...when they would be forced to travel together to retrieve the emerald sword?

Thank goodness for her ability to travel through the Ether.

The sooner they retrieved the sword and destroyed it, the better.

Elena was the only one at the table who picked at her food. She was as slight as a former ballerina would be. Not to mention she'd been sitting at tables to eat her entire life. Anna, like Ivan and Soren, was only now rediscovering what it was like to have an array of delectable food placed in front of her prepared for consumption. It wasn't strange that they should all concentrate on chewing and swallowing, but their lack of pleasure was.

Anna barely tasted the perfectly browned roasted meat or the crusty bread. It all turned to dust in her mouth whenever Ivan looked up from his plate. The sword's Call sounded deep within her hollowed chest. It pulsed with her heartbeat. It inhaled and exhaled on her every breath. As the alpha, how could Ivan not hear it, too? Her mother had known. She'd seen the echo of it in her daughter's eyes.

The thread of enchantment between her and Soren seemed to sing. He sat right across from her, ignoring it. If either of them gave it permission, the connection between them would click into place and become complete.

Instead, they chewed and swallowed and did their best to ignore the powerful magic that was as uninvited in the room as she was.

"Patrice has done wonders with the team of cooks I've hired for the kitchen. We suggested she might want to retire, but she's been baking almost nonstop with the new appliances," Elena said. When no one responded, she continued calmly, as if she was used to talking to herself. "We're doing all we can to help everyone with the transition to modern life. It's challenging but not impossible." She looked pointedly at Soren's tunic, but he kept eating as if he didn't notice.

Anna wanted to tell her that it was more complicated than clothes or table manners. It wasn't just habit they were trying to overcome. It was post-traumatic stress. It was heartache. It was severed companionship that could never be mended.

Before she realized what was happening, Anna's hands began to tingle in response to her stress. If her gloves had been off, the glowing veins would have given her away. As it was, only Soren noticed her sudden stiffening and panicked tension as she tamped back down the inadvertently summoned power from the Ether.

"Thank you for dinner, Elena. Everything was delicious. But I've traveled a long way and I'm exhausted," Anna said. She dropped her utensils and stood abruptly. Her chair was knocked backward, but she let it lie where it had fallen. She held her hands in front of her, clasped with threaded fingers, and backed toward the door.

Ivan stood.

It was the polite thing to do. It was also dangerous. Because Anna's power responded as if to a threat. Beneath her gloves, the power threatened to burn to the surface of the hands that sought to contain it. She'd tamped it down. It didn't matter. She'd yet to master complete control of her abilities and Ivan was the greatest potential threat she'd faced. Even greater than the feral white wolf.

Whether she saw Anna's fear or whether she felt Ivan's tension, Elena reached to place her hand on the alpha's arm.

He looked from Anna to his wife, and his tension melted. He smiled and the wolf in his eyes receded.

Soren slowly rose to his feet as if he knew a sudden move would be dangerous. His eyes locked onto hers.

"I'll escort *Anna* to her room," he said. He spoke her true name as if it was difficult, as if every time he referred to her as "Anna" he also reminded himself to guard against her.

"Just like old times," Anna managed tersely.

No one laughed. It was a poignant joke. One that hurt more than it helped. She'd had less trouble controlling her *Volkhvy* abilities on her mother's island. Probably because no one there saw her as the enemy. And because she'd been far away from Soren. His nearness magnified the Call of the emerald sword.

"Come back to us, brother," Ivan said, as if he knew they planned a dangerous mission.

"Always," Soren promised. He circled around the table without taking his intent gaze off Anna. She stood, trembling with the effort of resisting the sword's Call and the Ether's energy. No one asked her to return. Not even Elena.

Chapter 5

Soren came to her side, but he made no move to reach for her arm or to extend his. He waited, watchful and still, until she stiffly thanked Ivan and Elena for the meal and turned for the door. If he had touched her, gloves or not, she might have glowed brighter than the candlelight that illuminated the room. As it was, she was able to force the power to recede as they stepped into the cool dark corridor to head for the spiral staircase that led to her bedchamber.

They had placed her in the tower room. Either for her own protection or for theirs. She wondered if the aviary on the roof had been modernized as well, but she wasn't comfortable enough to ask to see it or to go exploring. The roof had been Bell's sanctuary. They all seemed to think Bell was lost. Ivan and Soren treated her as an entirely new threat. The difference in perception stung because it echoed the doubts she had in herself.

So she stepped lightly up the winding stone stairway

with Soren by her side. She was glad she wouldn't have to see him in the place they had been closest. He had kept watch on the floor at the foot of her bed in the aviary for too many years to count. He'd been privy to her dreams and nightmares and all her quiet confidences in the dark when no one else was around.

The tower was a less personal space.

They climbed silently until they reached the upper room. There, the heavy old artisan-crafted door had been repaired and replaced on sturdy hinges after Ivan had crashed through it to save Elena from the witchblood prince Grigori. Its bottom half was polished oak. Its top half was scrolling iron bars in the shape of thorny vines and roses.

The thorns and roses were Vasilisa's motif. She had built the castle for her champion wolf shifters after all.

Soren stopped. Anna paused for only a second, expecting him to speak. When he didn't, she continued on. She opened the door, paused again and then closed it as he continued to wait in silence. Perhaps he wanted to be certain she was locked away for the night where she could do no harm.

Soft electric lamps lit the dark curves of the round room, and they reflected off the gem tones of the stained glass windows that had been retrofitted into the tall narrow openings of the windows that ringed the room.

The heavy door had clanged as it shut. There was an antique key in its lock. She waited for Soren to reach and twist it. But she waited in vain. Her relief was palpable. If he'd reached for the key, she might have had to stop him. He barely moved, only blinking and breathing as they stood face-to-face with the bars between them.

"There are people in this castle who haven't forgiven your mother for what she did to us. It's a mistake to consider Bronwal free from the curse. It's no safer for you to go wandering at night than it was before. Perhaps less so. Do you understand?" Soren said quietly.

Anna's heartbeat was loud in her ears. This wasn't concern for her well-being. It couldn't be. He must seek to hurt her with the knowledge that he wasn't the only one who didn't welcome her here. The curse was broken, but its effects lingered on. As Bell, she'd had the run of the place with her loyal red wolf by her side. They'd slipped throughout the massive structure, gleaning and foraging and exploring whenever they materialized. It had been a hard-knock subsistence full of deprivation and dust.

But, hard or not, it had been hers and his, together.

Standing there, looking at Soren's face through the bars of what would be her prison this night, with a full stomach and fine clothes and all the power of the Ether a finger flick away, Anna wanted to weep. Or to rail at the fate that had separated them forever.

"I'm tired. My only plan is to sleep before our journey tomorrow," Anna said.

He stepped closer to the bars, and she didn't back away. Her feet seemed to have rooted to the ground right when she needed them to be nimble and quick. He was only a foot away, and the barrier of the iron vines seemed like no barrier at all. His amber eyes were dark in the shadows. So dark they were almost black. They stood out against his russet hair and beard. She couldn't help it. Her gaze dropped to find his lips where they peeked from the red waves of his beard. It didn't matter that the direction of her gaze was barely telegraphed by the flicker of her lashes. Or that she disciplined herself immediately and brought her attention back to his dark eyes.

He had seen the look.

He had seen whatever desires the flicker of her lashes revealed.

Her cheeks heated. The rise in color would be starkly revealed against her pale skin. But she was no coward. She didn't lower her chin or look away. She faced him, and she watched as her interest in his lips and her blush caused his brow to furrow and his face to tense.

"It isn't your plans that concern me. It's your presence. Vasilisa is an ongoing threat to our safety even as she currently helps us to recover. We've experienced the volatility of her favor. How quickly it can change from love to hate. Your very existence as her daughter threatens us all," Soren said. "The curse was for you. Her power is in you. How far will you go for love? How quickly will your love turn to hate?"

She didn't need him to say it. She felt it in her tingling fingers. She'd seen it in her mother's actions. She'd endured their effects as much as Soren and all the other denizens of Bronwal.

"I won't apologize for surviving," Anna said. "Not even for surviving the revelation of my *Volkhvy* parentage." Her gut was cold and hollow, but there was a tiny flame in her chest where her heart used to be. Its stalwart flickering kept her going. She was afraid of her blood, but fear wouldn't stop her. It never had.

Losing Soren was bad.

But losing her courage would be worse.

"Who survived? What survived? You pulse with the energy of the Ether that ate us every Cycle. It was relentless. Unstoppable. It sucked the life out of us all, year by year, coming and going until so many were lost. I might never see my brother's face again. *All because of the Ether.* The power you channel is evil. There is no light. It all comes from Darkness. The Ether is a relentless vacuum we barely escaped, only to find its energy walks and talks beside us in you," Soren said.

"The Ether is no different than the sun or the tides. It is energy. How we choose to use it determines whether it is Dark or Light. Whether you accept that fact or not is no concern of mine," Anna said. Her words were true. Dark or Light—it was a choice, not an inevitability. She had to believe it. That was the only way she could go on.

"What will you choose one day, *Volkhvy* princess? When your back is up against a wall? With unlimited Ether at your fingertips, how will you restrain yourself when your own mother—a much more experienced witch—failed?" Soren asked. He suddenly reached for the bars and his grip was white-knuckle and fierce. The rattle of iron rang out and echoed down the winding stairs. Anna jumped in response, but she didn't retreat.

She searched his eyes for the faith in her she'd once thought unshakable. The red wolf had never doubted her, not once in centuries. Until her parentage was revealed. And then he had turned away. He hadn't looked back until now. Her presence forced him to see what she'd become. She could read nothing in Soren's gaze. She could only sense his heightened emotion through the tension in his grip.

"We shall see," she said. She could make no promises. That was what hurt the most. His doubts were echoed in her own thoughts. There was no way of knowing how she would handle the abilities her *Volkhvy* blood gave her. So far she had chosen careful control. Even with the Call of the emerald sword increasing the energy that pulsed in her. But the use of power was a slippery slope. She had her mother's example as an ever-present warning.

She jumped again when Soren released the bars as

quickly as he had grabbed them. He pushed back from them and dropped his hands to his sides.

"We leave at dawn. On horseback until we reach Cyrna. I won't step willingly into the Ether for you. No enchantments. No tricks. You might recall my survival instinct is as healthy as your own," Soren said.

The tingling in her hands turned to ice as he walked away. If they traveled without using the Ether, the trip would last for weeks rather than days. She was a survivor, but she wasn't sure she could survive being close to Soren for that long. The Call tormented her. But his nearness both tormented and enticed.

The magnetism between them was a cruel jest in a world determined to keep them apart.

Elena dressed for bed in one of her black wolf's favorite nightgowns. It was a diaphanous silk spun through with glittering silver threads that reminded Ivan of the lair where they'd first made love. They still escaped to his former retreat sometimes when the demands of bringing Bronwal back from the brink became too stressful.

The gown settled against her skin softly. Its thin white material wasn't much protection against the chill of their bedchamber's stone walls, but Ivan's big warm body would soon rectify that.

Bumps rose along her skin and her nipples peaked obviously under her gown, but it wasn't the cold. She was only anticipating her husband's touch.

Ivan Romanov was a powerful, considerate lover who made up for his years of forced celibacy by devoting himself to her pleasure whenever they could escape into each other's arms. She hadn't told him yet that their frequent lovemaking had resulted in a quickening deep inside her.

Elena gently ran both hands down to her stomach and

pressed her palms against the life that she and the alpha wolf had created together. Ferocious joy claimed her as well as a poignant need to protect her unborn child from the effects of the curse that still haunted his or her future home. Ivan would be a wonderful father—if he could temper his protective instincts, which would be even fiercer than hers.

She heard his step outside the door and she lowered her hands lest her instinctive maternal position gave her secret away too soon. She needed to tell him, but she was worried about her friend. At one time Anna had been Ivan's charge, but Elena knew her husband no longer saw the other woman as family.

Ivan was a good man, but he was also the alpha wolf, one of the legendary Romanovs, and he was sure to be proactive in protecting the heir to his throne. Elena had to break the news of his pending fatherhood to him, but she was concerned about Anna and Soren.

One dinner with them had shown her that the red wolf and his former companion had much to settle between them. She hated to compound their difficulties with an alpha wolf on the protective prowl.

Ivan came into the room with a furrowed brow and a distracted frown on his scarred but handsome face. In spite of her secret and her plan to improve his mood before she revealed it, Elena's heart leaped in her chest. The sight of her husband had always caused her breath to catch and her heartbeat to quicken. Even before she'd realized she was being Called to be his mate by the enchanted sapphire sword, she'd been drawn to him because of his heroic presence.

Walking, talking, making love or simply brooding as he was tonight, he was legendary. His shifting abilities had been written into his genes by Vasilisa's enchantment before he was born. He had been raised as one of her

champions, and he had lived up to that charge every day
and night since, even during all the centuries he'd been
trapped in the curse because of his father's betrayal. He
still believed in standing against the Dark *Volkhvy*. He just
wasn't as trusting of the Light *Volkhvy* as he'd once been.

Still, he'd never once given up. He'd never faltered. He'd
stood for decades, alone, after his brothers had given in to
their shift to escape the endless torture. Bronwal had been
trapped in a cycle that sucked them into the nothingness
of the Ether again and again with only a month of relief
every ten years.

Until she and Ivan had come together to face Vasilisa
and defeat Grigori, the witchblood prince. They'd broken
the curse. They'd fallen in love. The legends she'd loved
as a child, the sapphire sword and their stubborn determination, had triumphed.

But there was still much to be done to claim the happily-
ever-after they'd earned.

"You look as if you're a few seconds away from running into the night to howl at the moon," Elena said. She
walked slowly toward Ivan as she said it, giving him time
to notice the gown and the graceful movement of her naked
body beneath it. She'd been a ballet dancer before she became a warrior and a black wolf's wife. She knew how to
place each foot for maximum effect.

Her performance was rewarded by the sudden, intense
focus of her husband's gaze. His brow smoothed. His frown
eased into a smile. His hard lips softened and curved into
that special smile he reserved for her when they were alone.
She smiled in return as she came up against the wall of
his brawny physique. He was well over six feet and muscular as only a legendary warrior born in the Dark Ages
could be. Yet his massive arms wrapped around her delicate dancer's body with loving care.

He knew how to be passionate and gentle. Powerful and considerate. But even when he got carried away, she didn't complain. Russian ballet had been much harder on her than Ivan Romanov had ever been, even when he'd been an adversary training her out of necessity and resisting the magnetism between them.

Her body was petite, but it was powerful in its own right. She'd wielded the sapphire blade with muscles honed by years of precision and sacrifice. And she'd made love to her big savage warrior with every ounce of her skill and power. She always had, even when she'd thought each time they came together would be their last.

He'd avoided close relationships for years before she came to his castle, but with all his stoicism and control, he hadn't been able to resist her kiss and her touch.

Tonight, he didn't try to resist. He sank into her kiss as if she saved him by merely offering him her eager lips and tongue. It was a long while before they spoke again, but finally he must have sensed that she had things to say. He lifted his head and she allowed her hands to fall away from the long hair she'd loosened from the queue he often wore down his back.

His hair was as black as his wolf. The freed waves gleamed as they slipped through her fingers.

She almost pulled him back down to her mouth, because his lips were swollen from her hunger and his eyes sparkled, free of concern. But she needed to make sure he understood that his brother was in trouble.

"Soren doesn't know there are Light *Volkhvy* besides Anna in the castle," Elena said.

Ivan's brow furrowed again, but only slightly. His hands roamed up and down the curve of her back as if her waist and the slight roundness of her bottom below it soothed him. She understood. Her hands had fallen down to the swell of his forearms. They were strong and warm beneath her fingers. He was no longer a figure in a storybook of legends. He was solid. He was real. And he would be a father by the spring of next year.

"I warned them all to avoid him. They're necessary to Bronwal's recovery. It would take decades to modernize without them. You and I agreed allowing Vasilisa to help us recover is a necessary risk," Ivan said.

Suddenly, he scooped her up and carried her toward the bed in the center of the room. Would she ever grow accustomed to his grace? He was muscular but not musclebound. Whether it was the wolf in his veins or simply the sheer physicality of his long life, he was almost as agile as a dancer.

Elena wrapped her legs around his waist. The airy folds of her dress parted and fell away to allow her the pleasure of pressing her hot core against him. His large hands cupped her bottom. She held his shoulders, and his freed hair tickled her nearly bare breasts.

"But that was before we knew how Soren would feel toward all *Volkhvy*...even the Light. He's terrified for Lev. And devastated by what's become of Bell... I mean, Anna," Elena said. She tried to focus on what had to be said even as her husband lowered his face to her chest to nuzzle her nipples through her gown. His hot tongue flicked out to tease her, and the gauzy material was no barrier at all. She gasped. She arched against him and then moaned as she felt the heat of his lean stomach between her legs.

"Bell was our sister. His feelings are understandable. It's hard to see her as Vasilisa's daughter now," Ivan said. His breath was hot against the wet silk and her pink skin that shone through it.

Elena reached for his face. She cupped his stubbled jaw and lifted his chin so she could meet his eyes. They glittered in the soft light of the new electric lamps. She saw so much there. Desire. Love. Worry for his people. Concern for his family.

"Anna was a sister to *you*," Elena said. "But I don't think she was ever that to Soren." She watched Ivan as her meaning became clear. "He thinks he's lost her, even though she's right beside him to this day. I'm only surprised she was able to stay away as long as she did. She has more willpower than I ever had."

"But he hates *Volkhvy*," Ivan said.

"If he doesn't come to grips with his feelings for witches, he'll never accept his feelings for Anna," Elena said.

"He's devoted to Lev. He won't let anything or anyone come between him and saving our brother," Ivan said. "And I can't blame him. We might be allowing the Light *Volkhvy* to help us restore the castle and help our people, but we don't fully trust them. How can we? Vasilisa gave in to the Darkness when she cursed us."

"She thought your father had killed her little girl," Elena reminded him. His hold had eased so she could slide down his body to sit on the edge of the bed. She reached for the hem of his loosened shirt and lifted it inch by inch. He sucked in a great gasp of air when she leaned forward to kiss his stomach. As always, she found his scars and flicked them with her tongue. She saw his erection grow beneath his trousers. They would make love and it would be as much of a wish for happiness for others as it was for their own pleasure and relief.

"Seeing the potential for Darkness in a Light *Volkhvy* queen causes me to distrust Anna, too. She's Vasilisa's daughter, and she left with her mother without protest. She chose her path. We didn't send her away. She gave me no chance to invite her to stay. She made no effort to maintain her loyalty to us and to Bronwal. She turned her back. She walked away. I don't blame Soren for doubting her. I doubt her myself," Ivan said.

"You are a king who feels abandoned by one of his people. But, Ivan, she is here now because of her love and loyalty to us. As for Soren, he was Anna's closest friend and companion. At some point he'll have to trust her or lose her," Elena said. It was a terrifying thought, because she'd come so close to losing Ivan. Hearing him express his doubts over Anna also confirmed her earlier fears. He might overreact to the perceived threat when he found out about the baby.

He heard the fear in her voice. His strong hands came to cup the sides of her face. She tilted her chin to look up at him. It was a long, long way up. His hair shadowed his face as he looked down at her, but she was no longer fooled by the darkness. His scars, his stoic perseverance, his powerful body had all hidden a hurt man within the legendary monster. She had found him. She had saved him as he'd saved her. She had to trust him now. His honor. His integrity. Yes, he was a wolf shifter. The alpha wolf shifter in a triumvirate of three Romanov shifters created by Vasilisa. But he was also her heart's mate.

She could only hope Soren and Anna could stand against even worse odds than she and Ivan had faced. And she could only pray that once Ivan learned about the baby, his protective instincts wouldn't cause even greater complications for his younger brother.

It was a mistake to go to the roof. He went anyway. Taking a route he'd traveled on four legs more often than two. It was both strange and painfully familiar when he came around the corner of an eastern turret to face the aviary Bell had called her home. She'd chosen the inaccessible, easily fortified stone building with shuttered window openings as the safest place in a castle that had few safe places. It had been smart. It had also been telling. She'd been on top of the world here, but she'd also been separate from Bronwal itself, as if she never felt like she belonged.

No one had questioned her proclivity for retreat even before the curse came down on them all. She'd claimed the aviary as a child's playhouse long before she'd claimed it as a bedchamber. Looking back, he was sorry that someone hadn't questioned her need for a hideaway back then. It hadn't occurred to him. Not when he'd been a young teen. Not later when he was in the form of the red wolf. He'd joined her in the aviary as her nighttime protector during the curse without thought to what it meant for her to have always felt safer apart.

Had she instinctively known his father was lying about rescuing her during a Dark *Volkhvy* attack when, in fact, it had been his father who had destroyed the village and the human foster parents Vasilisa had asked to shelter her daughter?

It pained him to think that he hadn't done half as good a job protecting his companion as he'd thought.

Now she was back.

And she wasn't.

She would never truly be back again.

What they had had was even more lost to them, because it had never actually been.

She hadn't been an orphan given a sheltering home and a family to care for her. She'd been stolen, kidnapped and treated as a foundling when she was actually a princess.

The early-autumn night was cold in the mountains. His

breath came from his lips as a vapor that floated away in clouds around his head. But he didn't go inside the aviary. He couldn't stand the air of neglect and abandonment he might find. Instead, he pressed his back against the chilled stone of the turret's wall and allowed his body to sink to a sitting position. He wrapped his arms around his knees.

Cold was good. Alone was good. The star-filled sky above his head brought clarity. He tried to focus on those diamond studs of light and forget the witch's big green eyes. She looked at him as if she was hungry to memorize his features. Never mind that his overgrown hair obscured them. If the color that rose on her cheeks was any indication, she'd found what she was looking for.

She'd looked from his eyes to his lips and back again.

Just a look. Nothing more. And he'd been hard-pressed to stand his ground without pulling her into his arms or backing away. He'd felt her hand on his head a million times before. She'd given him the comfort of her touch and the companionship he'd so desperately needed when Lev had abandoned him. It was beyond cruel that he would want her touch now that he was a man, even though she was no longer the woman she'd been before.

Her touch would be no comfort.

He shuddered from a yearning that refused to be banished by the cold or by his best intentions.

Soren missed Bell, but there was no denying he desired the witch she'd become.

His desire was a foolish physical reaction he would fight until he destroyed the sword. Surely the enchantment of the emerald in the sword's hilt was the reason he was drawn to Anna, the Light *Volkhvy* princess. He wasn't a young pup to be drawn to a woman based on her beauty or the feminine curves of her body. He was wiser than that. His reaction to her was manipulated by magic, and he didn't need any more evidence not to trust it than the loss of his brother right when he'd been so close to bringing him home.

He should have prevented Anna from frightening Lev away. He'd been thrown by her sudden appearance after so many months. Soren fisted his hands and leaned his forehead on his knees to block out the infinite stars. He should have been completely immune to any old feelings he'd had as the red wolf. He should have driven her away before she could do any harm. Instead, he'd been shocked by his body's yearning to touch her, to confirm the pull he felt was mutual. His reaction to her as a woman had distracted him from the *Volkhvy* power she could channel.

He'd been completely unprepared to face who and what she'd become.

His shock had allowed what had happened. It was his fault Lev had disappeared again. It would be on him if his brother never returned.

Beneath the crystalline sky, by the harsh light of a thousand stars, Soren vowed he would not be caught unprepared again.

Anna changed out of the white dress that hadn't served her well. It did no good to wave the flag of truce with an enemy who didn't believe in parley. Soren was blinded by his distrust of witches and his distaste of the Ether. As long as she channeled its power, he would see her as tainted. Yet how could he expect her to be anything other than her mother's daughter—even if her mother was the Light *Volkhvy* queen?

She prepared for bed in new ways that weren't at all automatic for her. Hot running water and soft new sleeping garments might be a delight to her for the rest of her life. She appreciated the luxury and comfort, even as she braced herself against the discomfort of other sensations.

There was a filament of enchantment stretched between her and Soren Romanov. It pulled painfully from deep within her chest to wherever he had gone to pass the night. Like a string stretched taut almost to the point of breaking, the filament threatened to release if she moved too suddenly or breathed too deeply.

She was caught and held by someone who didn't want to hold her at all.

It was the sword that created the tenuous but inexorable bond in spite of her best intentions to let the red wolf go. She pressed both hands against her chest to try to ease the pain. For sleep, she'd allowed herself to remove the protective gloves. The tingle was slight now that she was alone. There were distant threats, but she was tired and her power ebbed low. As she pressed her palms against the pain, the natural body heat in her hands soothed her.

It would be a relief to sever the thread that bound her and Soren together. For a while, as the late-night world grew silent and the doubts in her head grew loud, Anna thought about her aviary. She'd retreated to the roof of the castle so many times. Did her aviary wait there for her still, even though nothing and no one else had waited for her?

The idea of running quickly through the sleeping castle on one of the routes she would know even in the pitch darkness was seductive. But this was no longer her home. She had been reduced to a guest. An unwelcome guest. Her aviary wasn't hers anymore.

Besides, the red wolf wouldn't be there.

It would be cold and empty, filled only with the echoes of a life that was no longer hers. Her pain increased with that vision of her new reality.

Would the sword's destruction really end her torment?
She feared the enchanted filament that bound her to
Soren Romanov wasn't entirely dependent on the emerald sword.

Chapter 6

His sleep was never deep. Soren's body had rejected the oblivion of the Ether for so long it couldn't rest. But he did shut down occasionally. He lost the fight to stay awake. Never completely. He tossed and turned. He called out from the abyss of half consciousness, where his fear of nothingness and cold taunted him with familiar, icy fingers.

With Anna nearby it was suddenly much worse. He'd been running for days. He'd experienced the loss of his brother all over again. He'd had to face Anna's transformation. As an enchanted Romanov shape-shifter, he was powerful. He had endurance unlike a regular man. But he wasn't indefatigable. Sleep came for him eventually. It always did. But even asleep he couldn't relax. He fought rest as if it was the Ether trying to pull him away from Bronwal and his family.

Or from her.

The witch was nearby and he couldn't leave her. His panic as he sank into sleep thudded his heart in his chest and made his breathing quick.

His nightmare was always the same. He wandered a vast nightscape forest. Alone. Sometimes as the red wolf. Sometimes as a man. But always certain that he was almost out of time. He never understood what he needed to do before time ran out. He only knew with certain dread that if the Ether took him, all would be lost.

This time he was the wolf. He padded the pathways of the nightmare forest on four paws. Then he ran. It was useless. The pathways were always a maze with no beginning and no end in sight. Like the curse, his nightmare trapped him and held him until the Ether could claim him.

But unlike the curse, he had no one by his side to help him face the dark.

It was that loss that made him howl at the moonless sky in his nightmare. He called and called for a woman who couldn't reply.

The next morning, Soren watched his brother approach. His spine stiffened, because he could see the dark thunderclouds on the alpha wolf's brow even before he crossed the courtyard. Soren planted his feet and braced his shoulders as he stood with the horses an old groom he barely recognized had prepared for him and Anna.

Something was wrong.

He hadn't expected to see Ivan again this morning. They had said farewell last night.

His hands tightened on the halters of the large mounts as they tried to toss their heads in response to the emotions of the alpha they could also sense as he came closer.

Ivan Romanov was in his human form, but there was no mistaking the gleam of the black wolf in his eyes. A hint of dawn was all that was needed to illuminate that flash of savagery waiting to be freed. Soren swallowed against the howl that tried to crawl up his throat to seek an emotional release. His red wolf was ferocious, but it bowed without his permission before his big brother, the alpha.

"Where is she?" Ivan asked in almost-pained tones.

Soren wasn't surprised he didn't begin with a "good morning." The shift rode Ivan Romanov. It tightened his muscles and hardened his jaw. Ivan had often looked as steely and fierce toward the end of the curse, when he'd had to fight off the black wolf every day. His brother was moments away from howling at the rising sun.

But why? What new threat did they face?

Soren was no longer Anna's protector, but his first instinct was to stand between his brother's imminent shift and the witch who was supposed to join him in the courtyard soon.

"She's meeting me here at dawn," Soren said. He exuded calm in spite of his inner tension. He met the black wolf's potential fury with ice and then tried to diffuse it. "That's why I'm holding two horses."

Ivan blinked and stepped back as if he'd only just noticed the giant destriers his brother held. Their reaction to the alpha's close presence had intensified. Soren had to tighten his hold on their halters. The warhorses were afraid. Ivan noticed their fear, and the wildness in his eyes subsided. Soren watched as the black wolf retreated deeper within his brother, leaving a calmer leader in his place.

"I won't ask where you're going. If you'd wanted me to know, you would have shared that information last night," Ivan said. Suddenly, he stepped to Soren and placed a heavy hand on his shoulder. Instead of rearing, the horses calmed. Perhaps they could smell the man now that he had controlled his wolf. Ivan met him face-to-face, gaze to gaze.

His seriousness was palpable. Soren's forced calm only got icier with the eye contact. His brother was building to something big. He could think of only one thing that would cause the alpha to leave his warm bed and meet him at the break of dawn. "Make certain she doesn't return," Ivan continued.

Soren was the red wolf. He heard the alpha's command in his brother's voice. He saw the black wolf deep down in Ivan's eyes. His whole body went numb from the cold of the calm he forced through sheer willpower alone.

Who had told Ivan about the sword?

The alpha was warning him away from an unacceptable mate. Soren agreed. Hell, *Anna* agreed. So why was his internal response a long, echoing howl of refusal? He tamped it down. He clenched his teeth. He held himself still, because if he moved a millimeter, it might become a shift to challenge the alpha's authority. Ivan's eyes widened. In spite of Soren's best efforts, his brother was wise beyond his apparent years. He looked like a twenty-five-year-old man. He was, in fact, much older. He must have sensed or seen Soren's visceral response to his order.

A noise interrupted before the standoff could erupt into violence. They both broke away from the stare to look up. Elena appeared at a window high above them. She'd thrown it open, and several ravens had lifted off from their sentinel perches on its ledge. White curtains billowed outward around her blanket-wrapped form. They were too far away to see her face, but the sound of Ivan's name drifted with the sound of flapping wings.

"She's pregnant, Soren. She's going to have a child. My child. Your niece or nephew. Anna isn't welcome here. Not anymore," Ivan said.

The shift that had risen to claim Soren subsided as shock claimed him instead. He took a deep, shuddering breath and closed his eyes. Ivan didn't know about the emerald sword's Call. He was protecting his unborn child. Soren opened his eyes again to see his sister-in-law at the window. She'd gone silent, but the wind still fluttered the curtains around her petite figure. She looked small and vulnerable, although Soren knew she was a fierce warrior quite capable of protecting herself. Her silent urgency at the window didn't negate Ivan's response. It only backed it up.

A baby at Bronwal.

How could Soren respond to that with anything other than a nod? Anna wasn't welcome at Bronwal. Ivan was only saying what he already knew to be true: Anna was a danger to the Romanov family. She was a powerful witch being Called by the emerald sword. A connection with that enchanted blade would make her even more powerful. Dangerously powerful considering her lack of control. It would be a mistake to ever trust her again.

Before dawn, the corridors of Bronwal were as deserted as they'd been the night before. But it was a different type of desertion than she'd grown used to in the past. The floors were swept clean and covered with colorful woven rugs. There was artwork on the walls—from restored tapestries to exquisite paintings. Torches had been replaced with electric lighting and the necessary wiring was discreetly placed behind rich cherry baseboards that softened the edges of the stone walls.

The castle was becoming a home—a large home, but a home nonetheless.

Bronwal was located in the Carpathian Mountains of Romania. There was rich representation of Slav cultures in the tapestry, carpets and paintings. Rich golds, reds and oranges were vivid compared to the dust and decay she remembered. She suddenly wanted to stay long enough to see the people of the castle as well—those she'd lived with for centuries and those who had reappeared from the Ether when the curse was broken.

It wouldn't be safe.

There were many who saw her the same way Soren did, and their antagonism might cause her abilities to flare up in self-defense. Her only safe option was to move quickly through the silent halls in order to meet Soren before the castle woke up.

The sword knew she was coming.

She'd woken to a strange sensation in every cell in her body. The only explanation for the increased resonance of the sword's Call was her intention to travel to find it. She was filled with a silent sound that vibrated along every vessel and vein. It wasn't the energy of the Ether. It was the emerald. And it felt like joy. When she left the tower room, a buoyancy she tried to fight fueled her steps.

She should dread this journey. She shouldn't want to see Soren again so soon. But her body jeered at her foolish head. She had every intention of rejecting the sword's Call. She agreed with the red wolf. The emerald sword must be destroyed.

And still her body rushed downstairs.

"The stables have been restored. I assume you remember how to ride," Soren said. He waited with two giant horses at the courtyard side entrance. He didn't wait to see if she protested the outmoded form of transportation he'd chosen. For all intents and purposes, she and Soren were outmoded, as well. People who had lived well beyond their natural time on earth.

Or that was what she'd thought before she'd discovered she was a witch. *Volkhvy* lived much longer than humans. Then again, the legendary shifters had been enchanted to serve the Light *Volkhvy* queen. They were long-lived as well, even now that the curse was lifted.

Soren was oddly silent as he swung himself up to mount a large-boned black destrier. The horse pranced beneath his weight when he settled in the saddle, as if it was unused to a rider. She'd ridden with the young teen Romanovs many times, but that had been many years ago. Had Soren looked so commanding and unapproachable on horseback then as he looked right now?

He'd tamed the wild waves of his red hair into a thick twist at the nape of his neck. His beard looked trimmed, but she allowed her glance to skim away before she could be sure, because she didn't want her perusal to linger. His clothes were more modern than she'd seen him wear before. His long muscular legs were encased in jeans. His broad chest and strong arms were covered in a zippered leather jacket. In the stirrups, his low square-toed boots peeked from his jeans.

Her horse whickered, saving her from becoming too distracted by a man her eyes were too hungry to ignore. She reached for the dappled neck of the gray-and-white beast and patted it before she reached to pull herself onto its wide back. They were riding horses that had probably carried knights into battle before they'd been sucked into the nothingness of the Ether because of the curse. They seemed no worse for wear beyond their nervous prancing, as they grew used to having people on their rematerialized backs once more.

"It will take hours to make it down the mountain on horseback," Anna said. She gripped the reins in her gloved hands. The power of the Ether was at her fingertips, but the animal beneath her felt safer. Slower but safer, despite the years that had passed since she'd ridden. Her use of power wasn't reliable. She had yet to gain complete control. That, combined with the Dark chill of the Ether that was imprinted on her nightmares, was enough for her to humor Soren's choice. She preferred to ride in the forest.

"And I will have my body the entire time. I'll feel the wind in my hair and the sun on my face. I've had my fill of disappearing. I never want to vanish, wondering if I'll see this world again or not," Soren said.

He didn't remind her that he distrusted her as much as he distrusted the Ether. To him, she and the Ether were one and the same. Instead, he nudged his horse into motion with a flick of his reins and a shift of his legs. The black leaped forward but then settled into a steady gait her smaller gray was able to mimic. She gave the dappled gelding its head and allowed the horse to follow the leader. In the long run, Soren would be following her to the sword. For now, she preferred he go first so she wouldn't have to feel his disapproving gaze on her back as they made their way down the mountain.

The countryside had changed. Nothing was familiar. She trusted Soren because he'd been roaming the forest and mountain for months while she'd been on her mother's island. Besides, once they had left the pass that led to Bronwal, they came upon trails that zigzagged all over the mountain, indicating the high traffic of sightseers and pleasure seekers. Only Vasilisa's enchantment had kept the castle mostly hidden whenever it materialized throughout its long cursed existence. Her magic would continue to keep it protected from the outside world if the Romanovs wished it.

They would never be ordinary citizens.

Whether or not Ivan Romanov shared his brother's views on *Volkhvy* magic remained to be seen. In time, he would be the one to decide if Bronwal and its people—including the Romanovs themselves—would still choose to serve the Light *Volkhvy* queen as champions against the Dark.

* * *

He and his brothers hadn't solely relied on the shift to fight. They'd been trained to fight with swords as soon as they were strong enough to lift the wooden practice weapons that bloodied and bruised nearly as well as the real things. They were enchanted champions who hadn't been coddled in any way. Soren had been born to the weight of that responsibility, and he had carried it until the curse came down.

But he had abandoned the emerald sword before Vasilisa cursed them.

He could still remember the cruel day his mother fell in battle. They had been called for far too late, and the race to reach her in time had been the most desperate of his young life. The Dark *Volkhvy* king had killed her. Even the enchanted sword she carried as Vladimir's wife hadn't been able to defend her against him.

The battlefield had been smoking from the blood of the *Volkhvy* dead when they finally arrived. He remembered weaving between the pools of black blood mingled with red from the Romanov guard that had been traveling with its queen and the Light *Volkhvy* prince when they were ambushed.

Vasilisa's consort had been the target. Soren's mother, Naomi, had died trying to save him. The power in her sword had died with her. Soren remembered the shock of seeing its gem gone as gray as his father's fur. It had lain inches away from her pale, bloody fingers where it had fallen away from her grasp as she died.

All the power at his disposal—in his ferocious teeth, massive paws and muscled body—had been useless. Even worse than that, his father and brothers had been useless, as well. The battlefield had been filled with death. He'd recognized many of the fallen—his friends, comrades, relatives and allies. The Dark had won that day. He could perfectly recall the sudden notion that the Romanovs weren't invulnerable. That they could fall and fail. His mother's face had been untouched. He remembered her still. She'd been a pale beauty in life. In death, her beauty was a horrible shock in the midst of all the ugliness around her. He'd said goodbye with a red wolf's nose against her cold hand. Naomi's death had been a deeply personal loss, but it had also been the beginning of losing his belief in his family's mission and the Light.

He had left the battlefield and traveled back to his horse alone. He'd shifted in the snow without thought to his nakedness immediately going for his own enchanted blade. In his saddle's scabbard, the emerald blade had waited to choose his future warrior wife.

Or had it already chosen at that point?

He wouldn't allow himself to think of Bell now. That day, when he'd pulled the sword free, the gem had blazed with green light, as if it was already Calling the woman who would wield it. He had ignored its glow. He'd walked to the edge of a ravine and thrown it over the side.

Soren could still see the blade as its weight and the force of his throw embedded it in the ice far below where he'd stood. The emerald shine of its gem had faded as he'd watched. He'd turned away when it failed to become as dark and gray as his mother's. He'd had to believe that in time it would die as his mother's had done. Even before Vasilisa had crafted the curse against them, he had rejected her magical interference in his life. He had rejected the danger he would pose to a woman who might choose to be his mate.

And Soren hadn't yet understood his father's part in the ambush. His belief had suffered an unrecoverable setback when he'd learned Vladimir had sacrificed his wife because he hungered for the *Volkhvy* throne.

Long before he discovered Bell was Vasilisa's daughter, Soren found out *Volkhvy* power corrupted. His father. Queen Vasilisa. Even his poor, betrayed mother, Naomi was as undone by the enchanted sword that couldn't save her as she was by her liege and her lord.

He'd never regretted his decision.

Even if Bell weren't *Volkhvy*, he wouldn't have wanted to expose her to the risk of wielding a Romanov blade. As her former champion, it tortured him well enough that he couldn't protect her from the threat she carried within her own blood.

They rode for hours, until by midday Anna's body screamed in protest from the unusual position and constant motion. Her training with her mother had been physical at times, but it had never involved horseback riding. And her years spent surviving in the corridors of a cursed castle had been all about ninja stealth on her own two feet.

When they broke from the woods into a small clearing, the open air was a fresh relief on her hot face.

"We'll stop here for food and water," Soren said.

Had she moaned? She might have groaned. There was no way the legendary red wolf needed a break. But she was too sore to even care that the stop would mean more time in Soren's company. Anna swung her leg over the horse's neck and dropped to the ground. Where she immediately crumpled into an aching pile of failure.

After that, everything happened too fast for her to absorb. One second her knees gave out beneath her. The next, Soren Romanov had jumped from his own horse to land beside hers. His hands were wrapped around her upper arms before she could protest, and he pulled her to her feet.

Unfortunately, she'd fallen for a reason. Her legs, so unused to wrapping around a warhorse for hours, weren't ready to support her weight. It was as if her knees didn't remember how to stand. The result was a full-body press with the man who'd automatically come to her rescue even though he hated her.

Anna knew he regretted it. She could feel the hard tension in him from his neck to his ankles. Her gloved hands had come up to grab onto him for support. His leather lapels were crushed in her fingers.

But it was his strong arms that held her up. His hands had dropped from her arms to her waist. He held her in a warm embrace. She could feel every inch of heated muscle in his arms, his chest and his stomach.

It was a mistake to look into his eyes. For the first time, they weren't hidden by wild hair or a dim hallway. They weren't hooded by mist or shadows. They glowed amber in the sunlight, fully revealed. He didn't jerk away. He didn't avoid her search. He met her gaze as if he, too, was surprised by the sudden ability to really see into her eyes for the first time.

The vibration in her cells suddenly had a name, and its name was Soren.

The Call of the sword only magnified what was already there, worked into her body and soul at creation by some unseen hand.

Soren's hands reflexively tightened on her. She could feel their power along with the heat through her fleece jacket and thin T-shirt. Her nipples pebbled. Her breath caught. The tingling in her hands increased as the moment became heavy with impossible possibilities.

His eyes didn't seem cool and guarded. They seemed… warm.

He leaned. Just a little. And the sun glinted off the crown of his head, where his clean red hair had been smoothed down. There were no curls left to catch the light. She blinked against the sudden russet halo and the spell of the chemistry between them was broken. He dropped his hands and stepped back. She swayed but willed herself to stay on her feet by pure determination.

"I guess it's been a long time," Anna murmured. She planted her feet more firmly on the ground and stretched her waist this way and that in order to cover her embarrassment.

Soren had fisted his hands as if they'd betrayed him by holding her. She avoided his eyes. She didn't want to see all the warmth gone and caution returned. She would do well to remember that she couldn't let the sword's Call or old feelings cloud her judgment. She needed to stay cautious, as well. She couldn't afford to respond to the pull she felt from Soren.

It was a lie.

His rejection was the truth.

They were going after the sword in order to destroy it. The mission was necessary. It was also the ultimate rejection of what they had and what they could ever be.

He took care of the horses as if centuries hadn't passed since animal husbandry was a part of his everyday life. He led them to a nearby stream and then hobbled them into a meadow of tall green grass. He didn't need to rest. It would be better if they completed this mission as soon as possible. He needed to end this.

But the horses needed extra care after being in the Ether, just as humans and wolves did. It was a process to get your legs back under you after you'd had no legs or body at all. He remembered well the days of each Cycle they'd all wasted remembering how to be themselves again. How to think and move and exist. No wonder there were those who disappeared for good with every materialization. The Ether drained more from a man's soul each and every time it devoured his body. Going and coming from the cold darkness caused a loss of self and over time the diminishment could become complete.

Even as he cared for the horses, he knew he hadn't stopped out of consideration for the sturdy animals. He'd heard Anna groan. He'd stopped for her. She wasn't used to horseback riding, and her muscles hadn't been hardened by centuries of running as a wolf. They'd woken before dawn and pushed on for hours. She hadn't said a word. She hadn't argued with him about how much more quickly they would travel by using her witchery. She hadn't asked why horses instead of a more modern nonmagical form of transportation.

The truth was he hadn't wanted to discuss their trip with Ivan more than he had to. Asking for one of the new ATVs would have opened up all sorts of other questions and revelations. As the alpha, his brother might feel obligated to stop them from destroying the sword. Although he had forbidden Anna to return to Bronwal, he might envision another mate for the red wolf down the line. He might see the strategic advantage to having another warrior claim the sword. Soren rejected that thought almost before it began. He might be disadvantaged with no warrior to fight by his side, but he wanted no mate.

Plus, he had his pride.

He didn't want to admit to his older brother that his memories of being trapped in the Ether had become nightmares for him now that he was free.

Anna had settled her hips against a half-fallen tree that leaned to form a convenient triangle with the ground and its trunk. He'd managed to ignore her stretching… mostly…and now she was still save for the occasional sips she took from a water bottle she'd taken from the pack on her back.

She would be a distraction if she didn't move at all.

Her red silk cloak was gone. Probably rolled and stowed away in her backpack. She wore a green jacket the deep, rich color of summer leaves and thigh-hugging black leggings that were the thinnest, smoothest leather he'd ever seen. There were machines now that mass-produced the clothing that people had worked weeks to craft in his time.

The result of her outfit was practical as well as torturous...for him, at least. He could see every curve and dip and fine line of her body without even trying. She was fully covered and alluringly revealed at the same time.

He tried not to notice. Not only because it was torture, but also because he had no right to appreciate the womanly curves of a person who was his enemy. He was furious with himself for touching her when she'd fallen during her dismount. She hadn't been hurt or in danger. He'd had no obligation. It had been the habit of centuries to spring during her distress.

But his touch had only increased it.

He'd seen the pain in her wide green eyes. They'd gleamed with a shimmer of tears in the bright mountain sun. He'd wanted to ease her pain. He'd wanted to ease his own. He'd almost been entranced with the idea of sinking into her and tasting the full swell of her blush-red lips. She'd licked them as if they'd gone dry and he'd leaned... but then she'd blinked against a flash of blinding sunlight.

The spell had been broken.

At least enough to allow him to gain control and back away.

Now he knew he wanted a witch's kiss. He wanted to taste her lips, to taste *Anna* as deeply as she would allow. The hunger for her shocked him all the way to the wolf that slept deep in his heart.

* * *

She didn't protest when Soren decided to continue on down the mountain. The simple stop had turned into a torturous waiting game. She noticed every step he took and every glance he sent in her direction. As a wolf, he'd been a constant shadow to her movements. As a man, his presence was harder to grow accustomed to. His height and breadth continually drew her attention. His masculine grace constantly startled her. And not only because she looked for the wolf she'd known in his every gesture.

Soren drew her attention because he was impossible to ignore. Like all the Romanovs, he was gifted with a handsome face and a powerful body. But with Soren, that power and attractiveness was paired with occasional moments of alluring approachability. He'd been a commanding presence on his horse at dawn. Now the sunlight still gleamed off his russet hair, but it was no longer smooth. Tendrils had escaped to hang in thick rivulets of curls around his face. They moved as he moved, drawing her eye, causing her fingers to twitch. His brows, eyelashes and beard were a lighter shade of reddish brown. They offset the amber of his eyes and a hint of his sensual lips.

And absolutely none of that was sane for her to notice.

Soren, the red wolf, had been hers. Soren, the man, never would be. It was even worse after their embrace, because she continued to notice every rise and fall of his broad chest even though he'd placed himself several yards away from her while she rested.

When he brought her horse to her, she moved to mount without saying a word.

Soren came within a few feet of her to hold the horse while she climbed into the saddle, and their gazes locked. She had to force herself to look away once she was settled, but that lasted only as long as it took their fingers to brush when she took the reins from his hand.

She still wore her gloves.

They didn't help.

An arc of power flared in a small jagged bolt of light between their hands. She gasped as the sudden shock turned pleasant, radiating through her body like an electrified caress. The sensation ended as suddenly as it had begun. The electricity dissipated into the air, leaving nothing but pleasure behind.

If Soren had lifted her hand to kiss her fingers, she would have experienced the same aftermath—tingling shock in all the right places that caused her to shift on the saddle.

She blinked, swallowed and tried to remember to breathe normally, while Soren simply looked stunned.

He dropped his hand away from hers and she gripped the reins to hide the trembling in her fingers.

"Control your powers, Princess," Soren warned. He'd fisted his hand. She wondered if he tingled, too. Her whole body still vibrated from that one arc between them.

"That wasn't me," Anna said.

He stepped forward and looked up at her face as if he would argue, but his move brought his body into contact with her leg. Through boot and leather pants she felt his hard chest. How was she supposed to ignore the man he'd become? Especially if they were bound to travel together until they could destroy the sword.

"Are you saying it was me?" Soren asked. But his voice had deepened, as if the contact between her leg and his chest had at least partially given him the answer.

"It's both of us. Together," Anna said. Her horse danced sideways away from Soren, and she didn't stop it.

"I'll keep my distance," Soren said. The bright sunlight

caused his lashes to make shadows on his cheeks as he lowered his lids and turned his face away.

"The farther the better, I should think," Anna said. She kneed the sides of her dappled gray and the horse trotted back to the path that would take them down the mountain.

Chapter 7

He'd seen the tracks before he brought Anna her horse. He'd found them as he walked around the clearing looking for a distraction. He couldn't ignore her. Not a chance. But he could stay busy. That was when he'd seen the obvious imprints of Lev's paw prints at the edge of the forest.

Lev wasn't gone.

Relief rushed over him until he thought he'd drowned in it.

Then, for a second, he froze, torn between the chance to find his brother and the age-old need to keep Bell safe. Since Bell was long gone, finding the white wolf had to be his top priority, given any chance of success at all. Lev was more important than the sword. *For now.* He wasn't denying the inevitable need to destroy the emerald sword. He was keeping his priorities straight. There was no other reason he would put off destroying the sword.

Certainly not one in formfitting leggings that made it hard for him to *concentrate*.

He hadn't had any sign that his brother was still in the forest yesterday. Now that he'd found fresh tracks, he had to try once more to bring Lev home.

He went for the large dappled gray destrier and led it to Anna. She had moved to mount without a word. He'd thought it was going to be quick and easy to follow his brother's tracks, but one second of contact between his fingers and Anna's had slowed him down.

His body still shook from her electric touch.

He was on his horse again and he'd taken the lead. He'd veered off onto a different trail and she'd followed without question. This was his mountain. He was familiar with every twisting pathway. He knew each hollow and glade. It was the tingling sensation in his every cell that was new territory.

They really needed to find the sword and end whatever was happening between them.

Volkhvy power was fueled by energy that came from the Ether. Anna shouldn't be able to use it to create a spark that caused a chain reaction of pleasurable pain to suffuse his entire body. His mind knew that. His body, however, had felt what logic denied.

The Ether was cold. It was a black hole you couldn't see or touch. One that devoured, and during that continuous vacuum, it expelled energy that witches could absorb and harness for their spells. At one time, regular folk had tapped into the power as well with mostly harmless hearth magic to help speed recovery of illness or growth of crops, to protect loved ones preparing to set off on long journeys, or to hasten their return.

But there was inherent danger in the *Volkhvy* race and what they could do with the power from the Ether. His mother was dead because of that power. His father had been corrupted by his lust for it. As the head of Bronwal, it was Ivan's responsibility to walk the line between trust and caution in dealings with the *Volkhvy*. Soren was far less willing to walk that line.

Anna had said it wasn't her. That the arc had been caused by their connection. If that was true, he was as guilty as she was if he allowed himself to enjoy the *Volkhvy* enchantment that bound them together.

He'd vowed to keep his distance.

He couldn't allow that promise to be a lie. Until he found Lev, he needed to ignore the spark caused by their connection. He tightened every muscle in his body against the tingling pleasure that lingered. He rode with clenched teeth and a ramrod-straight spine.

And his body still burned.

"We're riding into the forest, Soren. Deeper into the shadows. Are you sure you took the right path?" Anna said.

He should have known she wouldn't be a blind follower. Survivors never were. If there was anything of Bell left in Anna, the Light *Volkhvy* princess, she would always have her eyes open and her wits about her.

"There were tracks in the clearing. Fresh wolf tracks of a particular size," Soren confessed. "Lev's tracks."

He heard the horse behind his come to sudden halt. He reined in as well and turned halfway in his saddle. Anna was right—they'd ridden deeper into the woods where the sunlight didn't reach. In the velvety shadows, the woman behind him was cloaked in darkness. He couldn't read her expression. He could only see her porcelain skin and the sheen of ruby lips she must have moistened to speak.

"You said I would frighten him away, but now you're using me as bait," Anna said. "I'm dampening my powers and you didn't warn me about the tracks because you wanted to keep it that way."

"If I don't get him back to the castle, he doesn't have

a chance of reclaiming himself," Soren said. "He won't harm you."

"You're harming me by leading me into danger without giving me a chance to prepare to defend myself," Anna said. Her voice was quiet and accusatory. The hushed syllables made him flinch. He would have given Bell a choice, but he didn't trust Anna. He wouldn't allow anything to happen to her. He needed her to help him lure Lev out of the woods...whether she wanted to or not.

"From what I've seen, you don't need preparation. Those gloves are useless," Soren said.

"I wouldn't recommend you put that theory to the test with skin-to-skin contact, Soren Romanov. Not if the arc from earlier is still tingling in you the way it's tingling in me," Anna said.

Suddenly, they were talking about something other than finding his brother. He'd sensed the sensual possibilities in that arc of electricity they'd shared. And, yes, his whole body did still tingle, although he tried to ignore it. Some of his reaction to his thoughts must have shown even in the shadows, because Anna's hands tightened on the reins and her horse took a step toward his. Maybe she could see his face beneath the trees better than he could see hers. He controlled his features. He set his jaw and narrowed his eyes. He might be aroused by her suggestion of what would happen if they were suddenly skin to skin, but Anna didn't need to know.

"I won't take them off. I won't risk frightening him away again," Anna said.

He'd controlled his face. Now he controlled his body. He rejected the electricity because he had to. He had to focus on rescuing Lev. His brother would come for a witch. He was sure of it. His only choice now was to believe what Anna said and hope it wasn't a mistake.

* * *

Her physical reaction to Soren mocked her now that he'd admitted to leading her haplessly into the forest. She'd been distracted by the lingering effects of the arc between them, and she'd already been taken off guard by his nearness.

Fifty miles apart would be too close to ignore him.

But she was determined that she wouldn't be the one to destroy Lev's chance of a reunion with his family. So she kept her gloves in place and held even tighter to the reins to keep from reaching to remove them.

It was impossible not to feel betrayed.

The red wolf wouldn't have led Bell into danger without a warning.

Soren wasn't only physically different as a man. He was a complete stranger to her. One that couldn't be trusted in spite of instincts deep within her that said otherwise. She had relaxed her guard. There was no way around the truth. She had to learn how to see Soren as someone who was a potential enemy rather than a lifelong friend.

"I'll leave the gloves on, but it will be up to you to protect me from the white wolf," Anna said. She never would have had to ask the red wolf for protection. His constant, watchful presence had been a promise she didn't have to seek out or demand. Their circumstances had changed. She had to change with them.

"He won't harm you," Soren repeated.

This time she didn't reply. No matter what the white wolf did, he wouldn't damage her as much as his brother already had.

Suddenly, Soren jumped off his horse's back and whacked its flank to urge it to turn and run away. The great black stallion needed no encouragement. It had scented the white wolf on the breeze. Its nostrils flared and it reared up on its hind legs before it whirled to land facing the way they'd come. Anna held on while the gray pranced and whinnied in fear as it responded to its companion's emotion.

"Let them go," Soren shouted above the noise of hooves.

The black had lunged into a gallop and was quickly on his way to the sunlit clearing. Soren was beside her as she tried to dismount. Her urgency to avoid getting thrown by the frightened, prancing gray was too great to be cautious. She threw herself into Soren's outstretched arms. Even his strength couldn't withstand the force of the destrier's dance and her leap. Soren fell back from the gray with quick grace to avoid its hooves. He caught her and protected her in a controlled slide that carried them several feet away from the path on a tangle of weeds.

Once again, they were touching.

And even the white wolf's howl far in the distance didn't stop her from feeling the strength of Soren's arms and his body heat beneath her.

The scent of crushed greenery rose around them, but it was Soren's scent that filled her senses—evergreen boughs and fallen leaves, both woodsy and fresh. Her red wolf had always carried the scent of the Carpathian forest in his fur. On Soren's masculine skin, the scent was more seductive and sweet. She'd thought fifty miles apart would be too close. Now she was pressed against him with nothing but clothes separating them. The hoofbeats had faded into the distance and the forest had fallen into a hush around them. Her heartbeat was so loud in her ears she was afraid it would become audible to the man beneath her.

"I'm still going to destroy the sword. After we get Lev back to the castle." Soren finally spoke to break the stillness.

"If you don't, I will," Anna agreed.

The only way to protect herself from the insane urge to get as close to Soren as possible was to end the reason for them to be together. The sooner they destroyed the sword, the better.

Soren rejected her with his words, but he was also searching her face. His eyes tracked from her tousled hair down to where she'd caught her lower lip by the edge of her teeth. She wasn't the only one fighting their connection.

The white wolf was coming.

She was a witch and she was with his brother. No matter how savage Lev had become he wouldn't ignore the threat of *Volkhvy* in Romanov territory. Some conditioning to be a champion was worked into his flesh and bones. And his hatred of witches had been forged in him through a devastating loss that obviously drove him to the brink of madness.

But the sudden ululating cries of a feral enchanted wolf seemed a more distant concern than the man who held her. Soren shook. She had grabbed his shoulders as they fell. She didn't have the luxury of gauging their width, but the tension in his muscles was so extreme that his body trembled.

She looked up from her hands to his face.

And then she began to tremble, too.

Soren Romanov's gaze was no longer tracking over her face. Instead, he stared at her lips. The intensity of his focus carried the weight of a physical touch. Her mouth tingled and it was his pure Romanov magnetism, not her power. His hands tightened on the curve of her back. Only his fingers. He didn't pull her closer with his arms. He only held her tightly with his hands, as if it was instinctive and not a conscious choice. In the pit of her stomach, a hot coil wound tighter and tighter until, if it didn't ease, she thought she would faint.

Had he raised his face closer to hers?

Gravity pressed her splayed body against his broad

chest. Her breasts were flattened so that their heartbeats pounded against each other. But she was certain that his lips were nearer to hers than they had been before.

Anna tried not to breathe. She didn't want him to see her pant, and there was no way she could achieve regular respiration with their mouths almost touching. Crazily, she realized Soren was holding his breath, too. She searched his face as if she could quickly tell what might happen in the next second, or the next.

She wasn't going to kiss him.

The white wolf was coming closer, and all she could think about was the man who had cushioned her from the hard ground as she fell—only to become even harder and an even greater threat beneath her.

Because of how badly she wanted to taste him.

Once again her gaze went to his lips.

She resented the untrimmed beard that tried to hide the full swell of his mouth from her view. She could only see a hint of where her lips longed to press. A hint was enough to steal her breath and tighten something deep inside her. The coil had become a hot knot of desire where the earlier tingles had been. It tried to propel her toward the possibility of one lip-to-lip indulgence, one flick of the tip of her tongue.

He must have seen the hunger in her face.

"Anna," he breathed, and it was doubly seductive because it was the first time he'd used her real name without sounding as if he used it as a reminder that she was his enemy. It didn't matter that it was a reluctant plea. She barely had to lower her face before his hands came up to the back of her head and he pulled her the rest of the way.

One warm taste was all it took to shatter her completely.

She inhaled a gasp of surprise that tasted of the forest around them, but also the forest long captured in the red curls that had escaped his attempt to tame them. She reached to touch his human hair as their lips pressed together, deeper, again. She was no longer able to resist lightly threading her fingers through the silky strands, but when his mouth opened, she forgot his hair. His tongue met hers in a sudden stolen exploration. She registered his heat, the rough and smooth textures, the intimacy of sharing breath as he gulped for air, too, and then their mouths parted as if they both were shocked at what had happened.

Anna pushed back from his chest and rose in a scramble to her feet. At the same time, Soren stood. She struggled to breathe. Her cheeks were hot. Her whole body was inflamed. Soren's skin was flushed. He pushed his hair back from his face as if he needed to clear the way for oxygen to get through and fill his lungs.

Nothing could have prevented that kiss.

Not Lev coming closer. Not all the willpower in the world. It had been rolling toward them on a tsunami of inevitability since Soren had regained his human form and she'd come back to Bronwal.

Anna had been right. Skin to skin was devastating. There was no chance of recovering from lips to lips and tongue to tongue. He could barely breathe, and now he knew forbidden fruit tasted of mint and Anna's heated sighs.

From the second he'd landed on the ground with Anna sprawled on top of him, he'd been unable to make rational decisions. It wasn't the time for their first kiss. There would never be the right time for such intimacy between them. But there had been an inevitability he couldn't resist.

Their bodies melded perfectly together, even with no effort and no comfortable accommodation. Her lush figure——one he knew better than he should from their years of camaraderie—was a sudden pleasure of full breasts and intriguing curves against his human chest. Her lovely face—so familiar and dear to him at one time—was flushed and her lips were parted as her breath came quickly from between them.

And then she'd seen him looking at her. She'd caught her breath and held it as if she waited to see if he was brave enough to follow through with what his body told him to do.

She was there, in his arms, and he couldn't deny that he was overwhelmed with the sensation of wanting her there, needing her there, enjoying her there. It wasn't a leisurely moment where they were free to indulge or deny impulses with careful thought and the summoning of maximum self-control.

It was sudden, quick and hot. His hunger rose and, judging from her response, hers had, too.

Now the white wolf howled, coming closer and closer, but all Soren could hear and feel was his own frustration at the distance between him and a witch he wanted to kiss again. He should be glad the mistake had ended as quickly as it had begun. He should be glad she looked as if she regretted the momentary lapse of judgment and control.

Instead, he felt an echoing howl deep inside his chest.

He wanted to taste Anna again. Deeper and longer. He wanted to explore every inch of her curves with his human hands and indulge all the desires that arose, both hers and his, as a result of that exploration.

Yes. Skin to skin was devastating. But not because of the electric energy of the Ether that her *Volkhvy* blood allowed her to channel. She'd controlled that even as their lips met. It had taken great effort. He'd felt her trembling as she'd fought for command, but her control over her abilities had held.

As he stood facing her, it was the simple requited passion between them that devastated. The power of the Ether was nothing compared to their chemistry. He'd tried not to think of her since the night of the Gathering, when her parentage had been revealed. He'd tried and failed the minute he shifted to become a man. Their sudden separation should have been a reprieve. It had been torture instead. Now he found that being with her was a different kind of torture. Fantasy and impossible what-ifs had been replaced by the living, breathing reality of a woman he longed to touch in spite of her blood and his loyalty to his brothers. The kiss had been a mistake, but one he would long to commit again and again.

"That can't happen again," Anna said. The emerald sword sang *I told you so* in her veins, pulsing with the beat of her heart. They had both decided the sword had to be destroyed. The kiss only made the inevitable that much harder to accomplish.

"It won't," Soren said. He sounded so certain. Much more certain than he'd tasted and felt. His lips had been eager on hers, startled but willing and quick to know exactly what to do. How could such a wild, hard man have such a soft, sensual mouth?

She found herself looking at his lips. Even partially hidden by his beard, they drew her attention. He should be frowning. His mouth should be hard and angry. It wasn't. His lips were still soft and full. If she stepped toward him again, they would welcome her even if he didn't.

But then, his mouth changed.

"Get behind me and don't say a word," Soren said. Anna froze. The pleasure she'd experienced moments before fled, leaving her cold. The man in front of her no longer looked at her lips, and his mouth had become a tight, stiff line. He looked over her shoulder at a threat she could suddenly sense as the fine hairs rose on the back of her neck.

"He's here," she guessed. But she could already hear the breathing of the large, winded wolf that had appeared out of the forest behind her.

"I've come to bring you home, brother," Soren said loudly.

Anna tried not to jump at his sudden false exuberance. She decided to follow his instructions. He knew the white wolf better than anyone. If she couldn't use her powers, she had to survive in other ways. She moved forward, carefully and slowly, to place herself behind Soren. Doing so caused her to face the white wolf. Once she turned around, her heart began to pound and a wash of adrenaline flooded her body. Lev was an even more monstrous sight than he'd been before. His fur was more matted and dirty with dried blood. His teeth were bared. He filled the entire width of the path with his broad shoulders and widespread paws. Her hands tingled almost painfully in response. She ground her teeth against the instinctive desire to tap into the Ether.

"Lev. Come with me to Bronwal. You can lie by the fire and rest. Ivan wants to see you," Soren said.

The white wolf growled in response. He wasn't looking at Soren. His focus was on Anna. He stepped forward one pace, then another. She couldn't tap into her powers, and the sword was somewhere far away in the possession of the Dark *Volkhvy*. It wasn't a decision to reach for her former protector. It was pure survival instinct.

Without thinking, Anna reached to place one gloved hand on Soren's shoulder. She shouldn't have touched him. She sought an anchor and a reminder of why she couldn't remove her gloves. What she received was an electric jolt through linen and leather that caused her to cry out. Somewhere the emerald sword flared. She sensed it even if she was too far away to see, and a sympathetic flash of green sparked behind her eyelids.

Her cry only seemed to throw fuel on the flames of Lev's raw, savage emotions. The white wolf leaped forward. Soren reached for his brother's fur on either side of his head, but even as muscular and as strong as he was in his human form, he was no match for a giant enchanted wolf.

Soren's fists tightened and held, but Lev's jaw closed over Anna's arm before Soren could prevent it.

Her gloves weren't useless. The thick leather protected her from having her arm torn off by the white wolf's ferocious bite, but Lev's teeth shredded the leather. Her skin was exposed and unprotected. The tips of his teeth snagged flesh. Her blood was shed. Anna's power flared from the gaps in her glove.

Lev's bite loosened, and a brilliant flash of green light repelled him backward away from them. Through her pain, Anna saw Lev land hard on the packed earth of the mountain path. He didn't move. Not one of his giant muscles twitched. Her pain was too great to care. Driven by her agony, her power flared again. This time instead of using the Ether as a weapon, she used it as an escape. The white wolf didn't move as the world disappeared. Before Anna lost consciousness, she felt the frigid cold of the Ether's vacuum, and she heard Soren shout his brother's name.

Chapter 8

*T*hey often faced the end of the month in the same place, in the same way. They climbed to the ramparts of Bronwal and watched the sunset. Bathed in orange and gold, they looked out over the mountains. In time, after many sunsets, Anna would hold the scruff on the red wolf's neck where his russet hair grew slightly longer and thicker. She would burrow her fingers there and hold on as the rays flared brightly just before they faded away.

Like the sun, so solid and hot and real, they, too, would disappear with the last rays of light and heat.

Anna's tight grip was always his last sensation after all else disappeared. They both fought the Ether even after hundreds of years of being unable to stay. The stone they sat on. The immovable mountain they faced. All the people of Bronwal vanished around them.

Soren was the last to disappear, because Anna didn't let go of him. His molecules stayed together for her. He *fought for her. He struggled with his last fully formed thought to stay by her side.*

He always failed.

With all his strength and determination. With his powerful body and his large heart. With his teeth and claws and massive muscles.

He still failed.

The Ether took them every time, an inevitable frigid darkness in which he couldn't find her because there was nothing left of him for her to hold.

The Ether claimed them for only a few minutes. When they materialized again, Soren fell to his knees, but he didn't drop the unconscious woman he held in his arms. They were out of the forest. He recognized the ramparts of Bronwal around them. He cradled Anna close. He felt the solid ground beneath him. It had been over quickly, but he still trembled from the cold and the knowledge that he'd been consumed by the Ether one more time without his permission.

Witches could travel through the Ether, but to bring him along with her had been a spectacular feat of power. He was a reluctant passenger and she was injured.

It took him longer than it should have to rise to his feet. Anna was bleeding severely from her injuries. The front of his jacket was covered in her blood. It was a deep, dark crimson so red it was almost black. *Volkhvy* blood. That evidence of her witchy heritage didn't prevent him from noticing how pale her face was against his shoulder. If anything, the contrast startled him into action.

"Help me!" he shouted.

They'd materialized outside Anna's aviary. It must have been instinct that directed the use of her power. She'd brought them to a place where she'd once felt safe. His calls for help rose up into the sky, but no help came from the lower levels of the castle. His voice was hoarse and weak. He couldn't summon the red wolf's howl. He'd regained his bearings, though. The numbness of the Ether had faded with the onset of the adrenaline as he noted Anna's injuries. He made for the stairs as he murmured the kinds of things a man murmurs when he's trying to save a woman's life.

For now, it didn't matter that the woman was a witch or that his brother had tried to kill her.

Agony racked her body with shudders as Anna regained consciousness. She tried to brace herself against the pain, but she could only ride the waves of it as her teeth chattered.

Then she remembered the white wolf's lunge. She remembered his massive teeth sinking into her skin.

"No," she cried out. Gentle hands pressed against her uninjured shoulder and her forehead.

"You're feverish, child. Shush. Be still. I've cleansed and bound your wounds," Patrice said. The familiar voice of the old housekeeper who had taken care of Bronwal for centuries penetrated her fear and pain. Anna settled back and the firm hands released her.

But the pain was no excuse to keep her eyes closed.

Anna struggled to open her lids and focus.

Patrice bustled in all her usual ways, straightening bedclothes and muttering beneath her breath. The familiarity of her stout aproned figure soothed. But the empty room didn't.

"Where's Soren?" Anna asked. She tried to sit up again, but this time Patrice stopped her with a hand on her chest before she managed to rise off the mattress.

"He's outside the door. Hasn't left to eat or sleep since he carried you to me two days ago," Patrice said.

"What happened to Lev?" Anna asked. Her powers had flared in self-defense. She wasn't sure what she had done to the wolf that had bitten her, but dread nearly overcame her pain. She'd broken her promise.

"You'll have to ask Soren. All I know is that you used the Ether to escape and that man in the hall is none too happy about it. He's vowed to stay out of the Ether for the rest of his life, and Romanov wolves live a very long time," Patrice said.

"I didn't mean to. It wasn't a conscious decision. It was instinct," Anna said. She fell back against the pillows.

"That's the problem, isn't it?" Patrice asked. "We've all seen where a witch's instincts can lead." She moved away from the bed as she spoke, but she didn't seem afraid. She went about her business as if she merely stated a fact.

Anna didn't argue. Patrice was right.

"This time you took me through the Ether without my permission. What will you do the next time? Or the next?" Soren asked from the doorway.

Anna blinked to try to bring the big man into focus.

"I didn't harm Lev even though he hurt me," Anna said. It was a weak argument for her reliability. It fell on ears that had to be too recently chilled by the black nothingness of the Ether to be sympathetic.

"Lev has disappeared," Soren said. "When I went back to find him, he was gone. I couldn't track him. I have no way of knowing if you brought me here and sent him into the Ether never to return."

She could see Soren's concern for his brother eating away at him. And the worst part was she couldn't reassure him. She hadn't consciously chosen what she'd done. Maybe her fear had banished Lev. Forever. "You just said you acted on instinct. How can we trust that your instincts will never lead you astray? Your mother's led her into the darkness. So deep and so far gone that she hurt her own daughter in the process. My mother died because my father craved more of the power Vasilisa had used to alter his blood. *Volkhvy* power can't be trusted," Soren said, but his golden-brown eyes tracked from her face to her bandaged shoulder as if he cared about her injury. His focus lingered on the blood seeping from her wounds to color the white linen Patrice had used to bind them. There was concern in his narrowed eyes. He firmed his lips as if he stopped himself from expressing it, and then his gaze tracked down from her shoulder to her naked hands.

Her gloves had been removed while Patrice treated her injuries.

"I'm not going to hurt anyone," Anna said. She might be unsure of her abilities and she might still need training in how to harness and use them, but in that moment she was certain she didn't lie to him. She was determined that her words would be true.

"I know you're not, because I won't allow it," Soren said.

He stood between her and the rest of the castle.

Some part of his heart might still feel for her. He might be sorry that she experienced pain.

But he hadn't been standing outside her door for two days because he was concerned for her. He'd been guarding her. He'd been protecting the people of Bronwal against the *Volkhvy* princess in their midst.

She was as an injured and unconscious woman who'd been attacked, unprovoked, by a vicious feral wolf. But she was also a witch. Soren saw her as a danger to his family.

"What do you think she can do in this state?" Patrice interrupted. The housekeeper came from a time when boxing a child's ears was always an option. She looked as if she would be fully capable of boxing an adult's ears, as well. She stood near her patient with her fisted hands on her hips. Anna blinked moisture back when she realized the tiny round woman was standing between her and Soren as Soren stood between her and his people.

"It's okay, Patrice," Anna said. She refused to cause problems between the servant and the man who had once been Patrice's master. The old housekeeper might live in the modern world now, but it would be almost impossible for her to leave the castle to seek a life elsewhere. She would have to live out her days here. Anna wanted those days to happy. "I have extra gloves in my backpack. If you fetch them for me, I'll put them on."

"Her bag was lashed to the dappled gray's saddle when it arrived at the stable last night," Soren said.

"I'll go and see where the groomsmen put it," Patrice said.

"I'm glad Lev let them come home," Anna said as the housekeeper headed toward the door. Patrice paused beside Soren and glared at him, but he didn't lower his eyes. He faced her stoically, completely unaffected by her anger. The housekeeper huffed and stomped away, but not before she glanced back at Anna as if to say she had no patience with red wolves in their human form.

"Even with the gloves, you can't stay here," Soren said. But he looked at her pale face and the blood on her bandages again as he spoke. The pain in her shoulder and arm hadn't faded. In fact, it was even worse now that she was wide-awake. It seemed as if every puncture and tear the white wolf's giant teeth had caused pulsed with its own heartbeat. Not only that, but the tingling from the Ether's energy she'd grown used to channeling over the past months was virtually nonexistent. She was probably too weak from her fever to absorb the power she could usually tap into now that her mother had taught her how.

The gloves wouldn't be necessary. They would only be a gesture of goodwill. One that hurt her to make, because the need for the gloves was symbolic of Soren's renewed distrust now that she had proved she was her mother's daughter.

Did he truly hate the Ether that much?

While they waited for Patrice to return, Soren stepped into the room. Her pain would have distracted her from his movements if he hadn't continued stepping closer and closer to her bed. When she understood that he wasn't going to stop, Anna gripped the downy quilt in fisted handfuls on either side of her hips even though the move increased the pain in her shoulder. Soren noticed. Of course he noticed. His intense amber gaze seemed to see everything about her, but especially the emotions she tried to hide.

"I'm not going to hurt you," Soren said.

He had hurt her with every word, glance and touch since she'd returned to Bronwal. He didn't need to know it. She was vulnerable enough as is. She couldn't hide her physical pain from him. All she could do was hope her emotional pain was hers to experience alone.

"I'll leave as soon as I can," Anna said. "The emerald sword will have to wait until I'm fully recovered. I'm in no shape to confront the Dark *Volkhvy* right now. I can't... I don't feel the energy of the Ether at all," she continued.

For years, she'd thought she was nothing but a human orphan. She hadn't succumbed to the Ether, either physically or mentally, and that was some indication that she was special, but she'd never suspected she had *Volkhvy* blood. She'd been a tough survivor with an enchanted wolf companion. No more. No less. Until Vasilisa began to teach her how to summon the Ether's energy. Now she was hurt and she felt more vulnerable than she'd ever felt. She didn't have her red wolf or her *Volkhvy* abilities.

"I'm sorry he hurt you. I didn't protect you from him as I promised I would," Soren said. He had moved to stand directly beside her bed. She looked up at him and didn't know how to smooth his furrowed brow.

"You didn't know he would bite me. He never has before," Anna said.

"But you knew. Or at least you knew you weren't safe. You tried to warn me," Soren said. "Now you're hurt." Then something changed in his face. The tightness of his jaw eased. His forehead smoothed. "You don't feel the Ether. At all?"

His voice had dropped to a whisper. He spoke quietly, as if he feared his regular voice would wake up her *Volkhvy* abilities to come between them again. But she didn't expect him to reach and smooth her rumpled brown curls back from her face. She wasn't prepared for his warm, rough fingers to linger on her cheek or softly caress the curve of her jaw.

"I'm weak, but that doesn't change what I am. I'm still a witch," Anna said. Her voice was breathless. He'd stolen all the oxygen from the room with the intimate brush of his thumb on her chin. He looked deeply into her eyes and she almost succumbed to the weakness of wanting to close her lids and feel his touch. Instead, she forced herself to acknowledge the speculation in his gaze. His touch only lingered because there was no Ether-fueled spark between them.

What flared was fully human, with no effort on her part at all. For now, she was no threat to a castle protected by enchanted wolves who could eat a normal woman for breakfast.

"You're so pale. I thought you might die. If Lev had killed you…" Soren said.

Anna couldn't breathe. Between his words, she read more than her weakened heart could take. He revealed the possibilities that would have existed. The affection he might have felt for the regular woman she could never hope to reclaim. He had willingly touched her because there was no arc of energy sparking between his fingers and her skin. She allowed the touch to continue because she wanted to imagine what might have been.

If she hadn't been a witch and the curse had been broken so that Bell and her red wolf turned human could be together again.

His fingers were as soft as a butterfly's wings against her skin. She moistened her lips. She shivered as her flesh grew sensitive. First goose bumps and then a rush of heat rose in response to the masculine brush of his hand on her face. She consciously breathed, in and out, so she wouldn't grow faint. She was already light-headed from her injuries. His touch magnified that. Even more so because he was obviously savoring this stolen moment to enjoy the skin-to-skin touch they were forbidden to indulge forever after.

Because of his brothers.

Because of her blood.

She would recover. She would reclaim her *Volkhvy* abilities. But, for right now, he traced the lines of her face—cheek, jaw, chin—until he came to the swell of her moistened lips. He paused and their eyes met. Oh, there was a spark there. A completely natural spark needing no help from *Volkhvy* enchantment at all. It didn't repel him. In fact, he drew in a shuddering breath of his own, as if this was the spark he'd craved. One that didn't threaten his home and family but only his heart.

The full, rough pad of his thumb caressed her lower lip.

He teased from one corner to the other, and the tingling that claimed her came from the energy she and Soren created, no Ether necessary.

"Soren," she sighed. Her pain was a constant throbbing, but it was at the edges of her consciousness now. Pleasure supplanted it. She focused on Soren's touch. She drowned in his darkened eyes. She ached for him to kiss her before they were interrupted by Patrice or by the Ether's return. It would return. She was an injured witch, not a human. This was no solution to their problem. His willingness to touch her now was a bittersweet opportunity at best.

But it was one she couldn't reject.

When he slowly leaned toward her face, she didn't take the time he gave her to protest. She used it to anticipate instead. His lips coming closer and closer. The rising hunger in his eyes as he realized she didn't want to stop him. She gasped when his mouth replaced his thumb. His hand moved to hold her face, but it was a gentle hold, one she could have escaped if she'd wanted to.

She didn't.

She kissed him back instead, sucking on his lips and his tongue and thrusting her own into the silky sweetness of his mouth.

He growled, deep and low in his chest, and he pressed into the kiss as if he hadn't ordered her away from the castle only moments before. This was as close to Bell as she was going to come for him ever again. It was both tragic that he wanted her so badly without her powers and a thrill to experience how much he desired her. It was only temporary, and it was because his brother had almost killed her. But it was irresistible to senses that had craved his taste and touch for so long.

"I am Anna, the Light *Volkhvy* princess. This changes nothing between us. I will recover. We will destroy the

sword," she said against his lips. He pulled back enough
to open his eyes and look into hers. She was immediately
cold, but his eyes were still full of heat.

"I know," Soren said. "Right now I don't care."

Anna had almost died. He thought he'd already dealt
with the loss of Bell. It wasn't until he carried a dying
Anna with her blood soaking warm and thick into his shirt
that he'd known what a lie that had been.

In his mind, he'd imagined them almost as two different women—there was the girl he'd known for centuries,
his most treasured companion against the cold of the Ether
and the darkness of a cursed castle home. And there was
the witch, a woman who had the potential to destroy all
that he had reclaimed from the Ether—including the companion he'd once held so dear.

Only they weren't two different women. Bell had never
existed. The woman he rushed to save was the only woman
he'd ever known. Anna was simply more—more complicated, more dangerous, more enticing than before. It was
the allure that he couldn't understand. He might be an enchanted wolf shape-shifter cursed by the Light *Volkhvy*
queen, but he wasn't interested in flirting with a darkness
he'd already faced down for centuries.

And yet, he'd watched Anna as she slept, a deep, unconscious sleep, and he'd wanted her to wake. He'd willed
her to open her eyes with the same energy he should have
reserved for willing her away, far away, where she could
no longer threaten his family with powers she could barely
control.

His vigil should have been for Ivan and Elena and their
unborn child. He should have guarded against the witch
who had come between his feral brother and salvation
again and again.

Instead, he'd paced the hallway outside Anna's door, waiting for her to wake up. He'd railed at his brother's instinctive savagery against the *Volkhvy*. He'd fought the urge to hunt his brother down—not to save him, but to hurt him for hurting Anna. He'd stayed outside her door only because he'd longed to see her vivid green eyes again. He'd ached when she'd moaned or cried out as if her pain was his.

And once she'd regained consciousness, he hadn't been able to resist touching her.

He needed to feel her awake and alive. He needed to accept that Anna was the woman he'd always known. The temporary absence of Ether energy had allowed it. He hadn't risked encouraging the magical connection between them. He hadn't tempted fate or the sword's Call or the vacuum of the Ether.

He'd only tempted himself and Anna. She'd leaned into his hand when he'd touched her face. She'd trembled beneath his fingers and then, when he saw that he didn't increase her pain or distress her, she'd hungrily returned his kiss.

Their lips had melded.

Only lips. No Ether. No enchanted sword. Just his mouth and hers.

She looked up at him now as if she was shattered by the momentary intimacy. He understood. His breath came quick and his heart pounded. His body temperature had spiked, and he wanted nothing more than to kiss her again.

I am Anna, the Light Volkhvy *princess. This changes nothing between us. I will recover. We will destroy the sword.*

Understanding slammed into his chest. She thought he had wanted to kiss her because of her absence of power. Truth was, he'd wanted to kiss her all along. He'd proved that in the forest when he hadn't been able to resist a quick, hot taste. The absence of Ether energy only made it easier to do without his conscious interrupting.

"I wasn't sure you'd wake up. This is me being glad that you have," Soren confessed. "You. Anna, the Light *Volkhvy* princess. I have no misconceptions about who and what you are, but I'm sorry that Lev attacked you and I'm glad you survived."

Her uninjured arm came up off the bed. She'd released the quilt in favor of touching the side of his face. He still leaned over her. She easily ran her fingers along where beard ended and cheek began. Only that. And the simple touch caused him to freeze and combust at the same time. He didn't move. He didn't blink. The very air stilled in his lungs while she touched his cheek and looked deep into his eyes.

He closed them against her. Not to savor her touch, although with his eyes closed the feeling of her fingers on his skin intensified. He did it to hide behind his eyelids. This moment between them changed nothing. She'd said it herself and he agreed. She didn't need to see that it pained him to kiss her and then let her go. She was the same woman he'd always known, and that changed nothing between them because she was also a dangerous witch capable of using her *Volkhvy* power against his family. They'd suffered too much because of the *Volkhvy* already.

A light step sounded in the hallway, and Patrice came into the room with Anna's backpack in her arms. Anna dropped her hand and Soren stepped back from the bed, but not before the housekeeper noticed their intimate positioning. She arched a brow in Soren's direction, but she didn't mention what she might have disturbed. She simply walked around the middle Romanov and placed the back-pack beside Anna on the bed.

"I thought you might like to have the whole pack with you," Patrice said.

Anna reached with her good arm to claim the bag and looked inside it for her gloves. Patrice helped her unzip the pocket she indicated so she could easily retrieve the spare black leather accessories.

"If it will make you feel better, I'll wear these until I can leave," Anna said. She didn't look at Soren as she spoke, and her cheeks were hot. Maybe he would think it was her fever and not because she hated how badly she wanted to leave her skin uncovered. Not for witchy reasons. But purely in case she might be able to touch him again.

"You're flushed," Patrice said. She reached to help Anna with the gloves, but when she finished with her uninjured arm and moved to the one with bandages, she stopped. Her hands felt icy on Anna's forearm. "This arm is on fire and the bleeding hasn't subsided. I need to change these bandages already."

"You freshened those just before she woke up," Soren said grimly. He reached to touch Anna's arm, and his whole body stiffened in response. He looked from his hands on her fiery skin to her heated face. "Something is very wrong."

Anna didn't need to be told. The room swam before her, and her heart thudded painfully in her chest.

"Get back. Let me help her," Patrice ordered. She reached for some implements she'd left in a basket on a nearby table. It resembled a sewing basket until a closer inspection revealed the kind of equipment a triage nurse might employ...if that nurse had been trained in medieval times.

Using a large pair of scissors, Patrice cut away at the

bandages she'd wound so carefully only an hour ago. She cried out at the wounds she revealed. They weren't healing. In fact, they were much worse.

"Ivan needs to send one of the *Volkhvy* workers to us. Now. Ordinary methods are not dealing with the white wolf's bites," Patrice said.

She turned to look at Soren. He'd backed several paces away from the evidence that her arm wasn't healing.

"Elena is pregnant and he sent all the *Volkhvy* away," Soren said.

The bed seemed to whirl, but Anna grabbed the quilt again to hang on. So it hadn't been Soren who wanted her gone as soon as possible—it had been Ivan. Elena was expecting a baby. The news seemed much more important than her arm. Bronwal was healing, even if she wasn't. A fierce joy suffused her pounding heart. Because of the baby. Not because Soren had ordered her away in obedience to the alpha wolf. She was sure he would have wanted her gone, baby or not. She couldn't allow herself to hope that he would ever soften toward her. He might not want her dead. He might accept that she was the woman he'd always known, only more powerful.

But he would never welcome her back to Bronwal.

Besides, welcome or not, it wouldn't matter if she didn't survive.

"There's nothing more I can do. These wounds aren't infected, but they're not healing, either. She lost a lot of blood. *Volkhvy* blood. It will take a *Volkhvy* to save her," Patrice said. She had placed fresh bandages around Anna's shoulder and upper arm. The pain of her manipulations combined with Anna's dizziness was almost enough to cause her to pass out again.

Soren stood tall at the door. Even blurry he looked muscular and capable and almost as reliable as the red wolf.

He wasn't. He hadn't been since he'd shifted back into his human form. He was volatile, unpredictable and obsessed with the white wolf's fate.

He was also her only hope.

Ivan and Elena needed to focus on their baby. She couldn't expect them to help her, and Patrice wasn't even a real nurse. She'd done her best with the resources she had at hand, but she couldn't heal a witch.

"There are no *Volkhvy* in Bronwal to come to Anna's aid. So I'll take Anna to the *Volkhvy,*" Soren said.

Soren would never seek help from witches on her behalf. Hallucination meant that she was worse off than she'd imagined. She'd survived a curse with hardly so much as a cold. It was hard to accept that the white wolf who had survived with her—if not as a friend or a brother, then at least as an ally—had killed her.

Chapter 9

Ivan had wanted to destroy the mirror Vasilisa had used to travel from her island off the coast of Scotland to Bronwal. It was a powerful portal that channeled the energy of the Ether in a concentrated manner. The whole world belonged to the Light *Volkhvy* queen, but with the portal, in only one step, she could leave her home and invade theirs. Elena had encouraged him to leave it functional for Bronwal's sake after the curse was broken. The Light witches Vasilisa had sent to help them modernize and renovate the castle had used the portal to hasten their work.

Anna's only hope was Vasilisa's mirror. If Ivan had decided to go through with his plan to destroy it once he'd discovered Elena's pregnancy...

Soren put all thoughts of what he was about to do out of his head. He focused on the feverish, unconscious woman in his arms and the hope that the mirror was still in the chapel. Vasilisa had claimed the abandoned room as her audience chamber during the centuries that she'd come, once every Cycle, to see the Romanovs suffer for what their father had done.

Soren and Lev had always stood watch outside the chapel door while Ivan had been forced to face their tormentor for her pleasure. This time Soren approached the vaulted chamber alone. There was no time to tell Ivan what he planned to do. Besides, he couldn't risk his alpha deciding to stop him. Best to barrel ahead with his thoughts focused on saving the woman—the witch—in his arms.

The elaborately carved door was open when he finally reached it. Anna hadn't made a sound since she'd moaned when he'd picked her up from her sickbed. Patrice hadn't interfered. She knew this was Anna's only chance to recover. The route had been familiar to him even though he traversed it on two legs instead of four. He didn't have to look at the hallways and corridors—he navigated by habit. His attention had been wholly focused on Anna's pale face. Two bright patches of color high on her cheeks stood out starkly against her white skin. Her rosy lips and her dark brown brows also startled in contrast.

She would look like a perfect sleeping beauty if it weren't for the dark blood staining her shoulder and arm where her injuries had already soaked through the fresh bandages once more.

Near death, not sleeping.

They could never be together, not as the sword intended them to be, but the idea that she would leave this world before him, when he'd protected her for so long, was unfathomable. He could sense her letting go. He cradled her close to his broad chest and his pounding heart, but he couldn't offer his ferocious life for hers. The bone-deep awareness he had of her deteriorating condition propelled him toward the one thing he'd intended to avoid for the rest of his life: the Ether.

He held his breath as he stepped across the threshold of the chapel into the gem-colored light of the sun filtered through the stained glass windows that ringed the vaulted chamber. The soft light fell on Anna's face, brushing it with a colorful palette that didn't come from within.

His vibrant companion who had been the only light in the darkness of his existence for centuries was almost extinguished.

Soren looked from Anna's face to the mirror that stood in the center of the room. Ivan hadn't destroyed it…yet. He'd sent the Light *Volkhvy* away. He must have intended to close the portal for good once they were all gone. But not yet, thank God. Not yet.

Anna was too weak to take herself to Vasilisa's island. Soren had to help.

He was no witch, but Vasilisa had manipulated his family's genes. There was *Volkhvy* enchantment in his blood. He hoped his shape-shifter blood combined with Anna's *Volkhvy* heritage would be enough to help him use the mirror to get her to her mother.

Soren crossed the room in several large strides and stood in front of the glass. His and Anna's reflections shimmered as if he looked into water instead of a mirror's flat surface. He couldn't see their faces and shapes distinctly. He and she blended into one figure as the silvery ripples flowed and swirled.

"Wait," a loud voice said from the doorway as Soren lifted his leg to step into the vertical river of seemingly molten glass.

He looked back over his shoulder to see Ivan Romanov stride into the room. His elder brother's shoulders were almost as broad as the doorway. Soren's chest tightened when Ivan paused and crossed himself, even though the chapel hadn't been used for religious services since their mother had died. Ivan had been the one constant in Soren's life for as long as he could remember. He'd been the last Romanov standing even after Soren had followed his brother into a shift he'd thought would be eternal.

None of them would still be alive if it hadn't been for Ivan. And the curse wouldn't have been broken if it hadn't been for his mate, Elena Pavlova, the tiny dancer with a warrior's heart who had crossed the centuries and climbed a mountain to find the black wolf.

"Don't try to stop me, Ivan. She's dying. I have to save her," Soren said.

"Vasilisa can't be trusted. I'm not sure about her daughter. But I can't risk Elena and the baby. The mirror has to be destroyed. The portal has to be closed. I came here to close it," Ivan said. But he stayed where he was. He didn't cross the room. His hands were two large fists, but he held them down and still at his sides.

"Once I've taken her through, then you can destroy it. I understand. I want you to protect the baby and Bronwal. Protect Elena. It's what we were made to do," Soren said.

"You don't know what you'll find on the other side. Vasilisa's island is hidden from the outside world. You won't be welcome. She made us her champions, but we were never the same as the Light *Volkhvy*. We were her monsters. Her useful pets. Our father was wrong. He never should have gone against her to try to steal the throne. He shouldn't have destroyed the village that sheltered Bell. He shouldn't have kidnapped her," Ivan said. He stepped forward one pace, then two as he continued, "But he did it for a reason. He wanted more. He challenged the Light *Volkhvy* queen because being her champion wasn't enough. He wanted to be king. *You'll be in danger there even if you go to save Anna.* The curse might be broken, but Vasilisa is still the queen. She says she regrets what she's done, but she will always see us as a threat to her rule. So she will always be a threat to those we love."

Soren looked down at Anna's flushed cheeks. Her breath still came through her parted lips, but it was light and quick, barely noticeable. Ivan had paused again, but two more strides would bring him close enough to stand in the way. Soren was big and strong. The *Volkhvy* manipulation of his genetic makeup had caused him to be over six feet tall. He'd been born in a time when men regularly fought and died in hand-to-hand combat. His time spent in wolf form had only increased muscle mass that had already been developed over years of hard training.

Ivan was bigger.

But it wasn't his size that made him the alpha. He commanded respect and honor beyond his height and breadth because he was the head of the Romanov family, and he had earned that title over decades of continued dedication and determination. He was Bronwal. He was home. He had been home to Soren even after all hope of home was gone.

"I'm going. Destroy the mirror after I'm gone," Soren said quietly.

He defied his alpha to save the woman in his arms. He would risk his life for hers, too. Without pause. Soren accepted the inevitability of having to give her up, but he would never let her die.

"Let them go," Elena said. He and Ivan turned to face her. She stood in the kaleidoscope light of a thousand chips of colored glass forming saints' figures, holding the hilt of the sapphire sword in her hand. It wasn't drawn. The blade hung in a scabbard at her waist. Its sheathed tip reached beyond her knee. The sapphire winked with a gleam of sparkling blue that came and went with her every subtle move. "He has to save her. The emerald sword has chosen."

Soren's attention flew from Elena to his brother. Ivan's whole body stiffened. He turned back toward the mirror and the man who held the dying witch to his chest.

"That isn't why I'm helping her. I rejected the emerald sword a long time ago," Soren said. He turned to fully face Ivan and Elena. With his back toward the mirror, he spoke directly to his brother. "It won't choose my mate." His words were a promise, but he took a step backward. He wasn't lying. Anna would never be his mate, but he would always be her protector.

"The sword doesn't decide, Soren. The sword *reveals*," Elena said.

The cold embrace of the mirror began to absorb his body.

"No!" Ivan exclaimed. He leaped forward, and his leap, even in his human form, was a sight to behold.

It was the last thing Soren saw as he calmly stepped backward one more time into the swirling glass of the mirror's face. It flowed over him and Anna like thick frigid mercury. The high pressure of its sucking embrace stole his breath. It enveloped with a heaviness that was a squeeze, not a splash. As it flowed, it sought access. It rose up over his back and shoulders. Liquid filled his ears and spread up over his cheeks and beard to flood his nose and mouth with suffocating fluid.

He didn't fight. Anna didn't move. The silvery liquid flowed over her, as well. He watched as long as he could. He looked down at her face until his eyes were submerged and he couldn't see anymore.

Like a man who had filled his pockets with rocks before jumping off a cliff into a winter river, he merely accepted as the mirror swept him away. For Anna. He could no longer feel her against his chest. His body had become the liquid mercury that consumed it. The mirror took them, but it was the energy from the Ether it channeled that swallowed them, body and soul.

When she channeled the power of the Ether with her *Volkhvy* abilities, Anna was in control—or as controlled as she could be with her level of experience. She'd been as traumatized as everyone else by the Ether that claimed Bronwal again and again during the curse. She'd been powerless against the frigid vacuum that caused them to dematerialize. She hadn't known the ability to use the Ether's energy was in her blood.

Even unconscious, she felt when the power of the Ether swallowed her. She felt as the man who held her disappeared. That mattered more than her own disappearance, for some reason. It was a nightmare she had to stop, but she couldn't wake up.

Vasilisa had taught her for months on the island. In grueling training sessions, Anna had used every ounce of her strength to harness and then begin to manipulate the energy the Ether expelled. It was worse than playing with fire. It was inviting the fire into your soul. Except the power didn't burn. It filled and froze. The trick was in not letting the energy from the Ether's Dark vacuum crowd everything and everyone else out.

And, most importantly, keeping a warmth for humanity in your heart.

Her mother had lost nearly all that warmth during the centuries she'd thought her daughter had been murdered by Vladimir Romanov. It was only in discovering Anna alive and in seeing the witchblood prince completely filled by the Ether's Dark energy that Vasilisa had come back from the cold.

Power could fill to the point that it overflowed and consumed.

Anna tried to scream. She tried to summon the lessons her mother had taught her. But she'd lost too much of her *Volkhvy* blood. She was near death, and even the threat of her red wolf's annihilation couldn't wake her.

The Ether had always claimed them with an inevitability they had learned not to fight. She had often sat on the ramparts of Bronwal with her wolf as the sun set on the last day of the month during their materialization. They hadn't had to speak. *Farewell for now until we meet again and again and again* pounded in their hearts.

This time was different. She was too sick to understand why it was happening. She only knew Soren hated the Ether and he'd vowed to never be taken by it again, no matter what. She willed her dying cells to fight for him, to help him, but her abilities wouldn't respond.

The cool nothingness of the Ether would have been soothing. She hurt. From wounds seen and unseen. But her resistance caused white-hot agony to consume her instead. The last drops of the powerful blood she'd inherited from Vasilisa didn't help her help Soren escape. The last thing she knew before she vanished was agony—for failing her red wolf and for trying to reject the Ether that would save her.

Chapter 10

He materialized on the edge of a cliff with tears on his face, but the wind coming off the sea dried them. It was a stiff wind, stinging and harsh. His hair whipped around his face, each strand like a russet lash. He was able to see through the wild mane to the woman who had materialized with him. He hadn't let her go, by God. Even when he could no longer feel his hands and arms. In the Ether, you were nothing, but if you were strong you could hold on.

He'd always held before.

His nightmares rose from the fear of not being sure he always would.

He was on his knees. He got to his feet as the wind fell. The weather around him was suddenly still and calm. He'd materialized to a cold, windswept ocean, but he rose to the warm embrace of a magically created Mediterranean climate. He'd heard of Vasilisa's island, Krajina. She maintained its secrecy and artificial atmosphere with her

Volkhvy abilities. The mirror must have disrupted the spell long enough to deposit him and Anna, and then the spell had reformed. He'd had only a glimpse of a stormy sea. Now he looked out over a calm, sunlit bay.

Anna's skin appeared worse than pale. Her cheeks were translucent in the bright light. With all his strength, he was powerless to save her from the damage his brother's bite had done.

And still he held on.

He turned away from the cliff to search for the beings he couldn't trust. He had no other options. Nowhere else to go. He stumbled to a halt after several strides, because the Light *Volkhvy* queen rode to meet them.

He didn't recognize the creature that bore her on its back. No doubt there were other species beyond man and wolf that she'd tampered with in order to enslave them.

Like a horse, her cream-colored mount had four legs. Unlike a horse, a golden mane encircled its head, and its tail was a short starburst of similar gold bristles. Its shiny brown hooves were as big as dinner plates, and it stood taller than the black wolf would be if he were here. Soren recalled tales he'd heard as a child of a mythological beast called an Indrik, but this beast had no horn on its head and it made no sound. It also moved slowly, as if it was very old. He noted gray hair mingled in its gold mane and tail.

"You did this?" Vasilisa asked as the beast she rode halted and she slid off its back.

She was dressed in a long white gown that blended with the white hair flowing over her back and shoulders. The absence of color startled against the green vegetation behind her and the blue sky overhead.

"No," Anna said. The sound was so soft he sensed it more than he heard it out loud. He looked from Vasilisa to Anna's face. The queen continued to approach. She might strike him dead when she reached his side. But he could only care about how weak Anna sounded and what it must have cost her to speak.

"Shh, you're home. Your mother is here," Soren said.

Vasilisa stopped a foot away at his words. He could feel her intense attention on his face. But he didn't look at the queen. He watched Anna instead. For signs of life, to memorize her last breaths—he wasn't sure which. As he stared at Anna, four more *Volkhvy* arrived. They pulled a cart with large wooden wheels by two handles on either side. They were big and burly witches, but the cart moved inch by inch up the rise to the cliff.

"Lev attacked her. We bound her wounds, but they continued to bleed. There were no witches left at Bronwal. So I brought her to you," Soren said.

"Ivan hasn't destroyed the mirror," Vasilisa said. She was a breathtakingly beautiful woman. Her white hair was shot through with silver strands that caused it to shimmer and gleam in the sun. Her eyes flashed, dark yet bright. The sunlight glittered on her pupils, causing a silvery outline around the obsidian edges. Her face was unlined, but there was harshness to her high cheekbones and the set of her jaw.

She was unaged, but she didn't look young. Vasilisa somehow carried all the years of the curse on her shoulders. He noted the weight as she moved closer to touch Anna's pale face. She was no longer graceful. Every step she took seemed an effort to push against something trying to hold her back—guilt, time or the Ether's hunger? Had she used too much of its energy for too long?

"He let me use it one last time," Soren said. "By now it's crushed beneath his paws."

The queen's dark eyes quickly cut upward to look at his face. He could feel the weight she carried pressing against him. He didn't back down, although his first instinct was one of retreat. He stood. He cradled Anna against his chest and he met the Light witch's eyes. The cart came to a stop several yards away.

"You risk your life for hers," Vasilisa said. It wasn't a question. It was a statement of fact. His life was in danger on Krajina. His brother had attacked the queen's daughter. Once again, the Romanovs had tried to take the life of her child. If Anna died—and maybe even if she survived— he would be the first Romanov to feel the Light *Volkhvy* queen's wrath…again.

"Help her," he said. "You can deal with me later."

"Bring her. Quickly. As only the red wolf can," Vasilisa commanded.

In the artificial light of an impossibly warm sun, Soren froze. He'd vowed never to risk the shift again. He hadn't risked it even when he hunted for Lev over the hills and forests of the Carpathian Mountains. Two legs had been a hardship, but he'd needed the pain and difficulty to distract him from the constant nightmares…and his memories of Bell.

"You weren't wrong. She is dying. And I can't help her here on this cliff," Vasilisa said. She turned and pointed toward the interior of the island, where he could see a distant garden surrounding a sprawling Mediterranean-style palace of stucco and tile. How much of the Ether's energy did Vasilisa channel to maintain her hidden island home?

He had no choice. He'd faced the Ether and he'd returned to himself again. He would return to his human form again once he used his wolf to help Anna. He moved to place his burden in the cart Vasilisa's men had dragged slowly up the hill. It was no relief to let her go and step away. The back of the cart was lined with pillows and soft blankets, but he missed her against his chest. He couldn't feel her heartbeat or see her slight respiration. As he backed away, Anna looked like she was in the deepest of sleeps.

She looked like she'd never wake up again.

Vasilisa mounted her horselike creature. It was too old and slow to pull the cart. The big witches who had pulled it up the hill were already headed back down. Soren had already made the decision to shift. He blinked. The earth trembled. Down below, the sea churned as the island quaked.

The shift was brutally physical. It wasn't pretty. Bones shifted and reknit themselves into a giant canine form. Skin stretched and changed and, in his case, russet fur spread across his cheeks and chest, arms and legs until he was covered. The pain was intense, but so was the relief. The wolf was always there, deep within his heart. Every beat risked its escape. Every space in between beats was a moment's longing for the wild that could be.

The howl was inevitable. It was always only a matter of where and when, not if. It wasn't until he leaped for the front of the cart to position his giant wolf self between the handles that he understood the real danger: as the red wolf, the loyalty he felt toward Anna was as ferocious as it had ever been. It was less diminished by human reason. It was cemented in this physical form as muscle memory he would have to fight.

But not now.

For now, he unleashed it.

The cart was nothing to him. The tiny woman in it not much more weight than she'd been as a child. The only thing that slowed him down was the care he had to take over rocks and bumps in the terrain. Other than those, they flew.

Soren slowed when they reached the garden that surrounded the palace. The sprawling structure was located on a rise above this tangle. He carefully made his way around the lush rosebushes that grew in a wilderness of thorns. Once they arrived at the base of a winding stairway that led up to the palace doors, he stopped. The stairway was lined with black banners on silver poles. Each banner held white markings he couldn't decipher. Some language he didn't understand. It was Vasilisa who picked Anna up from the back of the cart and carried her upstairs. The creature she'd ridden had almost kept up with Soren in spite of its age.

If she hadn't really needed his speed and strength to pull Anna to the palace, why had she manipulated him into the shift?

Vasilisa carried Anna up the stairway. Her white skirts trailed behind her gracefully as if she floated upward, step by step. Soren followed. As he walked up the stairway, he reclaimed his human form. His physical wolf attributes— hair, fangs, claws—disintegrated and rose from his newly reformed human shape as a fine smoky mist. He ignored the pain.

The soul of the red wolf, unlike its accoutrements, settled deep in his chest to inhabit the dark reaches of his heart.

Between one step and the next, he reached for one of the banners that flanked the stairs to wrap himself in a makeshift robe. He was comfortable with his nakedness. As a shape-shifter, he would have to be. But he was entering Anna's mother's home. Until he could find something better, the banner would have to do.

He didn't feel vulnerable in his human skin, but he did feel exposed as he followed Vasilisa into a great hall with a high, arched ceiling and black iron accents on pillars and posts. He couldn't hide his concern for Anna as well as he'd hidden his nudity.

Vasilisa paid him no notice. She walked through the hall and into an antechamber that led to another flight of curving stairs. When they finally reached the top, they came to a large round room lit by streaming beams of sunlight that poured through a faceted glass dome that formed its ceiling. Only then did he stop. His gaze tracked over a myriad of keepsakes he recognized from years of familiarity. The shelves and tables in the room as well as the windowsills and corners were stacked with Anna's magpie collection from the Bronwal aviary.

This was Anna's new bedchamber in her mother's palace.

Like the aviary, it was bright and ringed with windows that were open to the air and sun. Through those arched openings, he could see the ocean far below. It kissed the sandy shores of Krajina with soft curls of foamy white. But Anna's bedroom also had heavy doors and shutters that when closed would provide a solid defense against intruders.

She'd always been brave but cautious. Bold but careful.

Vasilisa placed Anna on a large canopied bed draped with diaphanous clouds of ivory fabric and jewel-toned silken coverlets and pillows. It was a bed fit for a princess, and more than anything else he'd seen on the island, more than the luxurious palace or the magical beast or the enchanted weather, the bed made him acknowledge that the waif he'd known was gone.

Bell had made do with dusty, deteriorating bedclothes and the empty aviary with its rough stone floor. She'd looked out on cold sunset mountains. She'd shivered and starved and barely survived.

And she'd loved still.

"I am your maker and Anna carries my blood in her veins. The white wolf's attack was an abomination against the Light power I used to create him. That's why she won't heal without my help. The enchantment I worked to create the Romanov wolves was tainted by the darkness of Lev's violent actions against my daughter. His bite carried with it the Ether itself poisoned by his hatred as if it was a venom," Vasilisa said. "I can cleanse her, but I'll need your help."

"I'm no longer your champion," Soren said. He looked at the pale woman on the bed instead of the queen he addressed. The drape of the borrowed banner was forgotten to sag low around his waist and one shoulder, but it was the focus of his attention that exposed him more than his bare skin.

He couldn't look away. Or turn away. He could only tell Vasilisa with his words and actions that he was here for Anna, not for her, and even that was temporary. He would never be tied to the *Volkhvy* again.

"Be that as it may, you shifted to bring her to the palace, because you will always be *her* champion whether you realize it or not," Vasilisa said. She held one hand toward him with her palm facing up and fingers spread. She gestured for him to take her outstretched hand and waited.

His attention had left Anna at Vasilisa's shocking claim. The shift had been a test of his loyalty to her daughter. He was too surprised to protest. Besides, Anna was dying. Now wasn't the time to argue that he and her daughter had decided to destroy the sword that tried to bind them together.

"What would you have me do?" Soren asked.

If he could fight the poison with tooth and claw, he would. Whether or not it gave Vasilisa misconceptions about his and Anna's relationship.

"She's lost too much blood. We need to cleanse her wounds so they can knit," Vasilisa said. A slight sea breeze came through the windows, gently shifting the gauzy bed hangings and the queen's hair. The silvery strands sparkled with the movement in the sun. "There's no hate in you for her. We can use your blood to undo what your brother has done."

"No," Soren said. He didn't hate Anna, but he did hate the *Volkhvy*. He had to. Vasilisa had tortured the Romanovs for centuries. "My blood will only hurt her more."

"You know your own heart better as the red wolf than you do as a man, Soren Romanov," Vasilisa scolded, obviously impatient with his hesitation. "You came here so that I could save my daughter's life. Let's get on with it before it's too late."

Soren forced his legs to carry him to Anna's side.

"Anger at injustice isn't hate. You're angry and you have every right to be. But you do not hate as your brother hates. He is the one Romanov that I wronged the most. I can never make right what was done to him. I took his wife and child. I drove him into the wilderness of his despair. For that, I never expect forgiveness. But you…you don't hate as your brother does. One day you'll come out on the other side of your anger, and you'll find yourself much as you ever were."

Vasilisa took one of his arms in her hands. It looked impossibly large and savagely scarred and muscled compared to her pale, soft limbs and graceful fingers. But he misjudged her savagery based on her feminine appearance. When she sliced his wrist with a sharp, pointed ring of sterling silver thorns she wore around the third finger of her left hand, he sucked air in between his clenched teeth in surprise.

Crimson blood welled up from the shallow cut, and the queen urged him to move. She positioned his bleeding wrist over Anna's bandaged wounds, where her *Volkhvy* blood had soaked through. His blood formed a scarlet tear-drop before it fell to splash on Anna's shoulder. It hissed and bubbled as it soaked into the bandages. Several more teardrops of blood fell until steam rose from Anna's shoulder. As the steam rose, Vasilisa released his arm and began to speak in a low voice, muttering words in a language he didn't understand. Soren backed away as Vasilisa reached to place her hands on Anna's steaming shoulder. The glow she'd summoned wasn't green like Anna's. It was purple, like the color of the mourning dresses she'd worn for centuries.

Anna cried out, and Soren clenched his fists. He was helpless to prevent her pain just as he'd been helpless to save her from the curse her mother had worked or the impossible choices the emerald sword forced them to make.

Whether he hated Anna's pain or not, he had to save his brother. The white wolf's poisonous bite was only more evidence that Lev was nearly too far gone. Soren and Anna had no future together, regardless of what the queen might think or how she manipulated them with her magic.

His only future was in saving his brother and protecting his family from further *Volkhvy* manipulations.

Anna wasn't welcome at Bronwal.

And Ivan had every right to protect his wife and child.

Soren watched as the color returned to the Light *Volkhvy* princess's cheeks, and then he held the banner around his hips and slipped away.

Chapter 11

It took three days on the island for Anna to recover her strength. By then, her shoulder no longer needed bandages and Lev's bites had nearly healed. There were only pale pink marks where the ugly puncture wounds had been.

She hadn't seen Soren since the day they arrived. From beneath barely opened eyelids, she'd watched him shift to pull her cart back to the palace. She'd seen him sacrifice his blood for her. Even near death, she'd been struck by his large, naked form in the doorway to her room, covered only by a torn banner he'd draped over one shoulder and around his lean, powerful hips. The drops of blood he'd shed for her had shone brightly against his muscular forearm. She'd been dying, but he'd seemed so vulnerable in that moment, nearly nude and his lifeblood bared for her.

The healing had burned through her like cold fire. Soren's blood was the heat. Her mother's power was the ice. She'd opened her eyes within moments, but Soren had already backed away. She watched him leave the room. His attention had been focused on her face. He hadn't met her eyes. What she'd seen in his had shot more arrows into her soul.

He'd brought her through the Ether. He'd given her his blood. But he still rejected the idea of a *Volkhvy* as his mate. Lev's hatred for her was so great that his bite had turned venomous. Soren had saved her, but he wouldn't give up on his brother.

She wouldn't want him to.

And now, there was another Romanov to consider. Ivan and Elena's baby would be a fresh, innocent life at Bronwal. One that should live completely free of the curse and all the pain it had caused. She didn't blame Soren for protecting his family from her. She would rather err on the side of caution herself.

But that didn't make what they had to do any easier. Especially now that she'd kissed him.

Anna had almost died, but she could still remember Soren's full, lush mouth slowly tasting hers when she'd lost her powers. Her favorite window allowed a view of the beach in the distance. She sat on its wide sill, bathed by the salty sea breeze, and she dwelled on those remembered moments.

Soren, as a man, was big and real and tempting to the touch. When he'd leaned close, how could she resist? The kiss had been intensely physical—the flick of his rough tongue against hers, the velvety suction of his mouth, the nip of his teeth against her lower lip, the friction of his beard. She'd tasted the salt as his temperature rose against her lips. His body heat had radiated out like a silent confession. As if he was wordlessly pleading for the kiss to continue...or to become more.

And then she'd touched his face.

That beautifully masculine face she'd longed to see for so many years. His human features were older, wiser, harder, but more handsome than she could have imagined. Especially when his cheeks were flushed with desire for her and his lips were swollen from their mutual hunger.

She hadn't lied to him. The sword must be destroyed. She was Anna, the Light *Volkhvy* princess. One day she might even become the queen. She felt the promise of power thrumming beneath her fingertips even when she wore thick leather gloves. She couldn't deny her blood, nor could she reconcile it with his need to protect his family from her.

In a moment of panic, she'd transported them through the Ether after the white wolf's attack.

It had been an instinctive use of her abilities that violated everything Soren wanted for himself. She'd taken him into the nightmare world that had haunted him every night since the curse had been broken.

Her *Volkhvy* abilities were dangerous, and there was no guarantee that she would ever have them fully under control.

She wasn't sure if the sunset was real or borrowed from wherever her mother borrowed the false Mediterranean atmosphere. To anyone who might pass, the island was rocky and uninhabitable, a typical skiff of earth in the Sea of the Hebrides among numerous others. Its true nature was blanketed by its false atmosphere to hide the palace and gardens and all the inhabitants. Krajina was yet another show of her mother's immense power. Power Anna probably possessed herself. She tried to enjoy the sun's glow. Shades of pink, orange and vivid yellow painted the azure sky. It was beautiful, but also vaguely threatening just like Vasilisa herself.

Anna touched her lips lightly with fingers that tingled even when she hadn't consciously called on her powers.

The kisses they'd stolen would have to be enough. She only wished it didn't feel as if the memory of his lips would become a new curse. Heat spread from her mouth down to her tight chest and then seductively lower. Her nipples peaked against the satin of her ivory nightgown made blush by the reflected glow of the sunset sky. She would have to live for an eternity of lonely nights with only two kisses to sustain her.

She would never forget them. The Ether's energy might tingle her fingers, but the feel and taste of Soren permanently tingled on her tongue.

Curse seemed apt.

Soren wanted off the island. He'd paced its confines since Anna had woken up. It was no surprise that he preferred outside to in. He might be in his human form, but he still wanted the sun on his hair and the breeze on his skin. Plus, when he was outside running across the windswept valleys and hills or along the craggy shores, there was no danger that he'd find himself at Anna's bedroom door.

Was he avoiding her?

It was a stupid question. One he didn't even have to ask himself. Of course the less time they spent together, the better. She needed to heal so they could go after the emerald sword. He remembered the blade. He could perfectly recall the gem's green glitter in its hilt. Only now did he recognize the same green in Anna's eyes and in the power her *Volkhvy* abilities channeled from the Ether.

She needed to heal, and he needed to develop more self-control.

He'd kissed her. The horror of Lev's attack and her near death afterward didn't diminish the impact of tasting her lips—the heat, the hunger, the intimate blending of their tongues. The allure of finally having a man's body to join with her womanly one paired with the absence of her power had tempted him beyond any seduction he'd ever known.

They'd experienced one quick, hot taste.

Then one slow, deep exploration.

It would never be enough.

He'd ache for another kiss for the rest of his days.

Of course he needed to avoid her. He should get off the island and never return. But even if the mirror was still intact at Bronwal, he wouldn't be able to take such an easy escape. The emerald sword couldn't be ignored. It had to be silenced. He wasn't the warrior it Called. He couldn't hear its song, but he felt the connection it tried to establish between them.

Even if he saved Lev, he could never trust his brother around Anna again. He could never risk another white wolf attack. And he also had to shield her from Ivan's alpha protectiveness.

He had circumnavigated the entire island several times. Today he found himself at the entrance to Vasilisa's wild, tangled rose garden. It looked as if it had been tended and well manicured at one time. There was evidence of a plan in the shape of its layout and rock-lined pathways, but vines hadn't been pruned in so long that they had crept and wound into an intricately knotted, untamed display of greenery.

Even though it was the queen's garden, there was something appealing about its wildness on an island that was mostly rolling green hills above a rock-strewed shore and rugged coast. The tangle drew him, and he jogged along one of its spiraled paths. He couldn't avoid Anna forever. The memory of her lips followed him wherever he went.

But he focused on stretching the muscles in his legs and his breathing.

Until he came to the center of Vasilisa's rose garden and an impossible sight took his breath away. They'd told him that his brother's wife and child had been protected from the Ether and the curse. He'd wanted to believe it, but he couldn't bring himself to trust the evil queen who had tormented them all for so long.

In the center of thousands of rosebushes where the scent of lush blossoms weighted the air with perfume, a formation of rocks jutted from the earth, forming a natural centerpiece sculpture to the spiral path he jogged.

He stopped, spraying tiny pebbles out from under his feet.

He'd borrowed running shoes, shorts and a T-shirt from a well-supplied closet in the bedchamber he'd been given. Like the wardrobes in Bronwal, the palace had been in existence for ages and many different cultures and styles were represented in its art and textiles, in the clothing of its inhabitants and the offerings to its "guests."

A woman lay sleeping beneath the glass of a coffin-like compartment that protruded from the rock as if it had grown like crystals from the earth's heart. It was Madeline Romanov. He recognized Lev's wife and the medieval clothing she wore. The babe in her arms was held to her chest as if she'd simply rocked him to sleep before falling asleep herself.

"My mother is going to open the case and wake her. She promised. She only waits for the right time," Anna said.

Soren had walked forward to place his hand against the cool, rough glass. Vasilisa's power had crafted the coffin from the minerals in the rock from which it rose. The formation simply changed from dark granite to gray limestone speckled with mica to crystal to glass. The woman and baby hadn't aged. They hadn't changed. Madeline's hair hadn't faded or turned gray. The baby, Trevor, was in perfect repose, his tiny lips curved into a smile.

"This is the most beautiful and the most horrible thing I've ever seen," Soren said. His voice broke. He wasn't ashamed. It was as if he'd been transported back to a time when he'd been at the edge of manhood, only to have the world he'd been growing into ripped away.

He turned from his eerily unchanged sister-in-law to face the woman—the witch—who approached him, but his angry recriminations died on his lips when he saw the tears that trailed down her cheeks.

Bell had never cried. At least not where anyone could see her. He was sure that Anna was the same. His chest was tight. His gut was clenched. His brother had searched the entire world for his family, but they'd been kept here, away from him and out of sight. They'd been stolen in the same way that Anna had been stolen from her mother.

"She thought she was being merciful in comparison to what Vladimir had done to her child. To…me," Anna said. "She could have killed them. An eye for an eye. She thought your father had killed me. Or she could have allowed the Ether to take the baby. He wouldn't have been strong enough to resist. Madeline was her warrior, the bearer of the ruby blade. She spared her and Trevor out of love."

"If this is *Volkhvy* love, then the Romanovs are better off without it," Soren said.

He turned away from her as she approached and returned his fisted hands to the glass as if he would break it, but he simply held them against it as if he knew it was too late. That it should have been shattered long ago.

If this is Volkhvy *love, then the Romanovs are better off without it.*

She didn't flinch. It was a triumph. Besides, he was

right. She could feel the potential for that kind of love humming beneath her skin. Especially when she was close to Soren Romanov. It was as if her *Volkhvy* abilities magnified what was already there. Theirs was a passionate race. Her mother had proved it. Anna proved it every second she was in Soren's presence. Her tears had dried. Now her face was tight and the sea breeze made it feel raw. She came here often to be near Madeline and Trevor. She hadn't expected to find Soren lying across their coffin. Her mother *had* promised to free them, but Vasilisa hesitated, because she feared what the white wolf might do once they were released. He was unpredictable and no longer human. He might be too wild for his wife to reclaim.

"You knew I was trying to save my brother. To get him to come back home. Madeline and Trevor would help me. They need to return to Bronwal. He'll come back to himself once his family is home. I know it," Soren said.

He straightened. She'd come to stand beside him. There was no chance they would disturb the bespelled mother and child behind the glass, but Soren spoke softly, as if he thought they might. She whispered, too. Because the peace of the garden's heart seemed fragile. There was so much at stake.

"Soren, you're talking to the woman your feral brother almost killed. He tried to bite off my arm. He would have if I didn't tap the Ether to transport us back to the castle and out of his reach," Anna said. She wore a floral sundress and sandals. It wasn't her usual kind of outfit. It wasn't practical. She carried no weapons. It had been light and airy against her tender skin when she'd pulled it on.

The man beside her seemed to notice her for the first time. His focus had been on the shock of his discovery. Now he turned to her. Had she come closer to him on purpose to draw his attention? She wasn't sure. She only knew once his intense gaze fell on her, she wanted to run away. She had just recovered from a near-death experience. It wasn't only her skin that was tender. She was vulnerable all the way to the deep, hidden hollow in the pit of her stomach. But, worse, she still remembered his kiss, even now. With poor Madeline and Trevor sleeping under glass beside them, her eyes still fell on his lips.

"You're healing," Soren said. It wasn't a question, but he suddenly lifted his hand to brush aside the loose sleeve of her dress. His touch was light. Barely there. She trembled anyway. The heat of his fingers transferred from those calloused pads to her sensitive flesh. Especially when he softly grazed over the reddened places where his brother's fangs had punctured her skin.

She released a long, shaky breath, trying to hide what his touch did to the hollow inside her. It had become molten. Filled with fire where only emptiness had been moments before. His hand fell away. She didn't move to straighten her dress, because she was afraid her hand would shake.

"I'm healing because I'm stronger than a human. If he bit Madeline or Trevor…" She hated to say it, but it had to be said.

"Lev would never harm them," Soren said. He wasn't angry. He'd stepped closer while she'd been distracted by his touch. He looked down at her upturned face, as if he wanted to convince her that his brother wasn't a monster.

"I hope you're right," Anna said, softly. "But there was a time I thought he'd never harm me. His bite wouldn't be venomous to his wife and child, but it would devastate all the same."

They shouldn't be together. So close. So warm. Soren's cheeks were flushed above his russet beard, and his eyes flashed with amber flames. From her eyes to her lips, his attention tracked, and she suddenly held herself very still. It would be so easy to lean into his muscular frame. To offer her mouth up for his taking.

Madeline hadn't kissed Lev in hundreds of years.

Anna wasn't sure if that made her kissing Soren, here and now, more impossible or more necessary. They'd been kept apart for so many Cycles, even though they'd been together. She'd longed to see his human face, but her longing had included desires she hadn't even acknowledged to herself. She hadn't only wanted to see him. She'd wanted to be with him. To feel his human arms wrapped around her waist. To look into his eyes as their lips came together.

She'd experienced that now. And it was impossible not to want to experience it again.

"You're a witch. Madeline and Trevor are human," Soren said.

This time his voice rose to a regular volume. He had a deep timbre that was physical as much as audible. Standing as close as they did, she could feel the roughness of it as much as she could hear it. He was a man, but he held the potential for howls and growls within him, just out of range.

His bark was worse than his brother's bite.

She stepped away. They both seemed to collapse a little as oxygen whooshed in between them. It seemed as if the air had been unnaturally still as they'd stood face-to-face, wanting to touch but refusing to give in to their desires.

"So you think your brother was justified in his attack. That I deserved to be bitten," Anna said.

"I didn't say that." He'd fisted the hand that had touched her skin. Did he resist the warmth that had transferred from her shoulder to him?

"You don't have to say it. You feel it. But the red wolf leaped to my rescue. He didn't hesitate. It's your human form that sees me as a threat. Why is that, do you think?" Anna asked.

She wasn't wearing her gloves. He hadn't noticed until now. Perhaps he'd thought she was still too weak to channel the Ether. The sudden arcing green light on the tips of her fingers proved him wrong.

Anna knew he'd enjoyed their kiss. She also knew she was right about him thinking all witches, including her, were dangerous. He'd saved her after Lev's attack, but he didn't think Lev had been wrong to attack her. He trusted the white wolf's feral instincts more than he trusted the connection between them. Maybe it was enchantment that drew them together. Maybe enchantment only called attention to what was already there. Either way, he couldn't kiss her and then hurt her unless she allowed it.

His lack of confidence in her control made her more determined than ever to exercise it. Over her powers and over herself.

No more kisses would be much easier to implement than no more tears.

Chapter 12

Queen Vasilisa of the Light *Volkhvy* knew all about mistakes.

She would live with the shock of finding her daughter alive and traumatized by her own actions for the rest of her long life. Every time she saw Anna, she was reminded of what she had done. Not only to her daughter, but to all the people of Bronwal.

They had been her people, in spite of what their ruler had done.

She should have exercised more mercy and restraint, but should haves wouldn't set things right. Only action could begin to do that. She'd already offered all the help of the Light *Volkhvy* to Ivan Romanov and his warrior wife. The bearer of the sapphire sword had brought the black wolf back from the brink of madness, and now she helped him reclaim Bronwal from the deterioration the curse had caused.

But they would continue to need *Volkhvy* help.

It pained Vasilisa that the Romanovs had rejected her *Volkhvy* workers when Elena had discovered she was pregnant. She knew it pained her daughter to no longer be welcome in the place she had once considered her home, curse and all.

Anna's pain was her responsibility.

Helping those she'd hurt, including the Romanovs who refused her help, would only appease her own pain. She couldn't let their refusal stop her. They were distrustful. She couldn't blame them. She had turned their trust and loyalty to ash when she'd unleashed the curse.

They might never trust her again, but she could only hope and mend and knit together all the pieces her vengeance had rent asunder.

Soren Romanov. The red Romanov wolf. Lev was Soren's twin. They had been born only minutes apart and they'd rarely been separated since. Lev was the youngest brother, but Vasilisa favored the middle child, Soren, above all the others, because he had stood by her daughter's side for centuries. When he'd used the mirror portal to bring Anna to Krajina for healing, he'd stood on the cliff overlooking the ocean, but his eyes had been focused on her daughter's pale face. He had barely spared a glance for Vasilisa or her people or the surroundings.

And yet, he rejected the Call of the emerald sword.

He would deny his own heart rather than trust a witch, and that was Vasilisa's fault. She had tainted the Light *Volkhvy* with her Dark use of the Ether's energy. Now her daughter suffered for what she had done. Much like how Vladimir's offspring had suffered for what he had done.

Enough.

Vasilisa went in search of her daughter, because she had received a report that she was nearly healed. She'd also ascertained that Anna and Soren were avoiding each other. The red wolf rose every morning and ran the perimeter of the island in his human form, as if he still searched for his lost white brother. He wasn't searching. He was escaping. The palace must seem like a sumptuous prison to him, filled with *Volkhvy* who might go Dark at any time. Not to mention the enchanted connection between him and Anna.

The sword only enhanced a connection between them that was as natural as breathing, but the red wolf wouldn't accept that.

She found Anna in a stone folly built on a smaller rise just below the palace itself. The folly sat above the tangle of the rose garden, for now, but one day, decades in the future, the thorny vines would reach it and twine around its columns and its octagonal red-tile roof.

The center of the folly's construction was solid white stucco. Around the stucco was a circular portico that resembled a merry-go-round, but instead of horses there were only empty spaces between the columns that held the roof until a wider gap on the ocean-facing side. In the wider gap, Anna sat on a swing made of red-lacquered wicker.

Vasilisa's heart warmed when she saw her daughter— until she noted the longing on Anna's face. The young woman shuttered her emotions as Vasilisa approached, but not quickly enough. An observant witch with the experience of centuries behind her, Vasilisa wasn't fooled.

It wasn't only the Romanovs who didn't trust her.

"You are feeling better," Vasilisa said. She stood beside the swing rather than sit where she wasn't welcome. The wind off the ocean blew her day dress around her legs. It was shorter than her usual garments for convenient walking around the island, but it was still a design that would have been favored at the turn of the nineteenth century in the outside world. Its skirt was full but swept back in a bustle. A thousand ivory buttons fastened from its high-necked bodice down to just below her knees and along the insides of both of her arms. At her cuffs, her hem and her neck, puffs of snowy lace fluttered in the breeze. Vasilisa liked pretty things. She always had. And vintage clothing design appealed to her love of aesthetics.

Modern style was much too plain for someone who had lived through ages of much more intricate and artistic clothing.

"I am. Thank you," Anna replied. She continued to stare out over the rolling waves.

Vasilisa had apologized. A million times. Yet still she had to bite her tongue to keep from apologizing again. Words were meaningless. Apologies only went so far. She had to fix this, and the only way she could do that was to force the red wolf and her daughter to spend time together.

She'd made her share of mistakes, but she couldn't allow Soren and Anna to suffer any more because of them.

"I've waited until you were well enough to attend, but there are many *Volkhvy* on the island and your wolf's wanderings make them nervous. He has to make an appearance tonight. We'll have a dinner to celebrate your recovery," Vasilisa said.

She left no room in her tone for refusal. Anna finally took her attention from the sea. Her green eyes fell on Vasilisa's face. They were so cool they made even a queen shiver.

"He isn't my wolf, Mother. He never will be," Anna said.

But she didn't argue or refuse the invitation. She simply stood and nodded before slowly walking away. That was when Vasilisa noticed the black leather gloves back on her daughter's hands. The gloves were an affectation.

Not necessary at all or even particularly helpful in aiding her control of *Volkhvy* abilities.

Vasilisa stretched her arms out toward the sea. A heavy silver ring on her left hand winked in the sun. It had replaced the lover's ring that Vladimir had given her. The silver had been crafted with thorns that faced both ways, outward and inward to pierce her skin. She had worn it at first as a constant reminder of Vladimir's betrayal. It had come to represent more than that. She deserved the pain now more than ever. For her betrayal of the Romanovs and her own daughter.

She was the one who had made Anna fear her ability to channel the Ether's energy. Her poor choices and her temper and the curse she had worked when all her hope was lost had caused so much suffering.

Truth was, Soren and Anna were going to suffer more. Together or apart. The emerald sword didn't lie. They were meant to be. If they didn't come to accept it, they would always be hollow inside, as if a part of them was missing. But, worse, if they didn't come to accept themselves, the wolf and the warrior, they would be separated from their own hearts forever.

Nothing about this was going to be easy, but Vasilisa was well versed in hard. She turned to watch her daughter head back to the palace. Anna had wrapped her gloved hands around herself as if the weather was chillier than it was. Without the Ether's energy, the island would be like others in the Outer Hebrides, buffeted by the Atlantic cold and currents.

Perhaps Anna could feel a hint of that weather through her enchantment.

Or perhaps it was the red wolf's distrust that made her cold.

Chapter 13

She wouldn't wear green.

Anna paced the confines of her room in her underwear as she tried to decide on a dress for dinner. Her mother dressed for every occasion, even walking in the garden, and dinner would be no exception. It would be a grand, formal affair, and as much as Anna might prefer to show up in jeans—or, better yet, not at all—there was also a part of her that wanted to go the other way.

She'd dressed for Soren the night of the *Volkhvy* Gathering at Bronwal. She'd been drawn to a green dress that she and Elena had found while searching out something for the former ballerina to wear. At first, she'd put the emerald green dress back in the wardrobe where it had hung forgotten for centuries.

But she'd gone back for it later.

Elena had dressed in a white swan gown with graceful feather accents. She'd done it to reclaim the power an evil witchblood prince had tried to take from her by forcing her to become a caged swan in nightmares he controlled. She'd accepted the Call of the sapphire sword. She'd accepted Ivan Romanov's love. Together, they had defeated Grigori and they'd broken the curse, freeing Bronwal and all its inhabitants.

Except for the white wolf.

Lev was still trapped in the shift he'd used to hunt for his wife and child until he couldn't remember how to be human again.

And her.

She was trapped by her parentage and by the power of the Ether that flowed through her veins.

She couldn't accept the Call of the emerald sword. She couldn't accept a love that wasn't offered. Even if Soren had loved her in spite of her witch heritage, she would have to reject him because of it. He deserved to finally find happiness with his family, and they all deserved to be safe at Bronwal after all this time.

Anna had been drawn to green for as long as she could remember. She'd never known the emerald sword influenced her preference. She trailed her fingers over several beautiful gowns a *Volkhvy* servant had draped over the bed. None quite matched the green of the dress she'd worn that night. In the end, her preparations for the Gathering had been wasted. It had turned into a battle, not a dance. And any appreciation Soren might have felt when he'd seen her had faded immediately once the truth was revealed.

The red wolf had growled at her when she'd reached for him. The emerald gown might as well have been rags. Afterward, she'd retreated to her aviary and ripped the beautiful dress from her body, as if its color was a confession she was no longer brave enough to make.

No. She wouldn't wear green tonight. In fact, after

tonight, she would get rid of everything green that she owned. With a decisive flourish, Anna scooped up the green dresses and dropped them all onto a chair in the corner of her room. Then she turned back to the closet and riffled through its contents herself. She might be a princess, but she wasn't used to being waited on. During the last decades of the curse, she'd been little more than a servant herself.

She was glad she hadn't summoned help when she dug to the back of the closet and found a long, sleek dress crafted from layers of silk. The dress looked black until she pulled it into the light of the setting sun.

The orange glow of the sunset caused the dress to burst into iridescent shades of flame. The dark red silk had been dyed with an artistic touch that created multifaceted shimmers of color with movement and light—from nearly black to scarlet.

It reminded her of *Volkhvy* blood.

Wearing it would be an obvious statement of who and what she was, but it would also be bold in other ways. The thin, clinging fabric would hug her curves. The delicate shoulder straps and the deep V of its plunging neckline would claim her newfound sensuality.

Anna pulled the dress over her head. The closet was scented with sachets. The fabric held the faintest hint of rose petals in its silken layers. Once it settled on her curves, Anna had to reevaluate its origins. Vasilisa had a slim build compared to her daughter.

The dress seemed made for Anna's figure.

Only a little rearranging of the silk was required for the bodice to settle over her lace bra and panties. In the mirror, her legs flashed pale and smooth from the thigh-high slits in the dress that parted when she walked. Her skin was framed by silk that was ebony from this angle and scarlet from the other.

She had been the belle of the ball for only seconds on that night six months ago when her world had crumbled around her. Tonight, she would be Anna, the Light *Volkhvy* princess. She would be the witch who was trying to rebuild her world without the red wolf in it.

She dressed for Soren Romanov again, but this time, she also dressed for herself.

Ivan had planned to destroy the mirror. Soren was probably trapped on the island until Anna was well enough to leave. He hadn't tested that theory. He'd visited the mirror's exit point on every circuit he'd run of the island, but he hadn't tried to use it. He straightened his cuff links and rolled his broad, muscled shoulders beneath the thin white poplin of his formal shirt. He wasn't used to these modern clothes—strange fabrics and fasteners caused everything to take longer—and he was out of practice with clothing as it was.

He was well aware that deciding he was trapped wasn't the same as actually being trapped. He dressed for dinner all the same.

One of the *Volkhvy* servants had taken pity on his fumbling and helped him with his necktie and cuff links. Most of the *Volkhvy* in the palace had avoided him since he arrived. Either they sensed he didn't trust them or they didn't trust him. He'd managed the buttons and zippers himself, including the ones on the backs of his heels, which tightened his short black leather boots on his feet. He'd worn rags for so long. His clothes had been threadbare. His boots had been rough and faded. And that was before he had worn nothing but his wolf's pelt.

He had to admit he liked the sharp angles of the pointed

toes as the shiny boots jutted out from the lean legs of his tailored pants. The black trousers conformed to the muscles of his legs almost like the leather leggings from a much earlier age. But his dinner outfit was much more lightweight than anything he'd worn before. Even after he'd added the fitted jacket over the translucent material of the shirt, he felt almost as naked as he'd felt in the stolen banner.

Of course, that was probably due to the haircut more than the clothes.

He rubbed his hand over his practically bare jaw and chin. The razor had left a trim shadow of his former beard on his face, but that was all. His reflection startled with a view of the lower half of his face he hadn't seen in a very long time. He ran his fingers over his lips but stopped when the calloused pads of his fingers made him recall the softer sensation of Anna's mouth.

The same servant who had helped him with his tie had cut his hair. It flopped over his forehead now with a thick bang he pushed back in a move that had become a habit an hour ago. Elsewhere, his long curls had been buzzed down almost to the skin. His neck was cold, but he had to admit his appearance was more civilized.

He also looked younger.

The face that stared back at him from the glass would have been more familiar to him if it hadn't been so long since he'd seen it.

What would Anna think?

It bothered him that he thought about her as he dressed. Her thoughts on his appearance shouldn't matter. And yet, he'd placed himself under the razor and the scissors for her. He had to admit it. He certainly didn't care what Vasilisa or all her *Volkhvy* horde would think of him as he sat down to dine with his enemies. The palace was a sparkling showplace of fine architecture and luxurious amenities.

It was no place for a wolf.

If not for Anna, he would have dribbled soup in his wild beard and worn his typical forest-scented garb to the table.

When Vasilisa's dinner invitation had been delivered, he'd wanted to close his bedroom door in the servant's face. But he hadn't. Yes, Vasilisa was an evil queen. She was also Anna's mother. He had to work with Anna until the emerald sword could be found and destroyed.

He might as well dress for dinner.

He'd attended many formal functions as one of the Romanov sons. He could remember them, vaguely, like some sort of distant dream. Clearer in his memories were the times he'd patrolled countless *Volkhvy* Gatherings as the red wolf. He remembered the many times he'd stolen sweetmeats and cakes for Anna when she'd been Bell and hiding in her aviary rather than dancing with witches.

He'd taken her the choicest treats and best bites.

Tonight, he would sit with her and watch her eat a feast fit for a princess in an enchanted palace that was her home. One in which he would never belong.

She deserved the feasts she'd never had. She should have a palace after so many years in a crumbling, cursed castle. She must have been so desperate and lonely with only a wolf for a friend.

So, yes, he shaved. Then he felt sorry that he had.

Anna had dined in different rooms since she'd arrived six months ago. She'd eaten from a tray in her bedroom. She'd had breakfast in her mother's solarium many times until she'd come to enjoy the sunrise through the thousands of panels of glass. She'd also dined with the queen's closest retinue in a formal room decorated with cherry furnishings and lined with matching wainscoting. That meal had been tense. It wasn't until afterward that Anna had realized it was her first presentation as the future Light *Volkhvy* queen.

Tonight, the palace servants had opened up a ballroom off the entry vestibule. Anna had never seen the grand double doors thrown wide or the vast room beyond. The white table that dominated the center of the room was ten times longer than the cherry table in the dining room and twice as wide. Its scrolled legs ended in the shape of gilded paws, and the wooden drapes of its edges were festooned with carvings of the Romanov wolves.

The dinner was intended to honor Soren Romanov, but somehow Anna doubted he would feel comfortable with the display. He claimed he was no longer Vasilisa's champion, and who could blame him?

Above the table several chandeliers made from thousands of dewdrops of faceted glass shimmered with the reflection of the guests below. A string orchestra played somewhere out of sight, and their quiet music was accompanied by subdued conversations and laughter...until she entered the room.

She was heir to her mother's throne.

It was possible that tonight was the first time she'd ever looked the part.

Anna stood in the open doorway as every *Volkhvy* turned to face her. She couldn't help it. When the men bowed and the women curtsied, she started and reached for a blade that wasn't there. Hopefully none of the bowed heads noticed her instinctive reaction to a people that were once her enemy. Now she knew they were her people, but old habits died hard—especially old habits that had kept her alive.

As the men straightened and the women rose, a line of guests on the left side of the room began to part. They made way for her mother, the queen. One man paused in the center of the line. He was a tall lean witch with lank black hair that hung to his shoulders. He stood straight seconds quicker than the rest, and he boldly met Anna's eyes. He didn't seem to be afraid. The deference the other *Volkhvy* showed for Vasilisa was tinged with fear. Although she was the Light *Volkhvy* queen, Vasilisa had dabbled in Darkness for centuries. Her people hadn't forgotten.

"My daughter, Anna, the Light *Volkhvy* princess and your future queen," Vasilisa announced. Approval shone from her face as she looked at Anna. The dress had been the right choice as far as Vasilisa was concerned. Her smile warmed her eyes as she reached for one of Anna's gloved hands. She twirled and lifted Anna's hand as if in presentation to the people, and the *Volkhvy* began to clap.

Anna looked around the ballroom from face to face. The bold man had faded into the crowd. Most of the faces she saw she didn't recognize, but she did see fear replaced by genuine warmth as they all seemed to welcome her home.

"Thank you," Anna said. Her mother allowed her to reclaim possession of her hand, and she used the chance to smooth her skirts. That was when she noticed that the chandelier light had set her dress on fire with even more depth and tonal differences than the sunset. Her pale skin was luminous compared to the shimmering silk that shifted from charcoal to jet to scarlet to the deepest, darkest oxblood as she moved.

"And now we wait for the guest of honor," Vasilisa said for Anna's ears alone. "If he chooses to appear. I'm afraid he'll run away instead. He's been running since he brought you here. Soon he'll determine that four legs are better for running than two again."

"He'll be here. Soren doesn't run away. He's been chasing Lev for centuries, not running. He'll never give up. I wouldn't want him to," Anna said.

"But it's acceptable if he gives up on you? Why do you deserve less loyalty than Lev?" Vasilisa asked. "Because you have *Volkhvy* blood?"

Anna didn't reply. She couldn't. Because Soren Romanov had entered the room, and once again the guests fell silent. This time their fear was palpable, and it wasn't in deference to the queen. The red wolf was in their midst, and he was one of the few beings who could do them harm.

She didn't think. She didn't reason or plan. She simply walked toward Soren because the gravity of his soul pulled her to orbit around him. In the crowded room, his was suddenly the only face she saw. His tall, muscular form and familiar eyes would have drawn her if he'd been clothed in rags. In a tuxedo, with every care taken to groom and prepare, his presence was devastating.

He was all man with only a hint of the wolf glittering in his amber eyes, and—this was new—he looked at her with nothing but intense, masculine appreciation.

Anna managed to continue her approach when she noticed his approval without stumbling on her unfamiliar heels, but it took all her concentration and skill. This wasn't the ill-fated Gathering where he'd growled at her when he'd discovered her true name. He knew who and what she was, and he didn't turn away. The dress had been a bold choice and a rebellious one. She wore her blood as proudly as she could, and she embraced the sensuality his shift to a man had woken in her. He stood straight and unmoving. He didn't step toward her, but his gaze tracked her steps across the floor.

Suddenly, it seemed as if no one else was in the room.

She reminded herself again that this time was different. This wasn't the Gathering where she'd been nothing but a young woman longing for a wolf to become a man so that she could dance with him for the first time. She stopped several paces away from him. She took a deep breath and held it. She was the Light *Volkhvy* princess. She was Vasilisa's daughter in a room full of witches.

And he was a Romanov wolf.

This time she was royalty and she was deigning to offer him her favor.

She lifted her hand toward him. Unlike on the night of the final Gathering at Bronwal, it was sheathed in a long black glove. For a moment, she regretted the glove. She wished her hand were as bared as Bell's heart had been that night six months ago. Anna stood with her hand outstretched, and it seemed as if the whole world held its breath with her.

They'd already decided to destroy the sword. But Soren had brought her to her mother to heal anyway. He had traveled through the Ether with her in his arms, facing his worst nightmare to save her. She didn't expect him to accept the Call of the emerald sword any more than she could.

She only wanted him to take her hand.

Anna looked from his hand at his side up to his face. She met his eyes. There was a silvery glint in the amber where his irises reflected the chandelier's light. She couldn't read his thoughts. Not in his eyes or in his lips when she dropped her gaze to the mouth she'd longed to see—and taste.

And then he took the hand she offered.

He clasped her gloved fingers in both of his hands. He didn't speak, but he held her hand tightly, as if he wouldn't allow her to pull away too soon.

Never would be too soon. She wanted to stand with her hand in both of his for an age to negate his growl at the

Gathering, but suddenly the crowd came alive again at a gesture from the queen. Seats were taken and Vasilisa swept to the head of the table. Her dress was unmitigated white, a ball gown from a bygone era with full backswept skirts and a myriad of different-textured fabrics. Her bodice was encrusted with hundreds of sparkling diamanté gems.

Did she proclaim a truce with the Romanovs with her sudden penchant for white?

Anna looked back up at Soren. His lids hooded his eyes once more. His appreciation for her appearance had been shuttered. But he didn't let go of her hand. He simply dropped one of his hands so they could walk to the table together. It seemed that for this meal, at least, he would consent to be her wolf.

Chapter 14

Vasilisa sat at the head of the table. Soren halted when he saw that his place was set at the other end. It was a position intended to convey a gesture of respect for an honored guest. Rather than accept the gesture, Soren curved away from the chair opposite Vasilisa and toward the chair to the right of it intended for Anna. Anna stood awkwardly for only a few seconds before she took the honored chair he'd left vacant.

Now Anna and Vasilisa sat at opposite heads of the long banquet table and Soren sat at Anna's right elbow in a lesser position.

If the queen felt his decision as a slight, she gave no indication. Once all the guests were seated, she rose.

"Thank you all for visiting the palace this evening. Please enjoy your meal and this chance to welcome a Romanov back to the palace. The black wolf, the red and the white were Anna's family while she was...away...from us. They have earned my eternal gratitude," Vasilisa said.

She raised a fluted glass that a servant had filled while she spoke. "I only hope that in time I can earn their forgiveness."

Anna didn't raise her glass higher than her lips. Soren didn't touch his glass at all. But the rest of the table joined the toast, and as the queen arranged her skirts to sit again, the room seemed to breathe a sigh of relief. Soft conversations began up and down and across the long table as numerous servants entered the room with a first course carried on large silver platters.

Keeping with the Mediterranean style of the palace, the first course consisted of a selection of finger foods—fresh bunches of grapes, figs, olives and meats rolled with feta cheese. Anna had to force herself to copy the other guests as they chose dainty bites with silver tongs. It had been six months, but she had subsisted on the roughest of fare for so long that her mouth watered at the wide variety of textures and flavors presented for her pleasure.

She looked up after a particularly savory bite of cheese to find that Soren was watching her. She paused midchew as heat rose in her cheeks. Okay. So maybe she wasn't being as dainty as the other guests after all.

"I can remember when a stale chunk of Patrice's bread was all I could find you," Soren said.

"You used to stand watch while I gathered berries when we materialized in summer," Anna said.

"No matter what the future brings, I'm glad you're not hungry anymore. You deserve this after all the deprivation," Soren said.

"Eating won't make you a traitor to your family," Anna said. Soren hadn't touched his food, although he had filled his plate when the servant had paused at his elbow. Probably out of pity for the young man who waited with his heavy tray. "You'll need your strength when we go after the sword. It's only food. Not forgiveness."

"I was only distracted by your pleasure. I'll eat. My survival instincts are too well honed to use food as a statement," Soren said. He proved his point by making short work of the shaved meat and cheese the servant had mounded on his plate when Soren had failed to fill it adequately to the servant's liking.

And suddenly Anna's mouth went dry.

She completely understood how her pleasure in the food had distracted Soren from his own meal. There was a sensuality to the rich flavors and aromas after years of doing without. She was transfixed by Soren's pure physical enjoyment of the feast. When he lifted his eyes from his plate as he swallowed the last bite, their gazes locked.

His lips were moist from his wine. His amber eyes were warm. And as he held her gaze, he lifted one finger to his mouth and sucked the juice of a dark red grape from it.

The noise of the other guests seemed to go distant and hollow in her ears. The room hazed at the corner of her eyes. Her entire world narrowed to Soren's finger wrapped gently by his lips.

"You need to follow your own advice. What's wrong? I know you haven't eaten your fill," Soren said.

Anna's face grew hotter. She had forgotten her plate because she'd been distracted by him. Had he been distracted in the same way? Her face wasn't the only place that heated. A hot coil of awareness wound tight, low in her stomach.

And that hot knot of fire radiated outward to more intimate regions.

This wasn't a sexy, romantic dinner.

The room was filled with the Light *Volkhvy*. A dangerous mission loomed before them, one that would sever their connection forever. Vasilisa was her mother and, as far as Soren was concerned, his greatest enemy.

But the tension only heightened the feeling that they shared an intimate secret in a crowded room.

He had taken her hand even though she'd worn the bloodred dress to boldly proclaim her heritage. He teased her now even though the chemistry between them shouldn't be encouraged.

"Perhaps this is torture for you, as well? We're bound to be torn apart, and all I want is to taste the wine on your tongue," Soren said. "And the worst part is I can tell you'd like to do the same with mine."

His tone was casual. The second course was carried into the room, and he sat back to allow his first plate to be removed. It was replaced by a bowl of soup. Fragrant steam rose from the creamy liquid. A servant crumbled a pinch of fresh green herbs over the soup with a flourish.

Through the entire process, Anna sat, electrified by the images his words had brought to life. She licked her lips as her soup was placed and garnished. Her thank-you was rough and smoky as desire tightened her throat.

Soren looked deep in her eyes as he leaned over his bowl to dip up a spoonful of soup and bring it to his lips. Her gaze tracked from his eyes to his mouth as he opened to gently savor the steaming broth.

The steam rising from her own bowl felt cool against her heated skin.

"*Cruel* is an understatement," Anna breathed. She broke eye contact and looked around the table. Her mother was busy with the important dignitaries to her left and her right. Everyone else pretended not to be watching the queen or her daughter or the wolf of honor in their midst.

Pretended.

All eyes were on them. In between sips of wine and

soup, glances flickered their way continually, as if eye-lashes were insects on fluttering wings drawn to their flame.

"Oh, you see that, too? I'm more than the guest of honor. I'm the dinner show," Soren said. He sat back in his chair and drained his wine. "I have to decide if it's curiosity or caution. Or something more nefarious that should put me on my guard."

Although he'd been playing with the chemistry between them, Anna had no doubt that Soren was already on his guard and had been since he'd first stepped foot on the island. Certainly since he'd found his brother's wife and baby encased in glass. Vasilisa might have the best intentions to reform, but she was a powerful witch who exhibited questionable judgment…still.

"These are my mother's closest advisers and friends," Anna argued. And yet she suddenly remembered the witch with lank hair who had seemed to challenge her before he'd disappeared.

"Exactly," Soren said. He placed his empty glass on the table. Even in his tuxedo with his hair cut and his beard trimmed, he looked edgy, as if wildness was only a breath away. "I would be foolish to trust any of them and so would you. Vasilisa dabbled in Darkness for a long time. These are the people that stayed by her side during the curse. What does that tell you about them?"

Anna barely noticed the servant who took away her untouched bowl of soup. It had grown cold while Soren repainted the picture of the dinner party with a suspicious brush.

Surviving was their greatest commonality. She couldn't pretend he was wrong. Suddenly, the guests' glances their way seemed more intrusive. Were they being sized up by an enemy who bided their time to strike? There had to be some who regretted that the Romanovs had regained favor. Were there *Volkhvy* preparing to enjoy the main course who resented that the heir to her mother's throne hadn't been destroyed?

Anna surreptitiously looked from the corner of her eye until she found a shiny black head. Once she saw the bold witch, she couldn't believe he'd faded from her view and attention so soon. He barely touched his food and drink. He didn't speak to the witches around him. He stared at her. She had to force herself not to stand to face the threat his attention conveyed.

"As much as I resent *Volkhvy* enchantment, I see the warrior in your eyes right now. The emerald sword isn't wrong. If there is a witch in this room who would come against us, he or she has no idea that their beautiful princess is as much a danger to them as the red Romanov wolf," Soren said. His voice was pitched low, for her ears alone, and its roughness seemed to vibrate intimately along her skin. Although he spoke in warning, his admiration warmed as the soup never could.

Anna looked back at the man who sat beside her. He still watched over her, no matter how he might deny it. Why else would he warn her about a possible danger around them? He might intend to sever all ties with her once they destroyed the sword, but he had saved her life by bringing her here, and he tried to protect her still.

The main course arrived. The servers presented dark purple eggplant stuffed with spicy minced meat. The scents of cinnamon and black pepper rose enticingly from a colorful dish ringed by bright red sundried tomatoes.

But Anna had to force herself to pick up her fork and take a bite. She did it. As the whole room watched, she ate as if she hadn't a care in the world. She hadn't touched her soup, but she had to go through the motions of enjoying her dinner. She wasn't free to stare down the witch with the lank hair or glance suspiciously from guest to guest, trying to decide which ones had embraced the Darkness.

Vasilisa laughed and talked as if she wasn't worried. Perhaps she'd been a lonely, isolated queen too long. Perhaps the return of her daughter was too great a distraction for even her wisdom and power to overcome.

The Dark *Volkhvy* had claimed the emerald sword. Was it possible that they also wanted to claim the Light *Volkhvy* throne?

Anna had stunned him when he walked into the room. He'd paused to stare as she'd approached him in a dress that shimmered and silkily conformed to her curves as she walked. Her skin had shone like porcelain, perfection against the black red of her gown. The silk parted in two high slits well above her knees to allow her to move easily and gracefully across the ballroom floor. He'd been transfixed by her transformation from practical to glamorous. Her upswept hair fell in a waterfall of curls down her back that rivaled only the dress and her skin with its shine.

She'd reached for him.

There was no way he could miss the parallel to another ballroom six months ago.

She'd worn green that night. Emerald green. A color that matched the highlights in her green eyes and another emerald gleam he'd seen in a sword hilt years before.

The red wolf had rejected the daughter of the Light *Volkhvy* queen. It had been a visceral reaction to a betrayal that hadn't been a choice, but a chance of birth. Bell had always been loyal to him, and he'd repaid that loyalty by turning his back and running after Lev.

What other choice had he had? His family needed him. He had to keep trying to reach the white wolf. Lev needed to know that Madeline and Trevor were alive. And Soren had to help Ivan protect his unborn child.

But he took her hand. He held on to her warmth as if he was grasping at a lifeline dangling on the edge of a cliff. Her cheeks had flushed at his touch. Her eyes had moistened with emotion. And then Vasilisa had spoken. She brought him back from the edge onto solid ground. His foundation had been built by the queen's true dangerous nature. It had been built by Darkness.

He was fine then. He'd rejected the queen's overtures. He'd refused the place of honor. His spine had been stiff and his course clear...until Anna had started to nibble her food. Her pleasure had undone his best intentions. The room had disappeared to his senses. He'd focused on her mouth and her throat as she'd chewed and swallowed and suddenly he was on that cliff again, ready to jump off without any lifeline at all.

He could only thank his wolf's instincts for warning him that the dinner party wasn't the happy gathering that it seemed. If he'd been a simple man, he would have been completely consumed with his and Anna's obvious attraction and desire for each other. He wasn't. He was a man with the heart of a wolf, and while that wildness increased his passion, it also increased his awareness of threat.

There was a tension in the air that went beyond the physical and emotional tensions he and Anna battled together. It went beyond his conflict with Vasilisa. The hair on the back of his neck rose to attention. His shoulders tightened as if he prepared for attack.

He'd warned Anna.

And her reaction had proved that her dress wasn't what stunned him about her.

As he'd watched, she'd gone from a glamorous princess to a womanly warrior in the blink of an eye. He doubted anyone else could tell the difference. On the surface, she'd still glittered and shone. Her lips had curled into frequent smiles. Her hands had gracefully managed her utensils and her glass.

It had been her eyes that gave her away, and the tightening of her shoulders and her jaw. Imperceptible except to a man who had known her for centuries and a wolf that had joined her in battle many times.

He'd been stunned once more because of what her transformation did to him.

The emerald sword Called to her, and as much as he hated to admit it, the sword wasn't wrong—Anna was a warrior fit for a Romanov wolf. His body had reacted to the fire in her eyes that only he could see.

And he was still struggling to control his body's reaction now that dinner was over and the guests were mingling in withdrawing rooms filled with string music and quiet conversations.

He mostly stood alone.

Few of the Light *Volkhvy* were brave enough to approach him, and those that tried were quickly rebuffed by his gruff demeanor and his unwillingness to engage in meaningless conversation about the weather—for God's sake, it was enchanted—or the meal. He had barely done it justice.

He stood with his glass and he watched over Anna as he always had. Unfortunately, he couldn't rely on habit, because they'd both changed more in six months than they had in all the centuries they'd shared before.

She was a witch and a princess. He was a wolf. And a Romanov. But as much as he tried to tell himself that those things mattered, his body insisted that only the warrior in her eyes mattered tonight.

Anna laughed and talked and met anyone and everyone

Vasilisa presented to her. But he could tell by her movements that she was on guard. Her dress was slinky and the way it clung to her skin made him ache, but she might as well have been wearing armor. He could see that she was prepared. He could also feel her gaze over and over as she sought him out. The constant need to affirm that he was there to back her up should someone decide to attack made adrenaline course beneath his skin. It joined the desire that already flowed there.

The mingling of cold with flame caused him to tremble with the need to release one or the other.

No one attacked.

One by one and then in bunches and groups, the guests began to take their leave. Many floated by him with bows and nods…and assessing gazes. More than once a handshake sparked, as if the witch who offered their hand did it to remind him of the power he faced.

He wasn't worried. Not for himself. He stood in his tuxedo knowing his shift was only a heartbeat away should he need it, and he watched the woman he would face down the entire *Volkhvy* horde for, Dark and Light, should it come to that.

Acknowledging that didn't change what he intended to do to the emerald sword. His feelings for Anna only made it that much more imperative that the sword was destroyed as soon as possible.

He would die for her, but he couldn't ask his brothers or his brothers' families to do the same.

Chapter 15

Soren's intensity made her nervous, as did the disappearance of the lank-haired witch who had boldly watched her throughout dinner only to vanish afterward. Anna handled all the duties of her position, but she was ever conscious of the red wolf's amber glare. She smiled and laughed twice as much to try to cover for his obvious antagonism. He was right—there was no way to be certain which *Volkhvy* they could trust. But his default of not trusting any of them put her in an untenable position.

Especially when his penetrating glare was trained on her and she could tell that distrust wasn't the only thing he felt for her.

Because nervous wasn't the only thing Soren made her.

The bold witch was gone, but she met so many new witches that names and faces blurred in her memory. Only one name and face were constantly with her throughout the whole night—Soren Romanov. He was the wolf in the room that everyone tried to ignore. Except there was no ignoring a six-foot-four-inch medieval Russian royal with a broad, powerful build and muscles that made his tailored tuxedo strain at the seams.

He stood with his arms crossed over his impressive chest, and he glared. But he also watched over her in a room full of possible enemies, and the fire in his eyes wasn't only for a fight. He desired her. He'd told her so matter-of-factly at dinner as he casually ate his soup.

All I want is to taste the wine on your tongue.

Her head grew light with the memory, even though she'd been careful not to overimbibe. Soren was impressive in his defensive mode, but there was something about him confessing a vulnerability that stunned her. She had to concentrate in her heels to keep from stumbling on the carpet-strewed marble floors.

He didn't trust her witch blood. He fully intended to find and destroy the emerald sword that tried to bind them together, a warrior and her wolf. But he would protect her still, and he desired her. He craved her taste and her touch.

Anna straightened her long black gloves again and again. She'd chosen velvet gloves banded in deep red silk for tonight to complement her dress. No one seemed to think her eccentric accessories were odd. After all, she was the daughter of a woman who was known for her anachronistic clothing choices—gloves were nothing compared to hoops and horned hats.

The electricity caused by her interactions with Soren—from glances to outright sensual promise—almost seemed to outdo the charge of the Ether's power. Her heartbeat was quick. Her breathing more labored than it should be. But it wasn't because she was having a hard time controlling her abilities. It was because Soren stared and protected and shattered her defenses with his defensive posturing.

He had always backed her up. She'd been braver than she would have been as a teen girl in a cursed castle with an enchanted red wolf by her side.

She wanted to be braver still with the man.

More guests began to take their leave at midnight. Anna stood beside her mother and bade each and every one safe travels, never knowing which ones might wish her harm. Finally, the rooms were silent, save for servants using the Ether's energy to set things right after the crowd. Jewel tones of light flared here and there like brilliant fireflies trapped indoors, seeking each other in the night.

"Some of the guests have chosen to sleep in the palace. Servants are showing them to their rooms. Perhaps Soren could escort you to your room," Vasilisa suggested.

"He thinks some of the guests might be your enemies now that the curse has been lifted. He says some of them might still prefer the Darkness," Anna said. "There was one particular witch—a tall man with black hair. He seemed to have an intent focus on me."

"I thought I detected more than the usual edge of battle readiness in Soren. I appreciate his concern for you," Vasilisa said. "It doesn't seem to be the concern of someone who is ready and willing to let you go. Quite a few of the male *Volkhvy* were watching you this evening—perhaps he's afraid one of them will step forward to take his place?"

"Stop. You make light of serious things. I know you say that your enchanted swords only reveal the truth, but the truth is Soren will never trust *Volkhvy* manipulations. We will part. And soon," Anna said.

"You'll never part. Destroy the sword if you must. You'll only discover that you're bound without it. Partnership binds. Your partnership with the red wolf has been obvious to anyone with eyes all night long," Vasilisa said. "I have eyes and experience. You will be lost without each other as soon as you take the first steps away."

Anna turned her back on her mother and walked toward Soren. He met her in several strides before she could cross the room, as if he'd been waiting to join her all night.

"Some of the guests are staying the night. They've been given rooms in the palace," Anna said. She didn't reach for him. There was no acceptable reason to take his hand other than that she'd wanted to touch him again for hours. He didn't touch her either, although the air between them crackled with tension.

"I'll take you to your room when you're ready. You shouldn't be alone. Any one of them might wait for an opportunity to hurt you as your mother's heir," Soren said.

"Once I attain control of the full measure of my abilities, they wouldn't dare. But right now, I'm probably a tempting target," Anna agreed. "I'm not sure Vasilisa thought this through. She probably should have waited until I was better trained to invite so many powerful guests."

"She knew exactly what she was doing," Soren said. He placed a hand on Anna's elbow. Even the thick velvet didn't cushion her from the heat that flared from that simple contact. "She wants a daughter and a powerful pet. I'm going to disappoint her manipulations."

"Even if you're disappointed, as well?" Anna asked. But he didn't reply. He led her out of the room with his hand on her arm without so much as a glance at the queen, who watched them leave.

As they left the withdrawing room and entered the main arcade that wound to the base of the tiled staircase to the upper floors, the large arched windows that faced the sea were open to the night air. Anna slowed her pace, and Soren allowed it. His grip eased on her arm, and even he seemed to take a breath of the enchanted breeze.

"Your mother relies too much on the island as a defense. The palace is completely unfortified. Anyone could come and go from all the open doors and windows. This artificial climate is an indulgence," Soren said. But he paused near an open archway and a beam of moonlight fell on his face. The sudden illumination penetrated his defenses, because she could suddenly see him looking at her in a way he wouldn't have been looking without the cover of shadows.

His face was a Romanov face, with a strong, straight nose and angular jaw. His cheekbones were revealed now that his beard had been trimmed, and they were sharply cut as if from a perfect block of stone. But it was his lips that confessed in the sudden moonlight. They were softer than they'd been earlier. As full and gentled as they'd been when she'd kissed him days ago.

Anna didn't wait for logic to catch up to her intentions. She allowed herself to press up against the big male body of her wolf. The heels that had threatened her equilibrium all night now enabled her to press her mouth to Soren's. His lips were as soft as the moonlight said they'd be. She explored that one delicious vulnerability with her tongue.

"Anna," Soren growled against her mouth. But it wasn't a growl that was meant to repel. It was a hungry growl. One that warned of a devouring to come if she didn't back away.

"Yes," she whispered back. It wasn't a question. It was an affirmation. She knew what she risked.

He pulled her into the shadows of the archway's corner. He perched his hip on the ledge and she stepped between his knees. Their bodies melded. Her dress was no barrier; neither was the thin poplin of his dress shirt. Anna slid her hands beneath his jacket to feel the heated skin of his sides. He pulled her closer until her breasts flattened against his chest. Her arms wound around him to press against his muscled back.

And still her mouth clung to his.

She could taste wine on his tongue as she stroked hers against it. She remembered his confession from dinner, and she trembled as he licked deeply between her lips and his desire came true. Time had been their enemy and their friend. Now it stood still as they stole a moment away from the world. The intensity he'd radiated all night long was suddenly hers to taste and touch. She explored the heated ripple of his muscles until his shirt rode loose of his waistband and her hands found bare skin.

They both froze.

Soren hated her gloves in that moment. He resented their fear. She caressed his lower back, and the velvet only made him crave her actual touch more. Whether or not he trusted her abilities, he trusted her need to touch him.

Soren broke their kiss. He drew back and brought one of her hands to his face so that he could bite the tip of the middle finger on her glove. She gasped as his teeth closed on the velvet. But as he worked the glove loose to free her hand, Anna reached to stop him with her other hand. She cupped the side of Soren's jaw with a velvet palm. They were in the shadows, but the glow of the moon reached them just enough so that he could see the gleam of her eyes. They sparkled more than they should. The kiss or his willingness to get rid of the glove had upset her.

"We can't. Even if you trust me not to hurt you, I don't trust myself. The energy I channel is too much for me to control sometimes," Anna said. "I proved that when I took you through the Ether after the white wolf's attack."

Soren closed his eyes. He took a deep breath that shuddered his entire body with its release. His desire for her touch was nearly impossible for him to control. He should be glad that Anna had stopped him. But he wasn't. Suddenly, her fear of her power seemed a horrible thing. Similar to his fear of the Ether and being trapped in the shift. They were both haunted.

She was a witch. He was a wolf.

There was no escape from what they were.

He still held her hand to his face, but he had released the velvet from his teeth. She looked up at him, and he could tell she held her breath as he decided what to do. There was no choice. He would respect her wishes. Her skin was hers. If she chose not to share it with him, he would let her go and back away.

"I'm not afraid of your touch," he said. Then he released her hand. She drew it quickly back and cradled it with her other arm against her stomach. As if it might decide to caress him of its own volition.

"You should be," she whispered.

She backed away from him, and the balmy night had suddenly gone cold. Once again he wondered if their sudden separation opened him up to the island's true climate.

This time, the chill stayed with him as he followed Anna up the painted tile stairs.

Chapter 16

Soren caught up with her and took the lead by the time she reached her bedroom door. He opened it, but instead of stepping aside for her to pass, he crossed the threshold as if he was prepared for battle. His shoulders were stiff. His spine was straight. His hands were clenched, causing the muscles in his arm to bulge beneath his tuxedo.

Anna's abilities responded to his tension. Gloves or not, the power of the Ether flowed into her fingers beneath the velvet. A soft greenish glow shone through the fabric to join with the rising moon to illuminate the room.

It was empty save for her and Soren.

In her opinion, that was threat enough, although admittedly in a different way than the Dark *Volkhvy*.

Soren was still focused on making sure there were no intruders. He paced around the room. He checked curtains and behind the clothes in her closet. Finally, when no stone had been left unturned—or negligee, for that matter—he came back to where she stood.

"It isn't safe. Some of the guests can't be trusted, but even with my wolf instincts, I don't know if they're the ones who stayed," Soren said.

The very idea of the lank-haired witch prowling around her bedroom made Anna swallow hard in distaste.

"I'll close and lock my door and windows. I'll keep my guard up," Anna said. "You know I'm experienced in survival."

The glow beneath her gloves hadn't faded. If anything, it seemed to brighten as he took another step closer to her as she spoke. The energy from the Ether in her fingers was nothing compared to the electricity that arced between her body and his. There had been no visible spark when their lips and tongues had touched, but it had been there all the same.

The spark between them was green, as well. Every time she blinked, it shimmered with emerald facets behind her eyelids.

"You were never the target before. As your mother's heir, you might face a more determined enemy than we faced at Bronwal," Soren said.

As if he didn't realize what he did, he unclenched one fist and she drew in a startled breath as he brushed a curled tendril of hair from her cheek. She reached up to stop him before the simple gesture could become a caress. He allowed it. His hand froze in her gloved fingers. But it also combusted. Heat spread from that point of contact, and she could tell by his widened eyes that it spread through him, too.

There was nothing magical about the heat. He was a man. She was a woman. Wolf and witch didn't matter. Only their attraction mattered as the distant roar of crashing waves penetrated her room. Far away the ocean pounded the sand. In the quiet, moonlit shadows of her bedroom, her heart pounded with the same tidal inevitability.

"I have greater defensive capabilities than I had before," Anna said.

"You don't have to guard against me," Soren said. He eased his hand back and she let him go. Even if she did regret it the second their fingers parted.

"Don't I?" Anna asked. He was tragically attractive in this light in the intimate setting of her room. She'd slept peacefully so many times when he'd watched over her as the red wolf. But with his shirt loosened and his jacket rumpled and his lips swollen from her kisses, she suddenly wanted the man he'd become in her bed. She had to guard against the desire she felt for him. With every ounce of self-control she had.

"Never. I would never hurt you. I will always protect you from harm," Soren said. Fear tingled down her spine as she recognized the seriousness in his tone as a vow.

"Even if that means protecting me from a *Volkhvy* enchantment that tries to bring us together," Anna said. She suddenly knew a deeper truth than she'd known before. She couldn't believe she hadn't understood it from the start. It wasn't only his family he protected by refusing the emerald sword's decision. He was protecting *her*. She would be in danger if she accepted the Call, because the white wolf would never accept her.

He didn't try to touch her or kiss her again, but his dark gaze tracked over her face as if he would memorize her shadowed features. Her heartbeat had slowed. Her breathing had quieted. But in the stillness, longing seemed loud between them.

"Rest. We have a journey through the Ether ahead of us. Even if it only takes seconds, it will feel like eternity," Soren said. He was the one with the strength to back away this time. Her lips had gone dry. She had to moisten them with the tip of her tongue before she could speak.

"We've handled eternity together before," she replied.

Soren walked silently out of her room. He closed the door with a quiet but decisive click. Once she sensed his presence fade away down the hall, she went through the motions of preparing for sleep.

They had handled eternity together, but how would they face it alone?

Soren forced himself to walk away when he wanted to stay. He wanted to do much more than stay. He had experienced everything he wanted to do in a torturous stream of sensual fantasy as they'd stood face-to-face, not touching, barely breathing and caught in a purgatory of possibilities that would never be realized.

He'd seen desire for him written on her face even in the darkness. He'd taken the time to catalog every flutter of her eyelashes, every soft sigh past her lips. She'd swayed toward him. If he'd touched her again, the torture might have been over for both of them.

Or just beginning.

How could they destroy the sword if they succumbed to the attraction that pulled them together in spite of their best intentions to ignore it?

If he allowed himself to indulge in even a quarter of the fantasies he'd imagined in those perilous moments, he would never let her go. And he'd be a worse betrayer of his brothers than Vasilisa herself.

He walked away. The corridor to his room was long and flanked on either side by other doors. He had no way of knowing how many guests had stayed. There must be hundreds of bedrooms in the palace, and many of them stood in between his room and Anna's.

He managed to get all the way to his door before he stopped. He didn't open it. Instead, he raised his face to the arched ceiling, took a deep breath and then leaned his hot forehead on the cool cherry panels.

Anna wasn't safe.

Even if he had to endure a long night of misery, he had to go back and guard her room as he'd always done when he was the red wolf. It hadn't been a habit. It had been a sacred obligation. The emerald sword and her *Volkhvy* abilities didn't change the unspoken promise that had been between them from the start.

He would protect her even if his divided loyalties tore his body apart.

Anna knew when Soren was back outside her door. It wasn't a breath or a sigh. The floor didn't creak beneath his graceful feet. Maybe his shifter energy caused the molecules in the air to vibrate with his intensity. Maybe the distant Call of the emerald sword whispered a little louder in her soul. Or maybe she had been attuned to his presence or his absence for too long to stop now when she should.

She half expected the door to open. She half hoped to see his tall, masculine silhouette suddenly outlined by moonlight. Anna sat up in bed. The cool cotton sheet slid off her heated skin. If her thoughts about his kisses had manifested him, they stopped short of making him open the door.

She slipped from the bed.

The windows were closed and shuttered, as she'd promised. Her curtains were drawn. She walked in deep shadows to the door. She had taken off her gloves. They lay on the bedside table if she needed them. Never far out of reach. But she raised bare hands to the cool cherrywood and placed her palms flat and her fingers wide against it.

She wouldn't try to disintegrate the barrier. She wished it away and thanked the universe for it at the same time. It was far past midnight. She'd been reliving every second of his kiss since he'd left her alone. Only the solid cherry door kept them apart.

Anna leaned her cheek against the wood in between her hands. She wasn't trying to hear him breathe or listen for his heartbeat. She was only getting as close to him as their stark circumstances would allow.

The temperature of the wood compared to the flush of her face caused her to shiver. She wore a voluminous white silk gown that she'd pulled from a sachet-scented drawer. It had been wrapped in tissue and tied up with faded satin ribbons, as if it had never been worn since some seamstress had crafted it long ago.

Vasilisa liked fine things, and she'd shared them with her daughter. She'd filled the room with amenities, some vintage, some newly made. But Anna hadn't found a robe with the nightgown.

Her trembling was caused as much by anticipation as by the chill.

She could invite him inside. They were alone. There were no Romanovs or *Volkhvy* here to stop them. Everyone else was sleeping. It wasn't a conscious decision to step back and reach for the doorknob. Anna twisted it, and the metallic noise its movement made seemed like a confession in the dark.

She opened the door.

Soren was there. She'd had no doubt. But she hadn't expected him to look so handsomely haggard and worn. He'd removed his jacket and his tie. His shirt was loose, unbuttoned midway down his chest and untucked from his tailored black pants. His hair looked dark and wild in the shadows, even with his new trimmed style. A tousled fringe covered one of his eyes.

"No. Go back inside. Close the door," Soren ordered.

His voice was hoarse with emotion. It was warmed by past howls and a desire he no longer tried to hide. If she trembled, he shook. He was only standing there, but he looked as if he was buffeted by an unseen storm.

The tempest was inside him.

She recognized it, because it roared in her own chest, as well.

"The shift kept us apart for centuries. Together, but separated by tooth and claw. How can we let a door keep us apart now?" Anna whispered. Her voice shocked her. It was hoarse, as if she, too, had spent years howling. And maybe she had. Silently, desperately crying out to be free to run with the wolf she loved.

The emerald sword's Call was only an echo of her own cry.

Soren moved so suddenly she didn't have time to gasp his name. One second he shook in the hallway, refusing her invitation, and the next he leaped to scoop her into his arms.

She was curvy and she'd enjoyed fine food since the curse had been broken, but her body was no burden to Soren's big Romanov build. In fact, he lifted her high with strong hands on her waist and extended his muscular arms until she looked down at his upturned face. The sudden rush of movement made her dizzy in the dark, and she placed her hands on his broad shoulders to prevent the fall he would never have allowed in spite of her loss of equilibrium. He tilted slightly backward to take her weight with his broad chest as well as his hands.

And then he lowered her inch by inch down his hot, hard body until her mouth reached his lips.

They found each other easily even without a lamp.

This time when they kissed, there was no hesitation. She eagerly sank into his hungry welcome. It was more physical than it had been before. His rough stubble sensitized her cheeks and chin. She nipped and nibbled the full swell of his mouth that had been kept from her view for too long.

The taste of Soren was wintry sweet. She could still breathe in the Carpathian forest from his skin and hair. The evergreens, the snow, the fresh mountain air had all become a part of him. He needed no cologne. The scent of wilderness went with him everywhere he traveled, even here where the atmosphere was controlled.

Her wolf should be wild.

He'd been careful and watchful and vigilant for far too long. She could love him and set him free in more ways than one. They would destroy the sword, but first she would destroy the wall of control between them.

Anna tried to wrap her legs around Soren's waist, but her nightgown wouldn't allow the movement. She whimpered into his mouth and suddenly his strong hands gripped the fabric at her sides. She felt the silk bunching in his fists as he continued to plumb the depths of her mouth with his tongue.

And then the delicate material gave way.

Cool air washed over her bared legs, but her trembling response wasn't a shiver. It was need. Her cheeks were wet with released emotion. Their kiss had gone salty with tears and perspiration.

"I'm here. I'm here," Soren murmured as he gentled the deep kiss into long, leisurely tastes. One after the other.

Soren let go of her gown, and she wrapped her freed legs around him. His hands came up to support her bottom and press her heat against him. Nothing could have prevented her from rocking against his erection. He bulged out the front of his trousers until the thin, slim-cut material revealed the solid length and heft of his excitement. Soren rewarded her undulations with a groan that was almost a growl.

She had opened the door. She had invited him inside. No one had to know. They had stolen moments before. Why couldn't they steal one last night?

Chapter 17

"The black wolf would never approve of this assignation. But what of the queen? I'll wager she'd be very happy if her daughter brings at least one of the Romanov wolves to heel," a voice interrupted them from the corridor. Soren had hooked the door with one of his ankles in order to pull it shut, but he froze and Anna ripped her mouth from his.

She and Soren weren't naked, but she felt completely exposed as a dozen *Volkhvy* approached from the hallway's shadows. She recognized them from the dinner party, but none of them had been seated together and none of them were the lank-haired witch she had most feared. She didn't remember any of their names. Like the lank-haired witch, they had faded away after dinner without staying to be introduced, but, unlike him, they had reappeared. If the tone of the witch who was obviously in the lead hadn't clued her in on their antagonism, the flanking maneuver of their positioning would have. They approached as enemies, covering the corridor's exits and extending their hands as a witch does before he or she summoned Ether energy.

"This is a mistake," Soren growled at the approaching witches. This time his emotion wasn't sexy. It was intended as a warning. He let her go when she loosened her legs and she slid to the floor. But Soren didn't allow her to stand where she'd dropped. He stepped forward. He placed his muscular frame in front of hers.

Suddenly, Anna wanted the emerald sword with a ferocity that startled her. She had other powers at her disposal. She'd never trained with a blade. But it was missing from her hands. She could almost feel its hilt in her fingers. She fisted her hands around nothing and stood with impotent rage in the sword's place.

"That's what it looked like from here. A mistake," the *Volkhvy* continued.

"A very hot mistake," another *Volkhvy* added. The older woman smirked at her own joke, looking Soren up and down as if she would like the chance to climb him herself.

"Hey," Anna protested. She stepped from behind Soren, and without thinking she summoned a flash of energy from the Ether that morphed into the shape of a glowing green sword in her hands.

"That's new," Soren said. He didn't try to block her again. He accepted her beside him.

The *Volkhvy* in the hallway responded to Anna's sword-shaped energy. The corridor exploded into multiple shades of jewel-toned light as they all summoned energy from the Ether.

"They stole my sword. I have to make do," Anna replied.

Soren didn't argue as she suddenly claimed the sword they'd both agreed should be destroyed. He simply shifted. He hadn't meant their kiss was a mistake, of course. He'd

meant it was a mistake for the Dark witches to attack the
red Romanov wolf.

The whole palace quaked with his shift. Dust drifted
from the ceiling and several glass panels fell with a tin-
kling crash, but the *Volkhvy* still advanced. Anna was a
survivor. She'd fought many battles during the curse. She'd
used whatever she could gather and grab. But this time,
she used the suddenly manifested energy sword as if it
was the real blade she'd never wielded.

The first *Volkhvy* who'd spoken went down beneath
her "blade" with a scream. Witches weren't easy to kill.
Energy from the Ether gave them long lives, and it also
healed them from grievous wounds. But Anna's "sword"
was made from the Ether's energy. It disrupted the connection between the Ether and the witch she stabbed. Black
blood flowed from his lips as he disappeared. He might
recover within the Ether itself, but that would take time.

Hopefully a long time.

The red wolf's bite was another matter.

He had been an enchanted champion of the Light
Volkhvy queen. She'd manipulated his genes with the Ether
before he was born. Although she was no longer his queen,
Volkhvy who must have allied themselves with Darkness
in order to attack a Romanov wolf and the queen's daughter still fell beneath his teeth.

They'd fought side by side before, but this time Anna
used all the power of her *Volkhvy* abilities to help Soren.
The older woman who had jokingly called their kiss a "hot
mistake" was much more experienced than Anna. But she
retreated before the blows of Anna's energy. The shredded
skirt of Anna's nightgown proved to be as useful in battle
as it had been in lovemaking. She moved with grace and
no hindrance of material as she landed blow after blow

against a bright citrine energy shield the *Volkhvy* woman had created.

Finally, the hallway fell silent except for the loud sizzle of Anna's electric blows and the woman's cries each time their energy connected. The *Volkhvy* fell back on one knee, and still Anna kept advancing until she lifted her sword over her head and brought it down onto nothing. The citrine had fizzled and disappeared. Her green sword plunged through the *Volkhvy*'s breast, and the woman retreated into the Ether.

Only then did Anna turn around.

Her green sword flickered and winked out as she faced a bloody scene.

The red wolf had been busy, too. There were half a dozen *Volkhvy* traitors who would never be able to retreat to the Ether for healing again. A Romanov wolf bite made for a much worse injury than an Ether-energy blade.

Soren came to her on four legs. He pushed his bloody snout into her outstretched hand. Of course, she reached for him. She always would. Even when she shouldn't.

"Well. This has been a long night," Vasilisa said from the archway of the stairs. She surveyed the damage Soren's shift had caused in the tile and the ceiling. She stepped off the stairs and into the hallway, carefully avoiding the bodies and steaming blood on the floor.

Anna noted that the queen had a matching robe for a nightgown that was similar to her own ruined garment. Automatically she reached to pull a ripped sleeve up on her exposed shoulder as her mother approached. Soren whined. The red wolf wasn't feral. But he wasn't human, either. He'd just attacked and killed *Volkhvy* he didn't trust. Now another *Volkhvy* he didn't trust was in the same hallway. She reached to place her hand on the top of his russet head. He fell silent. But he didn't retreat. He stood by her side.

"You were right, Soren. There were traitors in our midst.

I can't thank you enough for protecting my daughter, the future queen, from their treachery," Vasilisa said. Other *Volkhvy* had begun to poke their heads out of bedrooms. A troop of servants arrived to clean up after the battle.

She and Soren had never been alone. *Volkhvy* had surrounded them. Even if they had hidden behind her closed bedroom door, they would have had to face possible revelation in the morning. No one who had seen them together would believe they'd spent a platonic night.

Her arms ached from the fight. She'd used muscles to wield the energy sword that she'd never used before. It had seemed to come naturally to her, but now her body protested. Her forearms twitched with spasms, and her neck and shoulders screamed.

"You knew this would happen," Anna said. She wasn't only talking about the traitors or the battle. Her mother had wanted her and Soren to spend time together. But now it was obvious that she'd wanted them to connect as intimately as possible.

I'll wager she'd be very happy if her daughter brings at least one of the Romanov wolves to heel.

Vasilisa looked from Anna's face down to where her daughter's hand rested on top of the red wolf's head.

"They said that you'd want me to bring the red wolf to heel. Are you matchmaking, Mother? Is that why you provided the red dress? Is that why you insisted on a dinner?"

"I'm older and wiser than I appear," Vasilisa said. "I've made many mistakes. Some of them unforgivable. But in this, I'm guilty of nothing more than wanting my daughter to be happy."

The queen turned away. She lifted her skirts and stepped over the puddles of blood in the hall. Anna felt Soren move away from her hand, but she watched her mother until the

queen's back had disappeared up the stairway before she
turned around.

The red wolf was gone.

Anna couldn't blame him.

As the servants cleaned up the dead *Volkhvy* with no
more emotion than they'd shown when they tidied after
the dinner earlier in the evening, Anna retreated to her
bedroom. This time when she shut the door, she leaned
her back against it as if she would hold the whole dark
world at bay.

Her arms still trembled.

She hugged them around herself and closed her eyes.

She and Soren hadn't been allowed to steal a single
night, and she should be glad. Anna wouldn't allow Vasilisa
to use her to manipulate Soren back into being the queen's
champion. He should be free. And he would be. Even if it
broke her heart.

He ran because he could. And because he had to. The
night was still young for an enchanted wolf. He had bound-
less energy even after the battle and restlessness caused
by what might have been. Four legs became two as he ran,
and the shift didn't slow him down.

In fact, he ran faster as he became a man with a man's
needs.

He should be glad they'd been interrupted before they
could make a mistake that would haunt him for the rest of
his days. Trouble was he would be haunted anyway. He
slowed and stopped near the dark ribbon of a freshwater
stream. He'd splashed through it before. This time he used
the chill waters to wash away sweat and blood—his own,
as the *Volkhvy* blood had already evaporated from his skin
like smoke. He slicked his hair back out of his eyes. Then,

as the dirty water flowed away, he drank his fill of water from his cupped hands.

The moonlight illuminated the island around him, but he could still see the lights from the palace in the distance. He'd left Anna alone. She'd been shaken. She'd been upset with her mother and the treachery they'd faced.

Soren rose and tilted his chin toward the sky. He closed his eyes. He could still see Anna wielding her energy sword. The vision would stay with him forever. She'd been unstoppable. *Volkhvy* had fallen to her, left and right. In nothing but an ethereal nightdress, she had fought like a warrior.

Because it was her destiny to be one.

Destroying the emerald sword would take that destiny away from her. It wasn't until now, as the adrenaline of battle bled away to leave him hollow and cold, that he fully understood he would also be robbed.

He had mourned the loss of the waif. Now he knew he would mourn the loss of the warrior, as well.

Chapter 18

She was tired and sore to the bone. Her body ached with every heartbeat, or maybe it was only heartache that resonated outward with her *Volkhvy* blood as it pumped through an organ that was useless save for circulation.

She loved Soren.

Her mother was right.

But her love had to be denied.

They had been nothing but companions for centuries, a girl and her wolf. In truth, they had always been more. There was a connection between them and it was one that could never be severed, not even with the sword's destruction. But their connection couldn't be indulged. Not now when she'd seen time and again how fiercely Soren fought against it. And not ever if she wanted to avoid becoming too powerful to control her abilities.

Anna turned the hot-water tap on full blast and sat on the edge of the large claw-foot tub in her bedroom's bath.

As the steam rose to fill the room with swirling, soothing fog, she remembered the way they'd had to heat water on the kitchen fire and carry it in containers to wooden tubs for bathing. It had been an arduous chore and, more often than not, baths had been taken in an inch or two of rapidly cooling water. To fill a tub for soaking would have been a pure, selfish luxury they couldn't afford in a cursed castle where the clock was always counting down as they ran out of time.

Volkhvy blood rose like black smoke from the skin to disappear into the Ether when it was spilled. She ran the tub full of hot water more to cleanse her thoughts and soak her sore muscles than to wash. Her hair had loosened and tumbled down from her dinner coiffure during the battle. She took the bulk of it in her hands and wound it in a pile on top of her head, where she pinned it with a clip she'd found in the vanity drawer. Her nightgown was already hanging from her shoulders. The fight had been too rough for the delicate material. With only a tug, she pulled what was left of it free and allowed it to puddle on the floor.

And then she thought of Soren.

Of course she did.

The steam had fogged up the room and the full-length mirror that sat opposite the tub. The ghostly reflection of her nude form mocked her in the glass. The bath wouldn't soothe her. Its heat wasn't the heat she craved.

Anna lifted a leg and stepped into the water anyway. What else could she do? Soren had run away from her again. He'd been right to run. When they were together, it was hard to remember why they needed to stay apart.

The water welcomed her with a hot embrace that made her gasp, then sigh as she sank down into the tub. She leaned back against the highest end of the warmed enamel and propped herself with her arms on either side.

She closed her eyes and knew it for a mistake as soon as memories of Soren's kisses came flooding back to life in senses heightened by the lack of visual distraction.

The hot water lapped just over the rounded globes of Anna's breasts. The rest of her was a pale, shimmering mystery under the steaming liquid as vapor continued to rise. Soren drew in a shaky breath to steady himself in the doorway, and the heat and humidity infiltrated his lungs with languorous, heavy air.

He grabbed the frame of the door with both hands to hold himself where he should stay.

"I came back," he said softly. Anna opened her eyes. He thought to reassure her, but she wasn't startled. Some part of her must have already known he was there. "It isn't safe for you to be alone. There's no way of knowing if there are others who might attack before the night is out."

"I can take care of myself," Anna replied. She hadn't locked the doors to keep him out. She'd hoped he'd return. Besides, her abilities protected her from a *Volkhvy* threat better than any lock and key.

She didn't sink deeper into the water. She didn't cover her nudity with her hands. She simply watched as if she waited to see what he would do. She didn't order him away. His grip tightened on the doorjamb without him consciously deciding that he needed to tighten it. The slightest hint of rose scent tantalized, because he knew it would be sweeter and muskier breathed in deeply from the skin of her neck.

"I know," Soren said. "But you shouldn't have to. Not as long as I'm with you. I'll fight by your side."

He couldn't promise that he'd be by her side forever. He could only promise that while he was with her he would have her back as he'd always done.

"I don't need a champion. You saw me. You saw what I'm capable of," Anna said. Her voice trembled. He could hear her fear. He watched as her jaw tightened against it.

His hands loosened. He allowed them to slide down the door's frame. Anna's eyes tracked his hands. Then her gaze flew to his face. She sat up in the water. She was no longer reclined. The moist pink areolae of her breasts were exposed.

"Then I offer no champion. Only a partner. Only a friend," Soren said. He didn't feel friendly. His body was on fire with need and anticipation. He hadn't consciously come back to the palace to finish what they'd started earlier in the evening, but he couldn't walk away.

She was a sultry vision in the bath. Her nipples were still barely submerged, but their peaked tips caused his lips to go dry. He hardened, and only then did he realize he'd come to her still naked from his shift. His erection was a confession that drew her gaze and caused a flush to rise on her damp cheeks.

"Only a friend?" Anna asked. Her lips curled slightly into a smile that was at once familiar and electrifyingly new.

And that was when he knew they'd won a fight with the *Volkhvy*, but his battle against his desire for one special witch had been lost.

Soren appeared in the doorway like a god fallen from the heavens. His tall, muscular form was as she remembered it from the day she'd almost died, but this time, she was fully conscious and able to appreciate every curve and angle. He was perfect, from his damp russet hair to his long pale legs dusted with darker hair. His angular face was graced only with a trimmed red shadow of a beard that highlighted his cheek and jaw—and the tension in his jaw as he held himself in the doorway.

He wanted to join her.

She saw the need in his hard face and his glittering eyes even before she saw it elsewhere.

His arms were braced and bulging with muscle. His knuckles were white as he held on.

But it was the direction of his gaze that caused her to melt. Her nipples hardened with need as he moistened his lips. His grip loosened and his hands dropped from the door. And then his penis jutted proudly from a nest of dark red curls.

Anna stood at exactly the same moment that Soren stepped into the bathroom. Water sluiced off her skin, but she didn't have time to shiver. Because Soren took several more steps. He paused beside the tub. He lifted one hand to her face. She drew in a shaky breath as he cupped her cheek.

"We aren't alone. There are guards stationed outside your door. They allowed me to pass," Soren said.

Anna imagined their shock when a nude legendary wolf had made himself at home in their midst.

"So we won't steal a night together," Anna decided. "We'll claim it. We'll take it. After all this time, we deserve a taste of what might have been."

"I would walk away now, if you wished it," Soren offered. His touch was gentle, but his body was hard with tension. Heat radiated off his naked skin as he held himself in check.

"One day soon we'll both walk away. But not now. Not tonight," Anna whispered. She met his gaze. Steam had dissipated. The water around her legs had grown cold. But she didn't shiver. The heat in Soren's amber eyes warmed her.

"Not tonight," Soren agreed.

Anna reached for him. Soren dropped his hand, and

she placed her palms on his shoulders. She measured their broad span for a stunned second. Then she looked into Soren's eyes. They had narrowed slightly with humor at her reaction, crinkling at the edges.

"I don't remember you being this…big," Anna said. Her face flushed as she thought of other ways he was big in addition to his shoulders. The crinkles at the edges of his eyes grew deeper. But then his humor disappeared. He leaned to place his forehead against hers.

"I would never hurt you," Soren said. "One of the reasons I run is to know myself again. To get used to this body. I work every day for precision and control."

Anna's heartbeat kicked up a notch. She knew. She saw. His strength and grace. His power and his perfection. Oh, he had scars. He had lived a very long time and fought many battles. But they only added a storied past to his perfection. Legends behind his handsome face.

"I want to know you," Anna confessed.

Soren stilled. His breath caught and his movement ceased. He continued, unmoving, as she caressed from his strong neck down to the rounded curves of his biceps. She measured them on both sides with the spread of her fingers, which didn't reach even halfway around. Then she paused to hold his obvious strength in the palms of her hands.

Only then did he release a long, slow exhale. He lifted his forehead from hers. She looked up at his sudden movement away from her. But it was only temporary. When her chin lifted and her lips became accessible, Soren leaned in again to capture her lower lip. He suckled it while he watched her reaction and then when she gasped, he bathed it with his rough, moist tongue.

"I'm yours. For tonight," Soren said against her mouth as he released her. The intimate offer caused a hot coil of desire to suddenly tighten in the pit of her stomach. Her chest also tightened, but she ignored that darker emotion in favor of pressing her mouth to his for a deeper taste.

He'd sensitized her lips with his suckling. His tongue had shattered her equilibrium. She was light-headed even before the crackle of the Ether's energy arced from her mouth to his. The jolt was only an amplification of the chemistry that already existed between them. But it enhanced, from the slide of their tongues to the tingle in her nipples to the fire at the juncture of her thighs.

Soren cried out his pleasure in the slight electric pain of the arc that must have enhanced what was already happening to him, too.

"Tonight might kill me," he growled. She tasted perspiration on his lips.

"No. We'll die tomorrow and the next day and the next. Tonight we live. We savor," Anna said.

Soren reached for the towel she'd left on a chair near the tub. He wrapped her in its soft folds and lifted her into his arms. She didn't protest. She held on as he carried her into the bedroom beneath the stars.

It was dark before dawn. The moon had disappeared, and only the persistent twinkle of stars remained visible through the glass dome over their heads. Suddenly, Anna held tighter to Soren's neck as she thought of her aviary. And all the times they'd sat together on the ramparts of Bronwal beneath the stars.

"Is it too much? The difference in me?" Soren asked. He had paused in the middle of the room. The shadows hid his face but not his concerns.

"I could ask you the same," Anna said. "My answer is yes and no. You are Soren, the red Romanov wolf. You are the same in all the ways that matter, and you are new in ways that shake me to my toes."

She pressed her lips to his shoulder and flicked her tongue out to taste his skin. She licked his neck and then suckled where his pulse throbbed. He shuddered beneath the sensual attack. He brought a hand up to thread into her hair and hold her as she nuzzled and nipped his skin.

"You are wholly new to me, but that's because I didn't know you—all of you—before. You are a woman and a warrior and a witch. I thought you were my Bell, but you are Anna. Never to be mine, but precious all the same," Soren said.

Anna's eyes burned with unshed emotion.

He might not love her, but he didn't hate all *Volkhvy*. Not now. Not while he held her and felt her lips on his skin. He carried her to the bed, but he didn't lay her on it. Instead, just as he'd done when he'd stepped into the mirror, he turned to back up to the bed and sit on its edge. He lay back on the mounded coverlet. He took her with him into the soft bed. They sank together. The canopy's diaphanous coverings were translucent, but they still created a sense of privacy and retreat.

They'd found an intimate hideaway in a chaotic world.

"I've wanted you in this bed," Anna said. His arms loosened, and she was able to rearrange herself as she liked. She liked. A lot. There was so much man beneath her that she didn't know where to begin, but she naturally settled her heat against his flat, hard stomach. His erection bumped against her, fiery, hot and ready.

But he'd given her a gift, and she intended to collect.

"You're mine? For tonight?" Anna asked.

"Yes," Soren replied. He held himself still again. She could tell he was waiting to see what she wanted and wished. Heady anticipation filled her, hardening her nipples and pulsing between her legs. She arched her back and rocked against him, energy flaring along with her desire, arcing between their bodies everywhere they touched. "Yes," Soren repeated, this time breathless with need.

He was long and hard against her bottom. Thickened and slick. She was slick, too. Her excitement had quickened her core. She slid against his stomach as she undulated, and the sweet scent of her musk rose in the air.

"Mine," Anna said. And this time she wasn't asking for clarification or permission.

She slid off to lie beside him, but even as he groaned a protest, she claimed her wolf. She leaned over him to explore his naked chest with her lips. Although her heartbeat fluttered, she wasn't tentative. Nearly overwhelmed by the feast before her, yes, but not intimidated.

Anna took her time, but only in order to memorize every inch of him. She would never be able to make love to him again. Every kiss. Every caress. Every hot gasp she drew from his naked body had to be remembered forever.

She kissed around the hard swell of each pectoral muscle. Even though his muscles were hard, she could feel his heartbeat beneath her lips. She tasted the perspiration of his excitement. She rode the rapid rise and fall of his shallow breathing as she leaned into him.

The starlight wasn't enough. She couldn't see him as well as she'd like. She could only depend upon her lips to trace and her tongue to taste.

And her hand to follow.

She controlled her power. She only allowed the lightest of electric shocks to arc between her fingers and his skin. The green glow lit up the contours of his muscled chest, his rippled abdomen and the dip that led to...

Anna tamped down her power and took his hot erection in her hand. He was excited and well-endowed. He more than filled her hand with several inches revealed beyond the grip of her fist. Soren tossed his head back in abandon and jerked his hips up to thrust himself into her fist. She leaned over him to muffle his moans with her kisses. She licked his gasps from his lips and teased her tongue into his mouth. He reached to hold the back of her head and deepen the kiss while she stroked the smooth, steely length of him.

"Yes. Anna. Yes. Please," Soren moaned into her mouth.

He was an enchanted shape-shifter, powerful and dangerous and more than most women would brave. But Anna wasn't most women. She was a warrior. And it seemed like she'd been waiting for Soren to beg for her touch for a long time.

Anna rose up on her knees and Soren stilled again as if he knew what she wanted to do. He stopped thrusting. He fell silent. Until she leaned to take the head of his erection in her mouth. She closed her mouth over him. She licked and suckled and he cried out once more.

Suddenly, she was afraid of her hunger to please him. One night wasn't enough. It would never be enough.

But it was all she had.

Anna's fear fled.

She moved her hand out of the way so she could envelop him deeply. She took all of him into her mouth. And then she found a rhythm that made him call out her name. He took up most of her bed. He could fight a whole horde of Dark *Volkhvy*. But his sweet, salty pleasure was hers and hers alone. He was hers. For tonight. She brought the legendary wolf to earth, to fully inhabit his human body.

For her.

Always for her.

Soren shook as he fought his release, every muscle and every cell tensed against it until he collapsed back on the bed. Anna didn't protest. She allowed him to pull her back up to lie across his chest.

"If you kill me, you'll have to go after the sword alone," he teased. Her hair had tumbled down. If he drowned in silky rose-scented curls, he would die happy, but she didn't need to know that. He already tingled from the effects of her power. It vibrated beneath his skin, making him breathless the same way a rush of adrenaline would.

He didn't hate it.

That alone should make him get up and walk away.

"You like my power, but you don't like that you like it," Anna guessed.

"I've shifted twice in the last few days, but making love makes me feel very human. Maybe too human," Soren said. "I want this feeling to last."

The last was a confession. One he hated to make. Because it didn't matter what he wanted. Tomorrow they would leave the island to go in search of the emerald sword.

Chapter 19

When Soren's mood shifted, Anna felt the air in the room tighten with unspoken tension. He was a Romanov wolf. She wasn't the only one who tapped into the Ether to channel power. The Romanovs had been changed by the Ether's power. Vasilisa had manipulated their genes so that they became the powerful shape-shifters she needed to fight the Dark *Volkhvy*.

Soren's moods could literally rock the world if he chose to shift. And, apparently, he could rock hers even when he chose to stay human.

"This changes nothing. We're still going to destroy the sword. We have to. We have to keep your family safe from the Dark *Volkhvy*," Anna said. "From the ascendance of a new Dark prince...or *princess*."

"You're right and you're wrong. We're going to destroy the sword, but this still changes everything," Soren said. His hands grasped her arms and he lifted her off his chest and onto one of the pillows at the head of her bed. Now he leaned over her. She was trapped between his broad chest and the soft mattress. His eyes, so dark in the absence of light, met hers. She couldn't read any secrets in their glittering depths. Her only hope was that he also couldn't read hers. He was right. His kisses changed everything. More than kisses would restructure her world, whether or not he remained in it.

"This changes everything, but I can't stop. Not if you don't want me to," Soren said.

She didn't want him to stop. Now or ever. She settled for silence when speaking would reveal too much.

Soren kissed her and this time he was in total control of how long, how lingering, how deep and how slow he explored her mouth. Time stopped, but unlike when they dematerialized during the curse, they didn't disappear. She was more physical than she'd ever been. She was alive under his lips and in his arms. Her pulse throbbed in her veins. Her body throbbed along with it. Anna's eyes filled again. She was thankful for the darkness. Maybe if he tasted salt on her skin he would blame it on perspiration instead of tears.

She hoped in vain.

He drank the salty emotion from her cheeks with tender licks and kisses. He recognized her pain. He swam in it with her. He softly murmured her name. And then he smoothed a calloused hand over her jaw and tilted her chin as he tenderly kissed down to her neck.

Suddenly, her pain was overwhelmed with need.

She'd grown excited and wet when she'd suckled him. Now lust welled up again between her legs. *Yes.* This would make losing him harder, but she welcomed that later, greater pain if they could indulge in this connection now.

Soren's hand caressed down from her jaw to her chest.

He cupped the globe of one breast in the palm of his hand. He kissed her again as he gently thumbed her pebbled nipple.

It was Anna's turn to breathe a yes against his lips.

"Nothing else matters right now. Only this. Only touching you and pleasuring you and the two of us finally coming together," Soren said.

"Yes," Anna agreed. But it was more of a plea than an agreement. She lied. Losing him mattered. What she was meant to be mattered. But losing the sword mattered less than having him the only time they could allow.

Soren accepted her encouragement. He stroked his hand down to her trembling stomach, spreading heat all the way. Then he found the wet pulse between her legs. He dropped his hot mouth to capture the nipple he had ripened with his calloused thumb and, at the same time, he parted her intimate folds. He sucked and licked her breast as his fingers slid slickly over the tight bud of flesh that pulsed with her desire.

Anna cried out. Her hips bucked up to meet his touch, and she reached for the back of his neck to hold on. He lifted his lips from her breast to her mouth. He alternated between deep, suckling kisses and murmurs of encouragement. He seemed to savor her sounds of pleasure.

"We can't be together. But you're mine tonight. I want every tremble. Every sigh you'll give me," Soren said. "I want to carry this memory with me forever." His breath tickled hotly against her skin. Her tears had dried. His deft fingers owned all her attention. "Let go. Let me give you the ultimate pleasure. Give me your release."

She was shaking with tension. The salt on her face was no longer caused by sadness. Her body was flushed with heat. Her breasts rose and fell as she panted for breath and struggled for control. Her fingers slipped on his neck from the perspiration her excitement had generated. But she couldn't let go for him. She was holding the power of the Ether at bay...for him. She couldn't do both.

He'd never seen a woman so close to the edge of her climax but still holding on. Anna's wet heat engulfed his slowly thrusting finger, and her hips rose and fell to match the rhythm of his hand. The heat of her thigh was torture to his hardened cock as she moved, but he was determined to bring her to release before he settled himself between her legs. They'd been kept apart too long. He wouldn't rush their lovemaking now. He could sense that something was wrong even though she held him and moaned with pleasure. She arched for his hand, but he could tell she was holding back.

"What do you want, Anna? Tell me," he urged against her lips.

"I can't... The Ether's energy is all around us. It's gathering inside me. If I relax, I won't be able to control it," Anna replied. In the darkness of the shadowy room, her eyes had opened. He could tell because her emerald irises sparkled with the light of her power, barely held in check. The flecks of light illuminated her face. Her lashes were damp. Her cheeks were flushed. Her lips were swollen with heat and hunger. In that moment, he almost broke his internal vow to bring her to pleasure first. He wanted to take her, to join with her, to meld their bodies together.

But first, he had to trust her.

He'd paused the movement of his hand as she spoke. Now he gently pressed to claim her with his finger again. At the same time, he leaned close so that her sparkling eyes would illuminate his face. He wanted Anna to see his acceptance of her power. His desire for her to let go of all control.

For tonight. For him.

"I'm the red Romanov wolf. You don't have to control yourself for me. I was born and bred in the Ether's power. I want your pleasure. I want to bathe in your light," Soren said against her lips. He stared into her eyes. He saw them widen. He saw them brighten.

And then an emerald flash that would have sent a lesser man to the floor rocked him backward.

Soren held on to the headboard with his free hand. His muscles bunched and Anna's hold tightened around his neck. The burst of power didn't separate them. They stayed together as Anna's most intimate muscles contracted around his hand. She cried out. She called his name. It was the sweetest sound he'd heard in an age. His body tingled as her power infiltrated every cell. He didn't fight it. He basked in its glow.

And, finally, he allowed himself to settle between her parted legs.

Soren covered her with his hard, warm body and Anna gathered him close with her arms and legs. She needed his solid muscled back to anchor her to the earth. As their breathing synchronized, it seemed as if all her molecules reassembled in a slightly better position than they had been before.

She was whole. Somewhere the emerald sword shone. She was sure of it, even though she couldn't see it. Carnal connection had nothing to do with claiming her partnership with the red wolf. It was Soren's brief acceptance and pleasure in her power that caused the sword's glow and her feeling of perfect symmetry.

Then her legendary lover positioned himself so that their bodies could join, and suddenly Anna had a different definition of *whole*. The momentary pain was nothing compared to the tingling of her power that still pulsed beneath her skin. Replete seconds before, she immediately grew hungry for more when Soren began to slowly rock his hips between her thighs. She was slick to ease his passage.

But he had been her guardian for centuries, so she wasn't surprised when he softly asked if she was okay.

"I don't want to hurt you," Soren murmured against her ear.

Pain would come later. For now all she felt was pleasure.

"Nothing hurts. Not at all," Anna assured him. She lifted her hips to meet his thrusts. She quickened her pace to prove her point. Nothing did hurt. Not now. Pain and tears could wait. For now, she loved a legend and she could no longer wait to take him to the same heights he had taken her.

"Anna...Anna," Soren said. He claimed her with her true name and with the thrusts of his powerful hips. She held his shoulders and he lifted his hands up to hold her face. He cradled her jaw in both of his hands with impossible gentleness even as his rhythm increased. He was softly illuminated by green light. She saw the reflection of her glow in his eyes. He didn't close his lids against it. He held her face and looked deeply into her eyes. He'd taken her at her word. His movements grew stronger. He claimed her with his power as she'd claimed him with hers. The bed shook. Her world shook. She pulsed again with another climax. Her muscles contracted around his shaft, and a green aura of the Ether's energy lit the room as it rose from their entwined bodies.

Soren's body tensed above her. And still his hands remained gentle on her face. He finally closed his eyes as his climax claimed him, but he still had the presence of mind to pull out as he came. His seed was hot on her stomach. She only minded because she would rather have him inside her. He collapsed against her and she held him close, knowing the closeness wouldn't last.

Chapter 20

The sunrise painted the island in shades of crimson and gold. The lank-haired witch had never reappeared. No other *Volkhvy* had attacked. Beneath an aqua sky, Anna walked along the deceptively calm shore where craggy rocks belied the false atmosphere of a gentle Mediterranean breeze. The Outer Hebrides was actually storm tossed. Anna closed her eyes and concentrated before she opened them once more.

For a few seconds, she saw a true glimpse of the rough ocean breaking against the rocky shore. Sea spray burst high into the cold air, and the stinging sand it blew turned to needles against her skin.

And then the atmosphere calmed.

Her mother's enchantment held against her budding abilities.

The sun shimmered across the water, and its gentle warm light was a lie.

Soren had been gone when she woke up. She'd bathed and changed, expecting some word from him, but none had come. They had stolen a night together. No more. No less. And he'd been right. Everything was changed—for the worse. His silence and his distance flayed her skin in the same way the stinging sand driven by the stormy wind had now that she'd experienced the connection they could have had.

In her mind's eye, the emerald on her sword had gone dark. As lackluster and gray as the true sky had been moments before. Its fading light shouldn't hurt her. Not when her decision to destroy it had already been made. But *shouldn't* and *didn't* were two different things.

There was a hollow where her heart used to be. She should have grown used to it by now. But her brief wholeness the night before left her feeling less this morning than she'd felt yesterday, even before she and Soren had come together.

She had no time to coddle her feelings and coax herself back to full strength. Her pain had to be faced and worked through. Her difficulty would come in working through it with an audience of the one who was causing it.

He had basked in the glow of her power.

She had pleasured him as much with her *Volkhvy* abilities as she had with her body, and he had cried out her name. Only to leave her this morning before she woke up. It was for the best. He had given her time to rise and fortify her defenses. When she saw him again, she wouldn't blink, much less cringe at his distance.

Distance was the only way forward.

Her inability to control her powers while they were making love had been undeniably pleasurable, but he worried about her possible loss of control at other volatile times. Especially if his family was responsible for the volatility.

Both Ivan and Lev could easily provoke Anna's *Volkhvy* power into exploding merely by being themselves—the alpha with his leadership concerns and his protective instincts on high alert because of his pregnant wife. The white wolf with his wild unpredictability. Lev was currently savage. Soren could hope to civilize him again, but there would be no chance of that with Anna around.

And there was the concern even Anna echoed herself. That the emerald sword would make a witch too powerful for that witch to exercise control.

Their time on the island had been a reprieve. Their time in each other's arms the night before had been snatched from a universe that was obviously bound to keep them apart. Her chest might ache and echo with her lonely heart's stubborn beat. Her lips might be tender from remembered kisses. Her core might be sensitized from his touch and the frantic friction of their sex.

But her feet carried her, one in front of the other, from the shore to the palace. They would leave the island today to search for the sword. There was no other way forward for them.

And they couldn't go back.

He burned with the need to shift and run away. His human body couldn't contain all the sensations that buffeted it. Remembered sensations from the night before—Anna's soft lips on his skin, her hot mouth, the feel and taste of her nipple against his tongue—and current sensations, like the tenderness of his half-erect penis that wouldn't subside no matter how he willed it away, and the tingling in his cells that had barely subsided hours after Anna had flashed with emerald light.

Soren had asked for it. No, he'd *begged* for it. He wanted it still. Anna's power was the most intimate part of her.

The way she controlled and protected it from view made him crave to see her release it. He didn't want to merely tear off her gloves with his teeth. He wanted to shred them into a million pieces so she would never feel she had to hide behind them again.

He wasn't free to do that.

He was an enchanted shape-shifter and Anna's power had almost thrown him off the bed last night. The electric energy she channeled had shaken his body and lingered with him long after he left her sleeping. When Lev had attacked her, she'd traveled through the Ether to take them back to the castle, and she'd been wearing the gloves at the time.

Soren couldn't risk that kind of power, unharnessed, around his family, even if Ivan and Elena would allow it. Even if Anna's presence didn't risk frightening Lev away, Soren had to think of the baby.

They'd all been through so much in their lives because Vladimir and Vasilisa hadn't tempered their actions with the thought of the children their actions might harm.

He wouldn't make the same mistake. He'd been protecting others too long to stop now.

And he'd been protecting Anna the longest.

There was no use denying he needed to protect her from his family as much as he needed to protect his family from her.

Vasilisa visited Madeline and Trevor every day. It was only one penance she undertook for what she had done. But it was also a panacea because, for now, their unchanged faces hid long-ranging ramifications even she couldn't fathom.

They weren't actually sleeping. They wouldn't wake, refreshed and happy to greet the next day. Hundreds of years had passed as they'd been kept in a state of suspension. There would be a price to pay for all those lost years. She trembled as she ran her fingers along the crystallized glass. What if the cost Madeline had to pay for this refuge was too high?

Every day she visited, and every day she put off the inevitable. Eventually she would have to decide if she was truly sparing them from the danger the white wolf might pose or if she was only sparing herself.

For now, she waited.

She would delay as long as she could to ensure that Anna and Soren were given more time together. The mirror at Bronwal wasn't her only portal. She had numerous portals all over the world. But she hadn't informed her daughter, nor would she. Anna and Soren would have to travel the long way to the Dark *Volkhvy* who held the sword. Anna was still new to her abilities. The journey would tax her strength. Using the Ether would be quicker than traveling as a human, but it would still be slow.

Before Vasilisa woke Madeline, Anna and Soren needed more time to deal with their own awakening. She couldn't undo what she had done to them any more than she could undo what she had done to Madeline, Lev and their baby. She had inadvertently thrown Anna and Soren together for centuries. Now they were determined to part. Seeing her daughter lose the man she loved was a high price to pay for her mistakes.

Too high.

She'd lived with the pain of loss for too long to sit back while Anna suffered.

Vasilisa's hands glowed a soft violet as she continued to stroke the glass. *Soon.* The woman and baby beneath the glass weren't as deeply suspended as they had been before. There was a stirring within them that only Vasilisa could sense. First, she would give Anna and Soren a chance to change their minds about the emerald sword. But no matter their decision, she would have to free Madeline and Trevor. Lev posed a dangerous threat to her daughter, and he couldn't be allowed to hurt her again or come between Anna and Soren. Even if that meant Vasilisa would finally have to face the consequences of what she had done to the white wolf and his family.

For Anna, she had cursed Bronwal and its people.

For Anna, she would also set in motion what might become the culmination of her greatest mistake. There was no way to know how Madeline would wake or if Lev could be brought back from his feral state.

But Lev's personal tragedy might spare her own daughter from more pain.

Vasilisa was the Light *Volkhvy* queen, but she had dealt in Darkness for too long. She was no longer free to deal wholly in the Light. Her actions would always be touched by shadows. She could only hope that Anna would make a better queen.

Chapter 21

Soren found Anna dressed for travel. She wore dark green leggings and a matching fleece jacket as practical as they were distracting when they stretched and conformed to her curves with every move. Her brown curls had been tamed into a ponytail on the back of her head.

Discomfort stabbed his chest when he also noted the black leather gloves that covered her fingers before they disappeared beneath her sleeves. They weren't her only defenses. She barely glanced at him. Her face was stiff and her lips were pressed into a thin, tight line. Good. They needed to be on guard and closed off from each other as long as they were forced to travel together.

But his own tightness seemed to creak and strain once he noticed hers.

She wore a small backpack again.

He had found suitable clothes provided to him by the *Volkhvy* and he had to admit he was glad to be back in the tooled leather britches he preferred to jeans. They would provide more protection in a fight and more warmth as he was forced to traverse the Ether. He'd also chosen a thick homespun tunic and a leather jerkin that covered it like a fitted vest to his thighs.

"You look like a time traveler," Anna said.

He paused when she spoke, startled by the way his gut clenched as if he'd been punched. Her words were matter-of-fact. But the sound of her voice made him think of more sultry things she'd said the night before.

"Aren't we?" he replied. He pushed his thick bangs back from his forehead and turned to face her. Were her lips still swollen from his kisses? Or had she been deep in thought and worrying them with her teeth this morning? "You and I were both born so long ago. I'm not sure we can disguise that even with modern clothing. The years show in our eyes, don't you think?" he continued.

He met her serious gaze. The green of Anna's clothes brought out the flecks of emerald in her irises. Suddenly, he could barely breathe. His chest constricted, and he went molten everywhere else. He could too easily remember the vivid sparks that had shone from her eyes in the shadowed bedroom. And the way her power had seemed to claim him with tingling pleasure when their bodies had come together.

"I'm not sure others can see the years or if we just remember them too well. Every time I look at you, I see a medieval prince and a red wolf. They live on in your every gesture and word," Anna said. Her voice had dropped lower. The confessional tone didn't diminish the heat he struggled against. Neither did the way she glanced from his head to his feet, as if she was remembering him as only she could.

"Perhaps we can't unsee what we have seen in each other," Soren said. He didn't mean to refer to the night before. But the heat he fought against colored his words. He also didn't mean to step toward her, but his feet seemed to move of their own volition. He found himself looking down at her. They stood on the cliff where they had materialized from the mirror portal days ago. The sun had risen in a bright blue sky dotted with clouds so defined they looked like cloth.

"That's why we need to do this. We need to sever our connection once and for all. We need to protect your family from mine," Anna said. Her mouth had tightened again. She fisted her gloved hands.

Soren wanted to take her in his arms and kiss her until her lips softened against his.

He didn't, because she was right. The only way they could sever their connection was by destroying the sword. Perhaps then they could get on with the new lives they had found.

The red wolf wasn't pleased. It howled in his chest. It knew he had fully accepted what had to be done. The intimacy they'd shared last night made it harder, but it also made it more necessary.

As if conjured by her words, Anna's mother appeared in the distance. They stood side by side, waiting for her to approach. She probably could have traveled through the Ether to reach them in the blink of an eye. Instead, Vasilisa walked gracefully up the hill from the palace. She wore a simple white walking gown. As she came closer and closer, it gleamed in the sun against the grass.

She was alone.

"It's hard for me not to shift to face her. I'll always wonder what she'll do next," Soren said. If Anna made him tense, Vasilisa made him brace for battle.

"I feel the same. And she's my mother," Anna confessed.

Vasilisa finally reached them. Neither of them bowed

or curtsied to their queen. They waited silently for her to speak. Surprisingly, she didn't make a pronouncement. Instead, she stepped close to Soren and leaned in to speak for his ear alone.

"I wanted to bid you farewell," Vasilisa said. "Please take care that you don't undo something in the heat of the moment that is in all actuality your heart's desire."

Before he could reply, she had drifted away from him toward her daughter.

"I love you. Never doubt it," the queen said.

"I don't doubt it, Mother. But *Volkhvy* love can be... cataclysmic," Anna replied.

Vasilisa didn't speak again. She leaned to kiss Anna on one cheek and then the other. In response, Anna reached for Soren's hand. He gripped her firmly. His support was all he could offer. He couldn't negate her parentage. She wouldn't want him to. As cataclysmic as Vasilisa's love could be, it was still a mother's love. Anna had been without that for too long.

Besides, she was also *Volkhvy.* The fire in his belly and the hollow in his chest quietly whispered that Anna's love could be cataclysmic, too.

Anna knew what to do to ride the Ether. It was as basic as breathing, which was not basic at all. A million different nerve endings had to communicate their wishes to each other. Her job was to get out of the way.

Last night, Soren had urged her to let go and allow herself to climax in his arms. To let go she'd had to lower her walls against the Ether's energy. She'd had to welcome the power inside her. She'd had to willingly channel the blast that had built up behind her control.

When Lev had hurt her, she'd done the same thing instinctively.

This time, she consciously lowered her defenses to allow herself to tap into the energy of the vacuum the Ether created. It was that energy that she and Soren would ride for as long and as far as they could before she had to rest and recharge.

The Call of the emerald sword was a distant pinpoint on an unfamiliar map she would have to navigate. The sword and Soren's hand in hers were the only two solid things in the world to her as she stepped forward into the frigid nothingness. How many times had she disappeared into the Ether with the red wolf by her side?

This time she held her lover's hand. Once they reached their destination they would be parted, but, for now, they stood against the nothingness of the Ether the way they always had.

Chapter 22

Evergreen air rushed against Anna's face as she fell forward onto her knees. She'd traveled as far and as fast as she could. At first, the energy her *Volkhvy* abilities tapped into seemed to buffer her and Soren from the hungry vacuum of the Ether itself. But gradually she began to experience the inexorable pull of nothingness until it seemed like the Ether would eat her soul.

It was horrible and familiar.

She'd never consciously used her *Volkhvy* abilities to avoid disappearing for good during the curse. She hadn't known who she was or what she could do, but the power had been in her blood. She had reappeared time and time again with a fully functioning mind, unclouded by her time in the Ether.

Because she was a witch.

Perhaps she'd even helped Soren keep his faculties because they were constant companions.

Others had been less fortunate. Ivan had stood alone for hundreds of years before Elena found him. Lev had been lost for even longer.

Soren materialized as he fell. He collapsed on the ground beside her. Big and solid and not lost to the Ether, although he shivered as if its ice had penetrated to the marrow of his bones.

"H-h-hate th-that sh-sh-shit," he said as his teeth clicked together.

Anna shivered, too. She'd pushed herself to the limit of her abilities. Her vision was blurred, and a ringing in her ears made Soren's voice seem to come from far away. This was familiar, too. The first few moments of materialization after a long time in the Ether were always hard. She staggered to her feet and stomped them against the ground in order to increase circulation in her legs. She hugged herself against the cold.

Ineffectual when the cold came from within yourself.

The problem with being *Volkhvy* was that the Ether tried to eat you from without *and from within*.

"I. Hate. It. Too," Anna agreed. She clenched her teeth between each word to prevent a chatter. Soren pushed himself up from the ground at her feet. His big arms flexed and extended. His powerful legs obeyed his silent command. They gathered beneath him, and he stood much more gracefully than she had.

"Where are we?" Soren asked.

They were in an evergreen forest, but it wasn't the one they were used to. The trees were smaller and more tightly spaced together. Their needles were shorter and more compact. Their scent was sweeter. Anna could hear unfamiliar night sounds rising around them from creatures that didn't inhabit the Carpathian Mountains.

"Never mind. It isn't the Ether. That's good enough for me," Soren said.

The air was temperate. For that Anna was thankful. She wouldn't be able to travel again until she had rested and refueled. It really didn't matter where they were. It only mattered that she could still sense where they were going. The Call of the sword still pulled her in a definite direction.

Suddenly, Anna swayed on her feet. Soren's hand clamped down firmly on one of her shoulders. He moved his large body to stand against her back, warm and steady. He had noticed her sway even though he hadn't been facing her and his attention had been on the forest around him. Or so she'd thought. Her attention was always on him even when she gave no outward indication. She suspected his was on her, as well. She felt his focus. His attention hummed beneath her skin.

"You need to rest," Soren said. The rumble of his voice against her was as supportive as his physical strength.

He didn't move to pick her up. Thank God. Instead, he walked with her to the nearest fallen log where she could collapse. She sat while he prepared a spot for a fire by kicking out a hollow and lining it with rocks.

"The air isn't cold, but I need a fire after the Ether. You look like you could use one, as well," Soren said.

His practiced movements to start a fire mesmerized her. It was a skill they had all had to know once upon a time. Even during the curse, she'd often used flint to kindle a fireplace. She wasn't surprised when Soren pulled one from his pocket. It took much longer than a match and even longer than flicking a switch, but even before the first flames began to crackle, Anna was already comforted by Soren's actions. His deft fingers reminded her of the night before. His concern for her well-being reminded her of always.

They would have to say goodbye.

She would be cold without him, fire or not.

But for tonight they would sit together by this fire he'd made while the forest creatures sang.

They didn't sit together. Soren dragged another log into place across from her and sat on the ground with the log at his back. The large logs framed the heat from the fire and kept it from dissipating too soon. Soren had created a sheltered nook for them, but he also kept his distance.

Anna tried to be glad.

She focused on the water and the energy bar she'd taken from her backpack.

"Using your abilities saps your strength," Soren said in between bites from the bar she'd tossed him.

Talking about her *Volkhvy* blood was treading on dangerous ground. Her power would eventually drive them apart, no matter how well they came to understand it. Neither of them would ever fully trust it because of what her mother's curse had done to them.

"You know the Ether's vacuum," Anna began.

"Better than most," Soren interrupted.

"Exactly. We know the vacuum. I'm coming to know the energy that the vacuum expels. I tap into it. It channels through me, and it's converted to the shine you see. The power. That power can be used like electricity to fuel many different things. Travel through the Ether is one of them. But it isn't without risk. A witch can use too much power and dwell in the Ether too long. The energy can flood a witch who isn't careful. Until the vacuum eats from the inside as well as the outside," Anna explained.

She shivered and the remembered chill urged her to slide off her log closer to the fire. She sat with her back against the wood like Soren.

"The witchblood prince was flooded and consumed. He was eaten by the Ether," Soren said.

"Yes," Anna said. Her shivering increased. She recognized it as shock. They'd traveled through the Ether all day. She'd expended every ounce of her abilities to use the energy to protect them from the vacuum. But the cold had sunk deep into her bones. She had to reach the sword. She had to take it away from the Dark *Volkhvy*. Yet she risked the witchblood prince's fate if she rode the Ether's energy too long and she danced in the darkness of memories she'd rather forget.

She inched closer to the fire, but its heat didn't seem to warm her.

"Be careful. I'm not sure even a *Volkhvy* princess is fireproof," Soren said. He was suddenly beside her. He had risen and come to her when he'd seen her distress. Now he sank down next to her and pulled her against him.

"You don't have to hold me," Anna protested.

But her words were muffled against his warm, broad chest, and she didn't even try to stop herself from sinking into the body heat he offered.

"You're shaking. And if the Ether's inside you, I know why. The damn stuff on the outside is bad enough," Soren said.

His willingness to get close to her warmed her more than his body did. And his body warmed her a lot. She could already breathe in the difference on his skin and hair as the fresh forest atmosphere clung to him. Before she could think, she had taken two fistfuls of his leather jerkin in her gloved hands. The move parted his shirt so that her face was suddenly against his bare skin.

And then all thoughts of the Ether fled from her mind.

Her shaking gave way to stillness, his and hers. His chest stopped rising and falling beneath her cheek. She held her breath. One second dragged on to the next with neither of them moving. Then Anna broke. She nuzzled against his skin and pressed her lips to his chest.

"Anna," Soren sighed. He exhaled as if both the release of air and saying the syllables of her name was a relief.

His hands came up to thread into her hair. Her ponytail broke free and curls spilled down. His warm palms cupped her face, but he didn't push her away. He cradled her close. She took the gentle move as permission to flick out her tongue and taste the skin she'd bared.

She was drained of power. She was as close to being human in his arms as she would ever be. But he didn't glory in it. He worried. He wished he could recharge her abilities with sheer force of will.

Anna was a witch.

He accepted that. He no longer wished for what might have been if she'd been a completely different woman. Her abilities meant that they couldn't be together, but he wouldn't change who and what she was even if he could. He was grateful that he'd been able to get to know the real woman—her deepest strengths and desires—before they were forced to part. *Volkhvy* power might lead to inevitable darkness, but Anna wouldn't be herself without it.

"I'm not strong enough to let you go right now," Anna murmured against his skin. The butterfly movement of her lips against his chest as she spoke sent a frisson of excitement through him. He hardened, and his fingers tightened on her face.

"I wouldn't let you go right now even if you could," Soren confessed. He had buried his face in the curls on top of her head. He breathed deeply of her rose-petal scent. It had mingled with the forest air to become more fresh and wild.

"Last night was supposed to be the beginning and the end of us," Anna said. She had snuggled so tightly against him that his right thigh was between her legs. She was no longer shivering with cold. Her heat pressed to his muscular leg just inches from his hard cock was a siren's call he was only able to resist with supreme effort. He shook as he battled his desire.

And he grew harder still.

"This never ends, Anna. We never end. We have to walk away from each other. We have to destroy the sword. But this—you and I—we're paired for life. Even if we can't be together," Soren said.

He pulled her onto his lap to illustrate his point. She came willingly, grasping his hips between both of her thighs and settling her weight against his bulging shaft. His pants still contained him—barely. But there was no hiding what she did to him. He didn't want to. Soren wanted her to know how badly she was wanted even though he had to let her go.

After he'd helped her position herself straddling his lap, he returned his hands to her head. He held the back of her neck and looked up into her flushed face. She had let go of her tight grip on his clothes. She met his gaze boldly… and lifted her hands to slowly loosen the fingers of first one glove and then the other. His stomach tightened. His breath caught. He didn't move to stop her.

When the gloves were loosened, she pulled first one and then the other off each arm, inch by inch, and threw them on the ground. He already knew her power had been depleted. He also knew that the gloves were more for her peace of mind than an actual tool to control her abilities. She used them as a reminder that there needed to be a shield between her and the world to protect the world from harm.

He wasn't afraid. His quickened heartbeat was pure excitement. Her eyelids had lowered, giving her eyes a sultry cast as she watched him crave her touch.

Then her warm palms found their way under his shirt. She didn't need energy from the Ether to make him gulp a sudden gasp of air as the brush of her fingers on his chest made his erection harder. She used her palms to brace herself above him.

He might have been able to control himself if she had stopped there. Instead, with her bare hands on his chest, she undulated her hips to rub her heat against his hardness. He allowed his head to fall back and his eyes to close as pleasure pulsed through his body. He stroked down her back to cup her rocking bottom and moaned his approval of her movements.

"I'm warm now," Anna said. He opened his eyes and was rewarded by a vision of firelight dancing on her face and skin. Her hair glowed crimson and her eyes sparkled with reflected flames.

"You need to be warmer," Soren said. "I can help you recharge, Anna. When we touch, I can feel the emerald sword in the distance. Its energy flows through us when we allow the connection. I want to help you accept the energy and resist the vacuum of the Ether. Use my strength. Use me."

Anna froze even as she combusted at Soren's offer. Her beloved, muscular shape-shifter was beneath her. She held his powerful body between her thighs. The heated steel of his erection had inspired her to writhe against him. Now she paused. She could feel the pulse of his excitement through her leggings. His face was flushed against the darker russet hair of his beard. The waves of his bangs fell over his eyes, but she could still see the amber gleam of his irises in the firelight.

She could see he was earnest. He wanted to help her.

Her champion.

The seduction of his offer to indulge the connection between them stole her breath. She paused because it was too good to be true, even as it was so poignant that it slammed into her chest—no longer arrows to her heart, but a battering ram.

"I don't think we can. I don't think we should. If we accept the sword's Call only to reject it later..." Anna began.

"I won't risk letting the Ether have you," Soren vowed. "Not again." He sat up from the log he'd been leaning against. His move brought his chest against hers. The friction of her breasts flattening against his muscles sent arcs of pleasure from her nipples to the V between her legs. Her hands slid to his shoulders beneath his shirt. She held on for dear life as his mouth came within inches of hers. The closeness didn't help her to breathe any easier. "This is the only way we can be sure you can fight the Ether's vacuum until we reach the sword."

She was going to argue. He needed to know that his offer was dangerous. That once they forged the connection, it might be devastating to part. But the hot press of his lips against hers interrupted her before she could gather enough air to speak.

And then she didn't want to breathe anymore. She only wanted to taste and savor and fill the velvety, moist recesses of his mouth with her questing tongue. She devoured his groans of approval as she sank down into the kiss. She inspired more groans as she began to rock against his erection once more. His hands dropped back to her hips and he aided her movements with his strong arms. His fingers splayed and he cupped and kneaded her bottom until she was wet in reaction to his touch.

The rough linen of his homespun tunic parted beneath her eager hands. She didn't care that the fabric was vintage and irreplaceable. She only wanted it to be out of her way. The sound of it ripping spurred her on, as did the eager thrusts of his tongue against hers.

She pressed the torn shirt off his shoulders and then sat back. His palms had moved to brace against the ground on either side of his hips. He could no longer hold her. He was bound by his half-removed shirt and jerkin. The fabric held him in place halfway down his biceps and across his back. His broad chest and lean stomach were displayed beneath her. His muscles rippled with his heavy breathing. He could have easily ripped the shirt and jerkin off. But he didn't. His heavy-lidded eyes watched her to see what she would do. He waited, obviously excited, throbbing between her legs, for her to make the next move.

Anna's hand trembled when she reached to trace the outline of his beautiful face. He wasn't perfect. The sharp Romanov angles of his nose, cheekbones and jaw were more weathered than they'd once been. There were fine white scars here and there on his skin. She leaned to kiss one, then another and another as she cupped his whiskered chin. His eyes searched hers after her tender tastes. She didn't look away. She'd waited so long to see him again. Only to discover that she was seeing him for the first time. He was no longer the young knight he'd been. He was no longer the red wolf. But, somehow, he was both of them combined in an older, wiser, more hardened version of himself.

She'd waited hundreds of years only to be overwhelmed when he finally reappeared—more handsome, more appealing and more irresistible than he'd ever been before.

She was certain her appreciation shone from her eyes even though no power did, because Soren's widened as if he was surprised by what he'd seen.

Anna held his beautiful face and swooped in for another taste.

This time she pressed her lips to his and even though his arms were still bound by fabric he joined the kiss wholeheartedly with his hungry lips and tongue. He opened for her, coaxed her closer with sultry licks and then took her bottom lip between his teeth. She gasped at the shock of the sudden pleasure-pain, but then he soothed the nip with seductive suckling that caused a hot coil to tighten low in her stomach.

Her nipples tingled and peaked. The thrusts of her hips became more urgent and frustrated, and Soren's chuckle growled deep in his chest. She'd been wrong. He wasn't bound. She was the one who was tied by her need to join with him.

Anna drew back from his kiss to catch her breath. She leaned her forehead against his while she panted. Soren took the chance to nuzzle his lips into her neck. His hot mouth teased hungry, open-lipped kisses from the tender skin below her ear to the rapid pulse beating at the base of her throat. He interspersed kisses with teasing flicks of his tongue. Anna moaned and rode his erection while he caused her skin to go up in flames.

"This time won't only be physical, Anna. I want to join with you. Just once. I want to connect. I want you to answer the sword's Call. Will you do that for me? Will you join with me and claim your power?" Soren asked. "The Ether can't have you. Because you're mine."

"The sword is still too far away. I'm not sure I can claim it from here," Anna said.

Soren ripped his arms from the fabric that held them in

place. The pieces of his shirt and jerkin fell aside as he finally reached for her. He held her steady with both hands on either side of her face and looked deep into her eyes.

"It's already yours. And you're already mine. All you have to do is claim me to make our connection complete," Soren said.

He swam before her as her eyes filled. He wasn't only offering to help her against the Ether's vacuum. He was giving her his heart…if only for a little while. After all the years of waiting, a little while seemed like bliss.

Anna stood, and he allowed his hands to slip away from her as she rose. She stripped in front of the fire. He watched her every move. His gaze tracked her hand as she pulled the zipper of her fleece jacket down. Underneath she wore only a simple white lace camisole and bra. His attention was riveted as she unhooked the bra and pulled it and the camisole over her head. Her freed breasts were heavy, and her nipples were hard.

"You're killing me," Soren whispered. But still he waited for her to proceed.

Anna pulled her stretchy, formfitting leggings off her hips and down over her legs. She kicked them to the side. She stood above her legendary wolf wearing nothing but lacy white panties. They'd lived together for a long time. But she'd never been naked around him. Never once had she forgotten that he was actually a man.

"You have no idea how precious your curves are to me. I've tortured myself by imagining what it would be like to really see every inch of you, but none of my fantasies compare to this," Soren said hoarsely. She could still hear the howl in his voice. It roughened and graveled his tone. The vibrato of it teased against her naked skin.

She slipped her panties down while he watched her with a gaze so intense she could almost feel its caress along her legs as the lace fell. The sword Called from far away. Her abilities seemed dormant. But the pulse she experienced in a flush of desire that suffused her body was all Soren. She was wet and throbbing with need as she stood completely bare in front of him.

Soren reached for his waist. His leggings were handcrafted. They were laced at the fly. He slowly worked the knotted cord loose so that his erection could spring free. He had stretched and filled her last night, but it had been dark. In the firelight, she was able to see what she hadn't fully appreciated in the shadows of her room the night before or during his sudden appearance in her bathroom's doorway. His cock was fully engorged and the curve of it lay heavily against his stomach, thick and long and large.

Anna bit her lip and pressed her palm to her mound to quiet the throbbing there while Soren pushed his leather leggings off his hips.

"You can see what you do to me," he said. He looked from his erection up to her face. He met her eyes.

"You'll have to feel what you do to me," Anna replied.

It only took a couple of steps to bring her to his seated form. He stroked a hand up her leg when she paused beside him. Her leg trembled with pleasure beneath his gentle, calloused fingers. He alternated between watching her face to gauge her reaction and watching his fingers on her flesh. While he watched, he stroked them closer and closer to the chestnut curls between her legs.

Anna gasped and moaned with every tickling caress. Fire from his touch sank deep into her skin and spread. There was nowhere left that the Ether's cold could hide. He burned it all away.

And then he brushed aside the curls protecting her most intimate bud.

Anna cried out. Soren found her slick heat. His fingers

slid easily into her folds. She had to grab onto his broad shoulders to keep from falling, but the move brought her hips close to his face. Her knees gave out completely when he moved his hand and pressed his face where his fingers had been seconds before. She didn't fall. He held her in place with his strong arms and his hands on her bottom.

Then he licked into her and she called out his name.

"Soren."

"Always, Anna. Even when we have to part. Always," Soren murmured as he pleasured her with thrusts of his tongue.

She fell when she came. He couldn't hold her up any longer when her whole body went tense. But she fell onto his lap, where his hardened shaft was waiting. Anna positioned herself against him. She pulsed with aftershocks from her climax as she spread her legs and took Soren's erection inch by inch.

Now it was his turn to cry out her name as she claimed him. He pressed his face into the hollow between her breasts and she held him as she rocked them closer together.

"Not just physical, Anna. Accept the Call of the emerald sword," Soren gasped. He raised his hips to meet her thrusts.

"Yes. Yes. Yes," Anna said.

And then a blast of the Ether's energy flooded into every cell of her body. She cried out from the shock of the power as it filled her completely. From far away, she sensed the sword blaze to green life. The Dark witches who had stolen it were knocked back by its sudden gleaming power.

Enchantments didn't matter. Vasilisa didn't matter. Witches and wolves didn't matter. She and Soren had been forged for each other—by the curse. It had taken their destiny and crafted it into something unbreakable. They had faced day after day, decade after decade, century after century by each other's side. They had vanished and re-appeared together time after time. Time and distance and enchantment would never tear them apart even if they couldn't be together, because they survived. Their love survived. Anything. Always.

Anna found another release as her power engulfed them both. Her body convulsed around Soren, and she collapsed against his chest.

Soren cried out when his climax slammed into him along with Anna's power. His cry became a howl that rose up into the sky. Its resonant sound carried for miles. He didn't shift. He stayed a man for her. But the earth shook with his power and hers combined.

He lifted her and cradled her tight against his chest as he spilled his seed outside her body. They couldn't risk a baby, because even as they claimed their connection, they both knew they would always have to be apart.

Chapter 23

Soren left Anna sleeping by the fire. She'd cushioned her head on his discarded shirt, so he pulled up and laced his pants, then went shirtless into the woods. He found a game trail with no effort. Even in his human form, he knew all the red wolf did about field and forest and the creatures that lived there. He followed the trail to a crystal creek. He heard it before he saw it, a dark winding ribbon reflecting the glitter of stars.

He knelt and cupped several handfuls of the cold water up to his face to drink his fill. He tasted the bite of iron and minerals against his tongue, and he savored the liquid's richness. Much preferable to the plastic-flavored water Anna carried in her backpack.

Anna.

He stood and flipped damp bangs off his face. The freshwater hadn't soothed the residual tingle her power had left in his body. Nor did it soothe the hollow ache in his belly. He wasn't thirsty. Or hungry. Not for water or food.

He loved a witch, and he had to let her go.

The connection between them glowed green with emerald light behind his eyes every time he blinked. He was filled with it, and he'd never been so replete. The hollow in his gut wasn't real. He recognized it for what it was: dread. It was the phantom of future emptiness that haunted him and kept him from sleep.

By claiming the connection and helping her answer the sword's Call, he had ensured that their parting would have maximum impact on his soul. Ironically, it was his fullness that made him feel the future ache already.

Soren tightened the muscles in his stomach as if he prepared to take a punch. He flexed his damp fingers and fought the need to howl. No one could fix this. Not his alpha. Not a pack if he still had one to support him. There was no one to call.

A sliver of moon illuminated the forest around him. The shadowy, blurred edges of things didn't distract him from much more vivid visions of the passion he'd shared with Anna half an hour ago. She hadn't held the sword in her hand. She hadn't had to. She was Vasilisa's daughter, the Light *Volkhvy* princess. All it took was her red wolf's permission to claim the emerald sword that had been forged for his mate.

And he had given it.

He'd given himself to her with nothing held back, until now he wondered if destroying the sword to save his family would destroy him, as well.

Anna didn't sleep. She didn't know what to say when Soren left the fire to walk into the forest, and it was easier to keep her eyes closed than it would have been to watch him go. She only opened them after the sounds of his footsteps had faded in the distance.

The fire still burned, but the logs had settled and the flicker of flames was low to the ground. One of her gloves had landed too close to the embers. She didn't reach to save it.

The gloves hadn't stopped her. Her decision to claim Soren and the emerald sword had been made long ago.

"This never ends, Anna. We never end. We have to walk away from each other. We have to destroy the sword. But this—you and I—we're paired for life. Even if we can't be together," Soren had said.

The glove began to burn. Flames licked up from its fingers to its shaft. The leather curled in on itself as it began to disintegrate. But it wasn't the burning glove she saw. In the dance of flickering flames, she saw memories of Ivan, Lev and Soren. She saw them laughing, fighting and shifting. She'd grown up with the Romanovs. Their legend had been her day-to-day life.

Even after the curse came down on Bronwal, she'd still believed in the legendary wolves and their cause. She'd survived. She'd persevered, because she'd always believed that Soren and his brothers would triumph in the end. She'd thought she'd be a part of that triumph.

The curse was broken. Lev might still be saved and reunited with his family. Bronwal was rebuilt and a new Romanov heir was on the way.

But her part in the Romanov triumph was very different than she'd imagined.

Why had Vladimir spared her that day when he'd kidnapped her and killed all the innocents in the village who had been hiding her for Vasilisa? Had she been nothing but leverage to the gray wolf? Or had the enchanted beast sensed what the emerald sword would one day prove?

She was a witch, but she was also Called to be a warrior. The gray wolf had brought her to Bronwal. He had set into motion the events that would lead to centuries of torture, but if he hadn't something else would have led her to fight by Soren's side. It wasn't the loss of the sword she would mourn. It wasn't even the loss of purpose. She would have plenty to do as her mother's successor. She accepted her role as future queen, no matter how challenging it might be.

What hurt the most was that Soren needed her. Vasilisa had created the enchanted swords because her wolves needed help against the Dark *Volkhvy*. For all their size and power, they hadn't been made to fight alone.

Because she was a witch, Soren thought he had to sacrifice their partnership. She had agreed. Her abilities were too dangerous. She wasn't sure she could avoid misusing them as her mother had. She had accepted that she needed to destroy the sword in order to protect Ivan and Lev and their families.

But what about Soren?

He would have to fight alone once the sword was destroyed. Now that she'd answered the sword's Call and fully embraced the connection, Anna struggled with their mission. Soren needed a mate by his side to continue the fight against the Dark *Volkhvy*. And he deserved a partner he could trust.

The glove was gone, completely consumed by the fire. Anna felt as if she'd turned to ash herself.

She couldn't allow the emerald sword to be destroyed. But she couldn't retain her claim on it, either. Somehow she had to sever her connection with Soren once and for all—but save the sword so it could Call someone new.

Chapter 24

A howl sounded in the distance, rising and falling in an ululating cry that seemed to punctuate Anna's decision. It wasn't Soren's howl. He hadn't shifted. She would have known from their connection, even if she didn't recognize the way the earth shook every time a Romanov became a wolf.

She scrambled to her feet and gathered up her clothes. Her hands fumbled as she pulled on her underwear and her leggings. The howl had been too long and too loud to originate in a natural wolf's chest. If not Soren, there were only two other wolves it could be, and one of those wolves was with his pregnant wife at Bronwal.

Soren broke from the trees as she zipped her jacket into place. He slid to a stop when he saw she was okay. Dirt flew and then settled around his feet while they both held their breaths, waiting for another sound.

Anna's hands were already glowing. The sword and

her connection with Soren had recharged her power. Her abilities flared in order to protect her from the white wolf. It was *Volkhvy* instinct. It was survivor's instinct. But it was also a betrayal of her promise to Soren. She'd sworn she wouldn't scare Lev away again.

Another howl rent the air. Lev was closer. Louder. But even before the howl rose and fell to fade away in what seemed to be an expression of limitless sadness, Anna's glow faded, too. She tamped down the power she had instinctively tapped into. She pushed the Ether's energy back from where it came.

"I won't scare him away," she said. She braced with her feet apart and her hands fisted at her sides. This time she would keep her promise. She tried to ignore the terror that clawed its way up from her gut. Her shoulder throbbed with the memory of pain from Lev's bite. His hatred had turned venomous in her, and her body hadn't forgotten.

And still she stood without a single spark of green in her fingers.

Soren was shirtless. He stood in the pale glow from the sliver of a moon, his tension palpable. Their connection had given her more than enough power to kill his brother. She wasn't channeling it. She rejected it. But he must wonder how long her resolve would last if the white wolf attacked.

"Don't make promises you can't keep," he said. "I won't ask you not to use your power if he attacks. He almost killed you last time."

Suddenly, Anna had a grim idea of how she might release the sword. Going down under the white wolf's teeth would be a horrible way to die. Her chest tightened and her stomach turned to ice thinking about Lev's massive jaws. In spite of her best efforts to reject it, her fingers began to glow in self-defense.

Anna looked guiltily from her tingling hands to Soren's

face. His lips were set in a thin line. His jaw was tight. His body was tense, from his shoulders to his powerful legs to his feet planted firmly on the ground.

But his mouth softened and a half smile curved his lips when she met his eyes.

"He won't attack. He'll see what I see...a powerful witch warrior who could take him down with the blink of her eye. He's feral, but he isn't stupid," Soren said.

Anna hoped he was right. Her death might free the sword, but she wasn't ready to accept it as her only option to save Soren. Not yet. Her powers obviously agreed. She lost the battle to reject them. The glow in her fingers had engulfed both of her arms.

"Your eyes are beautiful when they sparkle with emerald light," Soren said. He stepped toward her. He didn't stop until they were nearly touching. His broad chest was only inches from her face. She tried to tilt away to shield him from the light in her eyes, but he reached to hold her chin. He gently tilted her face upward. Anna could see the reflection of her eyes in his. "Your irises look like faceted gems reflecting the firelight, but I know your Light comes from your power. Our power. Combined."

"I'll frighten your brother away," Anna warned. She'd had a lot to learn about channeling the power of the Ether before. Now she channeled even more power, and she was still a novice witch. If she protected herself, she might do more than frighten Lev. She might hurt him.

Or, even worse, kill him while Soren watched.

But it was too late. Her power had risen up at the threat of the approaching wolf, and she couldn't tamp it back down. She looked into Soren's eyes. He had narrowed his in response to her light, but he didn't look away.

"Lev found me this time. He'll find me again. I can focus on luring him back from the wild after we retrieve the sword from the Dark *Volkhvy*. You can go back to your mother's island, where you'll be safe, after we destroy the sword. Then I'll save Lev," Soren said.

He sounded calm and logical, as if he wasn't planning on sacrificing his future chance at happiness to protect her and his brother. A pang tightened her chest when she realized he hadn't even considered that the sword might bring him another mate if she was out of the way. He championed everyone but himself.

"You're recharged. If we travel through the Ether, Lev won't be able to follow on our heels. His is a wandering journey, not a direct one," Soren said. He placed his hands on her shoulders. "Take us to the sword."

He leaned to kiss her, and her energy flared in response. Not in defense. He was her mate, and her energy recognized their connection. Her power flared to engulf him in energy, too. A soft green aura expanded outward from her body to wrap and twine around them both.

Anna saw only a glimpse of the white wolf as he leaped into the clearing before she and Soren disappeared into the nothingness and cold.

Chapter 25

Anna had thought they might need to travel through the Ether many more times before they reached the Dark *Volkhvy* fortress, but the power from her connection with Soren and the fear of the white wolf propelled them the rest of the way.

This time when they materialized, they both fell forward onto hard, rocky terrain. The impact knocked the air from her body and grazed the side of her face where her cheek slid on the ground as she fell. She tasted blood. The fall had also busted her lower lip. She bathed it with her tongue as she struggled to draw air into her shocked lungs.

The emerald sword is near.

"Are you okay?" Soren asked. He was already up. The impact had barely made him pause. He reached out his hand toward her and she managed to take it, although everything was blurry in front of her. She blinked. She focused as he pulled her easily to her feet.

A mountainous landscape swam into view all around them. As did a sprawling home on the side of a sheer cliff about a mile away. It had been crafted of cement and glass. There were no obvious doors, and a few seconds' observation revealed that it was more fortress than house. The cement curved attractively, but it also walled off the glass high from the ground. It took her a second to understand that the odd rainbowlike ripples on the glass were in fact reflections of the eerie atmosphere that hung above the canyon the cliff faced.

"It's the Ether. It's visible here," Anna said. Shock and wonder filled her voice, but it was also colored by horror. The power of the Ether buffeted her senses. She couldn't imagine choosing to live so close to its manifested presence. Although the energy it expelled probably helped to fortify the building bathed in its light.

"Ivan said the witchblood prince lived near the Ether. He grew up in this atmosphere," Soren said. Anna could tell he felt the Ether's power, even though he wasn't a witch. She moved closer to him, instinctively wanting to block the rainbow light from touching his handsome features.

"We have to go to the fortress. That's where the sword is being held," Anna said.

Soren's eyes had narrowed when she'd positioned herself between him and the shimmering aurora borealis–like atmosphere. She stood facing him with her back to the deceptively beautiful rainbow. He looked at it over her shoulder, and then his gaze came back to her face.

"How bad is the vacuum you fight in this place?" he asked.

He hadn't let go of her hand when he'd pulled her to her feet. His fingers tightened around hers as if he would hold her if the Ether tried to take her away. He looked as if he could. Not only because of his broad shoulders, muscular arms and powerful frame, but also because of the intensity of determination that shone from his eyes. The usual warm amber of his irises suddenly looked like chips of agate crystal, and his grip on her hand seemed unshakable.

It was an illusion.

No one could hold out against the vacuum of the Ether forever—not even an enchanted legendary wolf or the witch who loved him.

She could feel its pull, colder and stronger than she'd ever felt it before.

But she lied.

"I'm not going anywhere. Our connection will give me the power I need to resist the vacuum. I can use the Ether's energy without succumbing to it. At least long enough to retrieve the sword," Anna said.

She wouldn't reveal that she'd had another grim thought about how she could release the sword. Death or disintegration in the Ether—they were one and the same. To save Soren she would have to sacrifice herself. She just had to choose—the white wolf's hunger or the Ether's.

Soren knew Anna was lying. He could see the fight she waged against the Ether's vacuum in her body and her eyes. Her jaw was tense. Her shoulders braced. Her hand gripped his as if she dangled over the edge of the cliff he faced. He just wasn't sure why she didn't tell him the truth. He would spare her this if he could. He would give her the sword and his heart and pledge to her his teeth and his claws for eternity if he wouldn't also condemn his family to *Volkhvy* danger at the same time.

"If it wasn't for the baby, we would leave this place…"
Soren began.

"For the baby, for Elena, for Ivan and for Lev. And for
you," Anna said. "I won't leave until I've done what has
to be done. For all of Bronwal."

Suddenly, she spoke truth. He could hear the difference
in her voice. He could see the change blazing in her emerald eyes. He could hardly remember when they'd been
a soft hazel with only a hint of green in the firelight or
the sunshine. Her power was such a part of her now. He
couldn't imagine her without it.

They'd had to use her power to find the sword and to
travel to it. They would have to use her power to wrest the
sword from the Dark *Volkhvy*'s control. They would have
to use it to destroy the sword. In their lovemaking, he'd
had an intimate connection with her *Volkhvy* abilities and
the way she channeled the energy of the Ether.

Her power had pulsed through him.

But for all that, he couldn't forget what Vasilisa had
done. The horrible curse and the damage she had inflicted
with her *Volkhvy* abilities would haunt him for the rest of
his days.

Anna stood between him and the atmosphere that shimmered colorfully and coldly behind her. It was beautiful
and it was a horror, one he'd endured for more years than
most men lived. The contradiction of its nature was represented in the woman he loved. She was lovely, from her
power-tossed curls highlighted by the dangerous rainbow
atmosphere to her emerald eyes, from her soft curves to her
hard determination to survive. She was also deadly. Even
without the emerald sword, she was the queen's daughter. With the emerald sword magnifying her abilities, she
would be unstoppable.

What they prepared to do had to be done, even if it hollowed his chest and sickened his gut.

He would lose her, but she would live. And his family wouldn't be joined to a *Volkhvy* clan that had already tortured them for centuries.

Soren had the experience of centuries behind his perceptions. Anna fought to keep her intentions to herself. If he knew she was even contemplating sacrificing herself to save the sword for him, he would try to stop her. Her only hope of stopping its destruction was to move forward as if she still intended to follow their original plan.

"They'll know we're coming. The emerald will give us away," Anna warned. She would distract him with action until they had the sword. If they defeated the Dark *Volkhvy*, then she would worry about facing Soren's reaction to the truth—that she couldn't allow him to sacrifice any chance at future partnership and happiness because she was a witch.

And deep in her chest, her heart beat the question: *The Ether's cold or the white wolf's bite? The white wolf's bite or the Ether's cold?*

She shivered at the very idea of allowing the Ether to take her after fighting against it for so long.

Her love for Soren was the only reason she could even contemplate such a fate.

"Oh, they'll know we're coming by much more than that," Soren said with a dark smile.

His hand loosened and slipped from hers. He backed several paces away. His move placed him fully in the glow of the Ether's light, and the eerie shimmer illuminated the intention on his face. Like the windows of the fortress, Soren's amber eyes reflected the rainbow. His russet hair was tipped on the sun-lightened ends by gold and lavender and blue.

He was fully the legend she knew and loved in that moment before he shifted.

Anna's heart expanded—not torn, not shredded after all.

And then the sudden shaking of the earth tossed her to her knees. She stayed, kneeling on the hard ground, while she watched Soren shift into her giant red wolf. Her body screamed with empathy as he cried out with the pain of his limbs and spine and face morphing into the massive canine shape, so familiar, so beloved, but even more so now that she loved the man.

"Soren," Anna said as he leaped and landed in front of her on four paws.

The shift was horrible. The result was perfectly beautiful either way. Whether Soren went from a man to a wolf or vice versa, he was breathtaking once the shift was complete. The red wolf nuzzled her hair as if to say "Hello." Anna thought maybe Soren breathed in her scent in a deeper, more appreciative way with his wolf's nose than he could with his own.

She reached for his russet scruff and fisted both hands in it to help raise herself to her feet. She'd made such a move hundreds of time before. They danced a dance of familiar partnership as she stood and he made way for her beside his large shoulder.

"You know what we have to do," Anna said. He didn't know. Not really. Her intention was still a hot, hard secret in her chest that rose up into her throat every time she tried to speak.

The red wolf turned his face to look at her, as if he heard something in her voice that Soren hadn't been able to hear as a man. She forced herself to look into his amber eyes. She placed both hands on either side of his enormous head.

"Retrieve the sword," Anna said.

That was one part of the mission on which they both agreed.

What she chose to do after was her own decision as the woman who wielded the sword.

Chapter 26

When he became the red wolf, everything was simplified and more complex at the same time. He senses were heightened to a degree that filled his brain with sights, sounds, odors and tastes. Because of that overload, his analytical functions stepped aside.

The red wolf was a creature of instinct and perception.

He didn't think. He *felt*.

He stood beside Anna with her hands in his scruff and he felt her heart beating, her lungs expanding and contracting, and he could feel the power of the Ether flowing beneath her skin. She was his partner. His companion. More so than she'd ever been. The heart that beat in his massive barrel chest beat for her.

He could also tell that something was wrong.

He was Soren. Soren was he. But Soren intended to destroy the emerald sword, and that was where the red wolf's instincts diverged with the man's. Would he rip open his own chest and throw his still-beating heart to the ground? No.

Anna was the red wolf's, always. She was also the always of the man. But Soren had lost himself to analytical thinking. The man didn't trust his instincts to lead him on the best path.

Still, the scents he received from Anna were confusing. The energy from the Ether burned his nose and stung his eyes. When she held him and looked into his face, it felt like she was saying goodbye.

But what she ordered was clear: *Retrieve the sword.* It matched with his instincts and overcame the burning and stinging. He blinked the moisture from his eyes and accepted the weight of his Anna when she climbed onto his back. She was larger than she'd been as a child, but she was still petite enough that she was no burden at all. When she held his scruff and placed her face close to his left ear, it felt like coming home.

"Take me to the sword, Soren," she said.

If the journey had been a thousand miles, he would have burst his heart to make it. For her. The Dark *Volkhvy* fortress was much closer. He gathered himself and sprang into a run, ever mindful of the precious rider on his back.

Anna allowed herself to feel the exhilaration she'd always felt on the red wolf's back. His leaps were twice the length of a horse's stride. Hardened muscles that had been crafted by the enchanted manipulation of his genes before he was born drove his speed.

But his giant heart was all Soren's.

He carried her toward the emerald sword he'd helped her claim the night before. It didn't matter that he also wanted her to destroy it. He had proved his love, saving her from the Ether by celebrating their connection. It didn't matter that he still couldn't trust her. She wouldn't allow his distrust to hurt her anymore. She had lived through the curse with him. She felt the same distrust for *Volkhvy* blood even though she now knew it flowed in her veins. The sword was hers. She could never allow herself to keep it. Even if Soren had trusted her with his family's lives.

She would never trust herself.

The red wolf was solid and warm beneath her. The fortress came closer and closer. Soon they would battle the Dark *Volkhvy* who had stolen the sword that had been made for her hands, even though she'd never held it. Anna held Soren instead. She buried her face in his russet fur one last time.

He had no name that he could remember. All he had was a gnawing hunger inside him that could never be filled, no matter how he hunted and fed. He was haunted by dreams he couldn't understand. He ran from visions of humans who called him Lev. Worse than that, he ran from visions of a woman who called him "beloved" and a tiny mewling babe at her breast.

He ran. He hunted. He killed. He fed.

But he hadn't killed the witch.

She had survived.

He didn't have a name. He only had visions he couldn't understand. But he also had one more thing: a hatred for the beings who channeled the energy from the Ether that ate him.

He had fought its devouring hunger for as long as he could remember. Even after he couldn't remember why, he fought it. He wasn't sure why he had to survive. He wasn't sure why no hunt satisfied, as if there was always a quarry he hadn't managed to chase down.

He only knew from his first taste of the witch's blood

that her death would right a horrible wrong. That certainty drove him to follow her. To find her no matter the cost. His paws grew raw. His fur became patched and shabby. His bones showed beneath his skin.

And still he ran on.

As he ran, he left his visions behind until the only being he saw whenever he closed his eyes was the witch he had to devour in order to survive so his hunt could go on.

Vasilisa knew when her daughter claimed the emerald sword. As someone with a majority of her consciousness subsumed in the Ether, the tremendous power drain caused her to grow faint. She was walking in the garden at midnight when she stumbled. She almost fell. But long practice in the variations of the Ether's energy allowed her to right herself and walk on.

She merely changed her direction because something was wrong. Her daughter had claimed the emerald sword, but it wasn't in her hand. The connection Anna shared with Soren was still tainted by mistrust. Worse than that, the white wolf, in his savage way, was as tuned in to the Ether's energy as Vasilisa was herself. If she could sense her daughter and Soren so clearly, then so could Lev.

Vasilisa headed for the sleeping warrior in the middle of her garden.

She no longer had the luxury of time.

If Soren couldn't trust Anna, if Anna couldn't trust herself, they would destroy the sword rather than trust the way it bound them together. Without the sword's connection, her daughter would fall to the white wolf. Especially if she was too distracted to defend herself against him.

The only solution was to ensure that the white wolf was the one too distracted to attack.

Chapter 27

As they drew closer to the fortress, Anna rose up on the red wolf's back to survey their destination. The cement that had seemed to curve up over the windows from a distance actually formed balconies that flowed out from the glass in the shape of waves curling back into themselves. They would be an effective barrier against witch or human attack, but not against a Romanov wolf.

She didn't have to speak. Soren had already seen what he should do. Anna only had to tighten her grip to be sure she didn't fall off his back when he gathered himself and leaped onto the balcony that surrounded the first floor.

The red wolf slid several feet when he landed. Anna couldn't let go to raise her hands to direct her energy. She could only duck her head against his fur and allow her power to flare out and around her body. The glowing energy that engulfed her protected her from the shattering glass as Soren's momentum took them through it. Thousands of shards of glass turned to glittering diamond-like dust against the green force field she formed. The dust burst outward from the red wolf's body as he landed inside the fortress's walls.

"The emerald sword belongs to me," Anna said as the dust dissipated.

A contingent of Dark *Volkhvy* met their arrival as if they'd known exactly where they would be even before they knew it themselves. One stood tall in front of all the others. It was the same *Volkhvy* who had drawn her attention at the palace dinner. He had the sword. He wore it in a black leather scabbard that draped loosely on a belt at his lean hips. The emerald in its hilt gleamed brightly as his jaunty walk toward them jarred it to and fro. During the dinner party, she'd told herself that the oily black of his hair and clothes didn't mean he was a Dark *Volkhvy*, but it hadn't been his clothes that made him shine darkly that night. She could see the darkness in his expression more clearly now. She could see the oily weight of his hair was caused by an almost-liquid shimmer around his head, a barely visible dark halo.

It wasn't oil.

He and his retinue stopped a few yards away. The glass dust she'd created settled on his shoulders as a light snow.

"The sword is mine, *Princess*. And soon you shall be mine, as well," the man said. "Forgive me for not introducing myself before. I am Aleksandr. I rule the Dark *Volkhvy*, but soon all *Volkhvy* shall have me as their Dark master."

"If the sword is yours, why don't you draw it, Alek?" Anna asked. The red wolf growled deep in his chest. The glow she'd summoned to protect herself from shattered glass still suffused her body. She didn't send it away. There was no hiding who and what she was from the man who challenged her.

Aleksandr's hand hovered over the hilt of the sword as if his fingers were being repelled. He didn't seem to mind.

"Because you can't. Now that the emerald shines for me, it won't allow anyone else to wield the sword."

Anna swung her leg over the red wolf's back and jumped to the ground. Soren crouched to make the move easier for her, as he'd done a thousand times. Then he rose to his full height beside her. She reached to hold the fur of his scruff. Touching him gave her strength and steadied her nerves. She also hoped to hold him back from attacking the Dark *Volkhvy* until she was certain the time was right.

The witches they faced were too calm. Many had smiles on their faces. None of them looked afraid. Soren wasn't the alpha wolf, but he posed a great danger to *Volkhvy*. Their calm made Anna's stomach go cold, as if the Ether had crept its way inside.

"It was never my aim to steal the emerald sword... alone," Aleksandr said. He sashayed closer toward them, as if Soren didn't have teeth a foot long, ready to sink into his flesh. "I had to attend the dinner party that night. I needed to demonstrate my 'loyalty' to Vasilisa. But once I saw you, I was so tempted. I almost revealed my hand. *It was always you I wanted.* Anna, the Light *Volkhvy* princess. I couldn't act at the palace, where Vasilisa's power is in the very air one breathes. The attack that night was only to draw attention away from me," Aleksandr continued. "I would have had you before now if you hadn't been hidden by Bronwal's curse. Why settle for the blade alone when I can have the blade and the woman who would wield it? You will unlock the sword's power for me, Anna. And then I will rule all of *Volkhvy* kind. The Dark and the Light."

He stopped far enough away that Soren would have to knock her aside to leap for the Dark *Volkhvy*'s throat. Anna's fingers had loosened on the red wolf's fur. But not because it was time for him to attack. Her hand grew slack from shock. The unexpected revelation caused her energy aura to fade just as she could feel her face go pale and cold.

"The sword was bait for me," Anna said. "You knew I would come for it. All along I've been trying to protect the Romanovs, but I've been lured here as the key to their destruction."

The cold that had begun in her middle had spread outward. Now it wasn't shock that had caused her fingers to loosen on Soren's fur. Her fingers had gone numb from the cold.

There was only one place she'd ever felt such cold. The Ether. Aleksandr was somehow using the Ether as a weapon. Not its energy, but the Ether itself.

"I've had months to prepare for your arrival," Aleksandr said. "And now I welcome you with the Ether's kiss."

Aleksandr's pupils darkened, and the darkness spread until blackness entirely claimed both of his eyes. Anna cried out. Even her connection with Soren didn't protect her from the spread of the Ether that had begun without her understanding what it was. The cold filled her. Her green aura of power faded completely. It winked out as if it was a candle that had been snuffed by Aleksandr's hand. The gleam of the emerald in the hilt of the sword—her sword— at Aleksandr's waist also went out. Her numb fingers slid from the red wolf's fur.

Soren howled...but he didn't leap for the Dark *Volkhvy*. Aleksandr laughed.

"You should have brought an army, or at the very least your brothers. Or have they turned their backs on a wolf that would love a witch?" Aleksandr asked the red wolf with false concern. He showed how unconcerned he was by stepping directly up to Soren's frozen face. He reached to grip the red wolf's scruff in mimicry of Anna's hold that had slipped away. "I should thank you before I feed you to the Ether. If your family hadn't fallen apart after the curse was broken, I wouldn't have stood a chance."

He jerked his hand from Soren's neck, taking some of the red wolf's russet fur with his fist.

Anna's body was still fully materialized, but she couldn't move or speak. Aleksandr's cruelty was a desecration toward the legendary wolf, but there was nothing she could do. The cold had fully claimed her. She couldn't summon her power. The sword was close, but she couldn't move to reach for it. She strained with all her heart, but her muscles didn't respond.

Soren began to disappear without her.

His massive paws were planted wide, as if he would hold himself to the ground with their strength and weight, but they slowly began to fade. Anna wanted to scream, but her vocal cords were as frozen as the rest of her. She could only watch as Soren's russet body began to disappear. He growled and whined and cried, but he was caught in a vacuum he couldn't escape, just as he'd been every time the curse had claimed them together. Finally, his sounds ceased as his chest and head vanished into nothingness.

Her red wolf had never gone into the Ether alone.

Her last glimpse was of Soren's amber eyes. They met hers. Somehow. With incredible effort. His gaze shifted toward her, even when his body was nearly gone. Aleksandr laughed as the giant wolf disappeared. He threw the handful of hair he'd torn from Soren's neck onto the spot where Soren had been.

Then he turned to face her.

The *Volkhvy* were a handsome race. Their enchanted manipulations ensured that only perfection would be passed on from generation to generation. But evil joy and cruelty twisted Aleksandr's features into a caricature of themselves. His nasty smile and obsidian eyes ruined his symmetrical bone structure.

Anna struggled, but her effort wasn't rewarded by any outward sign that she tried to break free. She couldn't so much as blink as Aleksandr turned his attention to her. He was in no hurry. He brushed his hands together to rid them of any remaining hair as he approached. His black eyes tracked from her head to feet and back again. He wasn't checking her for signs of resistance. He was eyeing his prize. With the red wolf gone, he thought the battle was over before it had begun.

He was wrong. He had to be wrong.

His manipulation of the Ether controlled her entire body. The Ether that ate away at her inside froze her. But, in spite of her paralysis, one tear spilled from the corner of her eye to track down her cheek.

Aleksandr saw her emotion. He reached his hand up with one finger extended and caught the tear before it could slip from her face and fall to the floor. He looked down at her as he lifted the moisture on his finger, as if he would show it to her.

"My anticipation of this day fell far short of reality," he said. His smile widened. He rubbed his thumb and forefinger together and crushed the teardrop in front of her face. He'd come far too close in order to catch her tear, but she couldn't back away. She could only endure as his tall, lean body pressed against her side.

Anna's eyelids were suddenly freed to close against his evil enjoyment of her devastation. She was no longer as frozen as she'd been seconds before. She blinked, and during the brief respite she felt the hard shaft of the emerald sword against her side.

The white wolf might kill her. She might throw herself into the Ether. But she wouldn't allow Soren to die. This travesty wasn't an option. If she saved the entire *Volkhvy* race at the same time, so be it. Anna refused to accept that the red wolf was gone.

When her eyes opened again a split second later, they glowed with emerald chips of the Ether's energy. Her eyes and the emerald in the sword flared at the same time. Aleksandr cried out and tried to stumble back from her, but he seemed to move in slow motion. She easily reached and drew the emerald sword from the scabbard at his waist as he fell. Her hands closed over the hilt as if it had been made for her fingers—because it had. Before she was born, the sword had been forged by Vasilisa's enchantment for Soren's mate, for the warrior who would fight the Dark *Volkhvy* by his side.

Anna was a witch, but she was also a warrior. More than that, she was Soren's champion, just as he was hers.

Her power blazed. The whole room was lit by the emerald aura that glowed around her and the sword she lifted high in the air above her head. Aleksandr had fallen to the ground. The black in his eyes had bled away until only a network of black veins remained. He was tainted by his Dark use of the Ether, but he was no longer powered by it.

Many of his retinue had run away.

Anna allowed them to run, but she used a directed blast of green energy to mark them. For the rest of their lives, the treacherous former Light *Volkhvy* would carry the shadowy scorched mark of a bellflower on their foreheads. Aleksandr cried out as a bolt of her energy traced the mark on his forehead. Smoke rose from his skin.

She'd always used the bellflower symbols to show her the way through the labyrinthine corridors of Bronwal. Now the Light *Volkhvy* would use them to know friend from proved foe.

Once the traitors were marked, Anna's power didn't diminish. She turned and stepped through the broken window to stand on the balcony overlooking the canyon. The aurora borealis glow of the Ether shimmered in the air. Her power rose. Thousands of tendrils of green light flared out from her sword and her body, but it wasn't the source of its power that her energy sought.

Soren wasn't gone. He was only lost without her. Fortunately, he hadn't had to be alone in the Ether for long. As if her energy was a net cast into an icy, empty sea, Anna gathered Soren's consciousness with a million threads of energy that began in her own heart. She pulled him from the Ether. He materialized in the sky, held by her power, and his howl echoed throughout the entire canyon.

The glass in the fortress behind her shattered as his cry filled the air.

The green tendrils of her power slowed his fall toward the balcony. As he descended, he shifted. His naked human body was wrapped in her energy's embrace when his feet hit the ground.

Soren's eyes opened and met hers.

The green aura around her softened. She lowered the sword and placed its tip on the ground. She was glad of its support. She was the daughter of a queen, but she was only a novice witch. She had used all the power at her disposal to save Soren from the Ether. She was left shaky and faint. Anna blinked and looked around. She had a lot to learn. Fortunately, she also had a warrior's heart to guide the way.

It was her connection to the sword that had saved the day. He would have been lost without it. Even as Soren stepped toward her and gathered her into his arms, Anna suddenly knew what she would be forced to do. She couldn't allow the emerald sword to be destroyed. The red Romanov wolf must have his warrior mate—even if that mate couldn't be her.

Chapter 28

The fortress seemed deserted. It was eerily like Bronwal when they went inside. Her booted footsteps echoed through the empty rooms and halls. Several straggling *Volkhvy* saw them and ran away. The shadowy bellflowers on their foreheads stood out like ashy brands. Aleksandr had already gone. He must have realized she would bring the red wolf back from the Ether and that together, with the sword, they couldn't be defeated.

"I marked them. You'll always know who stood with Aleksandr against us," Anna said. "Our connection with each other and the sword broke his ties to the Ether. He must have been absorbing it for years, just like the witchblood prince. If I hadn't stopped him, he would have eventually been consumed by the darkness he allowed inside him."

"He channeled it into me. If it wasn't for our connection, I would have been lost," Soren said.

"Being *Volkhvy* is a balancing act. We use the energy the Ether creates with its vacuum. Tampering with the Ether itself, accepting it inside us, is suicide," Anna said. Her chest was tight. She'd fought the icy nothingness of the Ether's hunger for so long she wasn't sure she could stop even when circumstances forced her to, but she had to try.

Soren came to her. He carried a scabbard he'd taken from a suit of armor that decorated the main hall of the fortress. He'd claimed a crimson sash for himself. He wore it as a loincloth draped low on his hips. As he walked to her side, his powerful body was displayed nonchalantly, but even in her weakened state, he caused her mouth to go dry.

He was hers, but he wouldn't be for long. She tried to memorize his tall, muscular form, from his broad shoulders to his strong legs. She stared at his face, the one she'd waited so long to see. Her imaginings of what he would be like seemed childish now. He was no longer a fantasy. He was a living legend. She cataloged every quirk of his lips and every movement of his jaw. His eyes seemed both ancient and ageless. No one who disappeared into the Ether ever came back the same. But Soren was a living champion this world needed against the darkness.

It was imperative that she let him go.

"Here. This will help," Soren said. He wound the belt of the scabbard around her waist twice and buckled it in place. She'd been dragging the heavy sword behind her on the floor. He reached around her to take its weight from her fingers. His nearness sizzled her nerves, but even exhausted, she didn't want to let the sword go. Her fingers clung. "I'm only going to put it in the scabbard so you can hold it more easily," Soren murmured into her hair.

His body was big and warm against hers. So solid. She closed her eyes and opened her fingers to allow him to take the sword. While he moved to place it in the scabbard, she breathed in his forest scent and absorbed the feel of him as much as she could. Would she remember him when the Ether took her? Would her molecules ache and search for him even when her body was gone?

Anna gasped when Soren's mouth left her hair to press against hers. He kissed her gently. His lips were barely a brush of warm air, tickling and tasting but asking for nothing in return. She didn't reach for him. She was afraid if she twined her arms around his neck, she would never let him go.

"It isn't safe to destroy the sword here. You need to rest first. Then we'll travel back to the island. Once we're there, I'll shift and crush the emerald with my bite," Soren said. She opened her eyes. He stared at her intently. He wasn't fooled. He knew something was changed. He knew something was wrong.

He couldn't know she intended to save the sword and allow the Ether to claim her so that he could find another mate. She'd only just decided herself. His amber gaze tracked over hers. He searched the depths of her eyes for answers to an unspoken question. She tried not to do the same.

She already knew the answer. She had to break her connection to the sword. The Romanovs could never be tied to the *Volkhvy*, no matter what the sword had decreed, but they would need all the enchanted swords to stand against the Darkness.

Anna had depleted all the energy she could channel in order to defeat Aleksandr and save Soren from the Ether. She was pale and wan as they searched the fortress to be sure no traitors remained. In spite of her weakness, she kept her hand on the hilt of her sword as if she would still draw it if she had to. He fully believed she would.

The Ether no longer froze him, and he was too used to nudity to be uncomfortable with his lack of clothes. His discomfort was pure concern. His heart beat too quickly. His respiration was faster than it should be. They looked for traitors, but he also braced for a more personal attack of a different sort around every corner.

His brother was coming.

Anna's determined hold on the sword worried him, because it mirrored the stubborn negation in his own heart. He'd seen her standing on the balcony of the fortress with the sword raised high over her head. He'd seen the energy come to her, channel through her and then come for him. He'd felt her energy's electric, tingling embrace. In spite of the ice in his heart, the charged memory of Anna's energy still hummed beneath his skin, a pleasurable hum that reminded him of her kiss and her touch and the hug of her thighs on his hips.

There was no more time for lovemaking. They couldn't hold off the inevitable separation any longer. The white wolf was on his way. Lev would find them again soon, especially with their enchanted connection resounding and reverberating with every beat of their hearts.

He couldn't risk Anna bringing harm to herself because of the white wolf's distrust of the *Volkhvy*.

He'd connected with Anna on a visceral level in the forest, but their lovemaking had only begun to solidify what he'd already known. He didn't only love her. The struggle with Aleksandr had brought him to the truth: he trusted Anna with his life. That wasn't a new development. It was only new that he should face it for the first time since he'd discovered she was a witch.

He no longer distrusted Anna's *Volkhvy* blood. He'd seen that evil was a choice in Aleksandr and his followers, not an inevitability. Anna was powerful. More powerful now than ever before. She'd still chosen to mark the traitors rather than dissolve them in electric-green fire. She'd been a warrior before she'd known she was a witch. She'd fought the curse with the Romanovs for centuries.

Soren was devoted to his family. That would never change. But Anna's safety was his paramount concern.

And his trust in her changed nothing.

Lev would never stop trying to kill her. And Soren could never give up on his brother. So he had to let Anna go.

They still needed to reject their connection and destroy the sword.

Soren was right about one thing. She needed to get him back to her mother's island before she broke their connection. It might take time for the sword to Call a new warrior to fight by his side. Vasilisa might help to protect him until his new mate was Called if Anna insisted her own happiness depended upon it.

As nighttime approached, Anna discovered the value of a home overlooking the manifest presence of the Ether. She walked along the balcony of the top floor bathed in rainbow light and soaked up its energy like a plant in the sun. She kept herself carefully shielded against the Ether itself. She would open to it only when she was ready to leave Soren's side.

He currently leaned against the frame of one of the windows his howl had shattered. He'd found some clothing in one of the bedrooms. More was the pity. But even dressed in jeans and a plain white T-shirt, he was impressive. The thin cotton of the shirt stretched over his chest, and his biceps bulged from its sleeves. Modern clothing was made for men who found Pilates and free weights a challenge. Soren had been molded by a life challenged by much harsher things, including hand-to-hand combat on muddy battlefields.

His past showed in more than just his eyes.

She'd kissed his scars before, one by one. She wished she could kiss them again and memorize their every fine white line. He stared at her as if he'd like to do the same. She did have a few scars of her own. Their life during the curse had been hard and she hadn't made it through unscathed, even with an enchanted wolf companion by her side.

Anna caught herself fantasizing about how they could soothe past hurts, and heat rose in her cheeks...and elsewhere.

"It's working. Your color is better. Your cheeks are flushed," Soren said. He pushed away from the door and approached her. Anna stopped her pacing and stood bathed in the Ether's light. She liked how the multicolored light shimmered in Soren's eyes. It didn't disguise his thoughts. He wasn't coming closer to gauge her recovery. He was coming closer for the same reason she stared.

"Even before I could hear the sword's Call I felt connected to you, but it's as if the connection I've always felt is more tangible now. There for all the world to see," Anna whispered. Soren stopped, halted by her raw honesty, but then he proceeded. He came so close her breasts touched his chest before he stopped. He looked down at her upturned face.

"I love you. Destroying the sword won't change that. I told you before, we'll always be connected and I believe it now more than ever," Soren said.

The atmosphere around Anna seemed to expand and contract. Her chest filled with emotion and then hollowed with dread. She'd known. His confession only made her more certain of her decision to free him.

"You can't love me," Anna said.

She wasn't prepared for Soren to scoop her up and propel her into the curve of the cement wave that created the balcony on which they stood. It created a nook for their bodies, and he pressed her there in between his broad chest and the wall with her feet off the ground. He held her, high and hidden, away from the Ether's light.

"I can and I do," Soren vowed.

Anna didn't resist his angry passion. She reached for the back of his head and tangled her hands in the curls that were growing out at the nape of his neck. Her eyes had flared with flecks of emerald light. She could tell because the glow illuminated the frustrated desire on Soren's face.

"I love you, too," Anna said. "I always have."

She lowered her head to capture his lips in a kiss that wasn't slow or sweet. She was as frustrated as he was. She plunged her tongue to taste him deeply, and the resultant thrill that claimed her body was painfully bittersweet.

His hands had splayed on her back to protect her from the hardness of the cement. Now he used them to pull her closer. The sword blazed in its scabbard. The balcony was flooded with a green light that subsumed the Ether's rainbow.

It was a goodbye kiss.

Only Soren didn't know just how final she intended it to be.

She took them through the Ether without pulling her lips from his. Their tongues twined, and she continued to taste him rebelliously as all else disappeared. The sword would Call another. She would be gone. But he would always remember her. And, maybe, even if she never materialized again, she would remember him, too.

Chapter 29

The white wolf was waiting when they materialized on the cliff overlooking the false Mediterranean Sea that surrounded Krajina. Lev had never penetrated Vasilisa's enchantment when he was looking for his wife and child.

Until now.

Soren and Anna had appeared in each other's arms. Their lips were still pressed together. But at the presence of the white wolf and the sound of his rumbling growl, they broke apart.

"No, Lev. She's my mate. I won't allow you to harm her," Soren proclaimed. Anna couldn't help the thrill that rushed beneath her skin at his words. But she also felt despair. Lev was feral. He couldn't be reasoned with or dissuaded from the hatred that blazed in his bloodshot eyes. The pale gray of his irises was shot through with red. Madeline's had been the ruby sword. Its light seemed to shine from deep in the white wolf's eyes.

Madeline's sword slept with her and Trevor. Its power hadn't glowed in hundreds of years. The gleam of ruby light in Lev's eyes caused a flutter of unease in Anna's stomach.

"Stop. He won't be able to harm me," Anna said. "Not where I'm going. And when I'm gone, you'll be free to help him."

She backed away from Soren, but all the while her gaze tracked over him. She would take a vision of him with her into the cold and dark. He had watched over her for centuries. His memory would watch over her still. She would never be alone.

"What are you saying?" Soren asked. He stepped after her, but the white wolf leaped to place his massive body in between the brother he instinctively trusted and the witch losing his family had made him hate.

"You've been right all along. We can't be together. But you were wrong about the sword. We can't destroy it. There will always be *Volkhvy* who choose the Darkness. The Romanovs will always need to stand against them. You can't be left without a sword or a partner to wield it. You can't be left to stand alone," Anna said. "We're going to let each other go, just as you planned. But I'm letting the sword go, too."

"No," Soren protested. It came from deep in his chest and sounded much like the red wolf's howl. Lev was startled and confused. He sidestepped and rounded to face them both with his back to the edge of the cliff.

"When I'm gone, the sword will have to Call another woman to fight by your side. A more suitable choice. You've always been my champion. But you need a champion, too. You can't sacrifice your chance at a powerful partnership just because I'm an unsuitable mate," Anna said.

"Is that why you think I'm doing this? Anna, I love

you. I love a witch. There is no better mate for me. There will never be another mate for me. I wanted to destroy the sword to protect you from Lev's venom and Ivan's anger," Soren said. "And if they won't accept you as my mate. If you're in danger from them, then I'll have no other. I refuse." Soren took another step toward her, even though Lev looked like he would attack at any second. "I'll destroy the sword if its rightful owner can't wield it," he continued.

Anna froze.

He'd already told her he loved her. She hadn't believed him. Not really. She'd thought the distrust he had for *Volkhvy* blood prevented him from truly loving her. Even when he'd urged her to accept the sword's Call to help her resist the Ether's vacuum, she'd thought he was being her protector, not her lover.

"I'm a witch," Anna said, as if anyone could doubt her heritage when the emerald light was shining in her eyes.

"I know. I feel your power pulsing beneath my skin. When we kiss, it vibrates in my soul. And I don't fear it, because I know you. I've known you for an age. I was thrown by the revelation at the Gathering. I'll admit it. My fear of the Ether colored my reaction. I will always watch my back around Vasilisa. But I trust you with my life. And with my family's lives," Soren said.

The last stabbed into her heart with its finality. Because nothing he had said changed what she had to do. It only made the loss of what they could have had harsher. He trusted her, but she couldn't trust herself. She would leap into the Ether with the certain knowledge that they could have been together.

But he had been right not to trust her with his family's lives. With Lev's life.

Anna turned off the flow of the Ether's energy with one unwavering mental push. The sword at her waist went dark. The green glow left her eyes. The ever-present tingling in her hands died.

"No," Soren said. This time his protest wasn't a howl. It was a hoarse whisper from lips swollen by her kiss.

Lev paced toward her along the edge of the cliff, emboldened by her sudden apparent weakness. She stood on the edge of a precipice with all her power gone. But it wasn't weakness. It was the ultimate strength. She rejected self-defense. She finally had total control of her abilities, and she used them to protect the white wolf even as he stalked her.

"I won't let him kill me, Soren. I know that would destroy you and your family. I'm going into the Ether instead. Once I'm gone, the sword will be freed. Don't destroy it. Allow it to choose a better mate."

It was even harder to let the sword go than it had been to cut off the flow of energy from its stone. Nevertheless, she did it. Anna released the sword. Her fingers loosened, and the sword fell to the ground. It landed at her feet with a dull thud. Lev paused again, confused by her nonaggressive stance.

"We did it, Soren. We survived the curse. Our love survived. For a while, I thought it had only survived in me, but now I see it survived in us both. And Bronwal survived, too. Help Ivan rebuild. He needs you. Elena and the baby need you. Madeline and Trevor need you..." Anna said, but she was interrupted.

She immediately understood what the ruby glow in Lev's eyes had signified and why it had caused a feeling of unease in her gut. As if her words had conjured Lev's wife from her coffin in the center of the garden, a familiar figure approached from below. Her bright auburn hair was whipped by the wind and bathed in ruby light. Her dress tangled around her legs as the artificial atmosphere created by Vasilisa disappeared. The baby was nowhere in sight. Madeline no longer cradled Trevor to her breast. Instead, she wielded the ruby sword, which no longer slumbered. The ruby in its hilt gleamed, sending beams of multifaceted light in every direction away from her windswept figure.

Lev howled. Rocks from the cliff's edge crumbled beneath his back paws and fell into the frothing waves far below.

The white wolf's howl was so loud it caused Anna to crumple to her knees. She pressed her hands to her ears as it continued. Soren wasn't as affected. He was the red wolf after all. He endured the howl, pushing through the shattered atmosphere it caused to fall by Anna's side at the cliff's edge with his arm around her.

"If you leap into the Ether, I'll follow you," he shouted above his brother's howling.

Madeline had continued her climb. She reached the top of the cliff. The ruby light glowed from her eyes. An aura surrounded her wild hair like a halo of red. She raised the sword high in the air. She was a medieval warrior princess raised from an enchanted sleep, but she didn't approach the white wolf as his wife.

She walked toward him like an avenging angel about to take his life.

Anna and Soren both understood what was happening at the same time. Madeline was connected to the white wolf. She had woken feeling his extreme fury as her own.

And part of the white wolf's fury was directed at himself. He'd been searching for his lost mate and his son forever. He hadn't been able to save them.

Soren was able to get to his feet first, but he reached immediately to pull Anna up from the ground. Lev's howl had died down to a whine. He crouched on the edge of the cliff, facing his long-lost love's approach. More rock came loose beneath his giant paws to tumble end over end before splashing into the water below.

"Madeline, stop. It's Lev. Don't you know him? He's your husband," Anna shouted above the wind and the waves.

"He'll kill her," Soren said. He let go of Anna, but she reached to grab his arm before he could run toward the other couple.

"No. He won't," Anna said.

And she was right. Rain began to fall. As it pelted against the white wolf, it flattened his fur and turned what was left of the ground beneath his feet to mud. More rocks were dislodged, and Anna cried out as the white wolf's back paws struggled to keep purchase on his dissolving perch.

But then Lev shifted back into his human form for the first time in centuries. The ground shook and a chunk of cliff fell away, but Lev's human form was lighter and smaller. He didn't fall into the sea. Mud and rocks fell, but Lev knelt on what was left of the edge of the cliff. His wife paused, confused by the disappearance of the savage wolf she'd been preparing to attack.

"Vasilisa said it might take time once Madeline was awakened for her to be herself again. She's feeling Lev's emotions, but I think *the sword* is driving her instincts, and I'm her sister-in-arms. She was protecting me from the white wolf," Anna said. "She's confused. It's been so long. She doesn't recognize Lev, but she can't kill the man she loved."

Her heart thudded painfully in her chest. Lev was separated from his prey by the woman who was supposed to be his champion and partner. But deep down he must have recognized Madeline. He hadn't attacked her. They had been separated for so long, but his endless roaming indicated he'd been searching even after he'd forgotten who he'd been searching for.

He'd finally found the woman he'd lost.

Madeline lowered the sword, but she still hesitated. The rain lashed down and plastered her hair to her face and body. Anna went to her. It was like approaching a ghost. The ruby light in her eyes had faded. She released the sword easily into Anna's hand, but she only stood stiffly when Anna tried to embrace her.

"Lev, no!" Soren yelled.

The white wolf had shifted into his human form, but he still had the same hatred for witches in his heart. He sprang toward Anna. He howled at the same time, and the sound contained all the pain hundreds of years of lonely wandering could bring. Anna didn't raise the sword. She didn't have time to step into the Ether, either. Nor did she summon her energy for defense.

She pushed Madeline in one direction. She threw the ruby sword in the other. And she stood to face Lev's attack.

Her love for Soren extended to his family. And unlike the queen, the queen-to-be honored the Light *Volkhvy* champions above self-preservation. It would be better to die than to harm a single hair on a Romanov head. But she didn't stand alone. The earth shook. The wind stilled. Suddenly, the red wolf stood on one side of her, and the Light *Volkhvy* queen stood on the other.

Chapter 30

Vasilisa had calmed the atmosphere, but it was Soren who halted Lev's attack. He met his brother's advance with a cold snout against Lev's forehead and a snarling maw inches from Lev's face. As a man, the white wolf was impossibly lean and hard. His muscles had seen nothing but relentless exercise for hundreds of years. He had the tall, broad Romanov build with none of the bulk around it. His eyes blazed with blue-gray fury and confusion.

But the red light from the ruby was gone.

His wet hair was tangled and wind tossed, but it was also streaked with white. The white streaks were new. He hadn't had them as a man centuries ago, but Anna didn't think they'd been caused by his extreme age. He still looked strong and vital and young.

The streaks were white, not gray. Anna thought either the shock of losing his wife or the shock of finding her again had drained the color from his formerly golden hair.

The ruby in the sword's hilt was dead and gray.

"You woke her too quickly after you said you shouldn't," Anna said.

"Yes. I did. It was the only thing I could do to help you against the white wolf," Vasilisa said. "Her connection to him actually woke her. I just stopped shielding her from that connection."

Lev fisted his hands and moved to go for the *Volkhvy* queen, but Soren growled and nudged him backward with his massive head against Lev's chest. It was a testament to Lev's strength that even the red wolf didn't budge him far. His bare heels dug into the ground, and his resistance caused two ruts to form.

Anna would have gone for her mother herself, except she was burdened by Madeline's weight. The other woman's knees had collapsed when the ruby sword was taken from her hand. She was only on her feet because Anna held her upright with an arm around her waist. It wasn't an easy feat. Madeline was a tall woman with an athletic build that hadn't been diminished by her long, enforced rest.

But it was Madeline's need of her support that made her anger toward Vasilisa kindle like green fire in Anna's eyes and deep within her chest. She knew without a shadow of a doubt that she wouldn't have done this. It was the first time certainty and confidence in her abilities filled her with a calm resolve.

Witch or no witch. Queen or no queen. She would love with all she had, but she would never hurt the helpless. And she would never value herself above those she ruled.

The queen didn't seem intimidated by the green glow of fury in Anna's eyes. She came to her daughter's side and took her precious burden. Madeline didn't resist. She went to the queen's hold easily, and Vasilisa seemed to take her weight with no effort. Madeline could suddenly stand. Anna wondered if her mother used her abilities to keep Madeline on her feet. If so, she couldn't help her in other ways. Madeline looked like she wasn't fully aware of what was going on.

Which wasn't necessarily a bad thing. Not when Lev Romanov looked like he was still more wolf than man.

Anna placed her hand on Soren's scruff. She held it to comfort him and to comfort herself. She also held on to keep him from overdoing the correction of his brother's aggression. The edge of the cliff wasn't that far away.

"You need to get him to Bronwal now that he's shifted. I'll take care of Madeline. Trevor is still sleeping. I'm waking him up slowly to give him time to adjust," Vasilisa said.

"You should have given Madeline time," Anna accused. Lev growled as if he still had fangs. It might have been because he agreed. It might have been because he hated the sound of Anna's voice.

"I had no time to spare. And now Lev Romanov is found. He is a human for the first time in hundreds of years. You can hate me for it," Vasilisa said. "I deserve no thanks after all I've done."

Soren whined. Lev had slumped back to his knees and Madeline had swooned in the queen's arms. Anna released Soren to touch Madeline's face. Her skin was cold and damp. In her state of suspended animation, she'd seemed moments away from her next breath and her next step. Now that she had woken up, she seemed near death.

"I wouldn't have done this," Anna said.

"I know," Vasilisa whispered. "You were going to go into the Ether to protect them all. When the time comes, you will be a far greater queen than I have been, and you will also be more loved than feared by your subjects."

Vasilisa walked back toward the palace. Madeline placed one foot in front of the other beside the queen, but she didn't seem to understand that she was walking away from the man she'd once loved and the sword that was rightfully hers.

Everyone but Anna forgot the ruby sword on the ground. She went to pick it up. Even though it wasn't her blade, it still responded to her touch. The ruby gave off the softest glow, and Lev's growls dissolved into silent seething tears.

Bronwal welcomed Lev back with subdued joy. The corridors were filled with servants falling over themselves to help a man who would have preferred to be left alone. He claimed the tower room, and no one dared to try to convince him otherwise. It became the new lair of the white wolf, who walked on two legs, but who was probably more savage than he'd ever been before.

No one was certain how much he understood about his wife and son. About where they were or how they were or if they would ever be able to come home. It had to be enough for now that he was home, where he could at least have a chance of recovering from his centuries-long ordeal.

Anna's part in his homecoming was told of far and wide. At first, Soren had told the tale to Ivan and Elena, and then Elena and Patrice took the tale from there. He had faced his brother and his pregnant sister-in-law first to be certain they understood what Anna had tried to do. And also to fight the alpha wolf if he had to.

He loved his family. He always would. But he loved a witch, as well.

"She was going to throw herself into the Ether?" Ivan had asked. The giant man had stood beside the fireplace in the great hall with his arms crossed over his chest. Everyone had known to disappear when his voice boomed out like thunder. Everyone but Soren. The red wolf wasn't the alpha, but he also wasn't afraid. The one thing he'd always feared—losing his twin brother—had been averted. He'd finally faced that possible loss, and he'd watched as Anna had almost sacrificed herself to be sure it wouldn't happen.

"And not to travel with its energy. She fully intended to give up her life so that the Romanovs could be safe and strong. She thought it was the only way to make sure that I had my brothers and the emerald sword by my side," Soren explained.

"And you stopped her," Ivan said. His forehead had been heavy and his lips tight. His frame had been stiff with tension.

"As you would have stopped Elena if she tried to sacrifice herself for you," Soren had said.

"My mate is not a witch, brother," Ivan reminded him. But some of the tension that had claimed him with Anna's sudden arrival at Bronwal had gone out of his body.

They stood in a room with thrones that had been reclaimed by a couple who actually loved each other. Vladimir Romanov had never loved their mother, Naomi. He'd sacrificed her to the Dark *Volkhvy* at the same time he'd sacrificed Vasilisa's prince consort so that he could seduce the queen. Being a champion hadn't been enough for him. He'd wanted to rule the *Volkhvy.*

The thrones had been washed and refinished with a fine cherry stain. The wolf heads on each arm and on the back overlooking the seat were now well lit by recessed electric lighting that revealed just how intricately the carvings had been rendered.

Bronwal had always been defended. But now it was cared for as it had never been before.

"I've always loved Anna. I've always trusted her. My fear blinded me to the fact that she's always been a witch. Her blood doesn't negate my trust. I'm only sorry that I had to almost lose her to see that," Soren said.

Ivan strode to his side. Soren braced himself. If the alpha still intended to send Anna away, he would have to choose to fight or flee. He fisted his hands, because his choice had already been made. But rather than a battle, Ivan offered a hand. He gripped one of Soren's shoulders, and the power in his squeeze made Soren glad he hadn't offered a punch instead.

"Elena said the swords know. She doesn't doubt her sister-in-arms at all," Ivan said. "She's looking forward to welcoming her as a sister-in-law." He looked thoughtfully at Soren's face, surveying his human features as if he would memorize them. Soren had changed even though he'd barely aged. He thought Ivan was noticing those differences, and when a smile broke through the alpha's concentration, Soren thought that maybe he'd passed some sort of test. "Considering what the sapphire sword has done for me... I can only welcome the warrior who wields the emerald sword to the family," Ivan said.

His bear hug had been almost as brutal as a full-body slam would have been from a lesser man.

Since Lev had claimed the tower room, Anna found herself back in the old aviary she'd loved. It was practically empty. All the keepsakes and necessary items she'd gleaned and gathered over the centuries were in the palace on her mother's island.

But the bed and all the other furnishings had been restored, and all the linens had been replaced. She found a giant bed filled with luxurious pillows and blankets. She exclaimed over a fireplace that didn't smoke and a bathroom that had been built onto the side.

Her aviary hadn't been shuttered and forgotten.

Maybe they hadn't intended for her to return, but they hadn't destroyed her place, either. She cuddled into the big bed after a long soak and thought about all the years she'd spent using her hideaway to escape her uncertain position at Bronwal. She'd been an orphan and a foundling. Vladimir's lack of affection and attention had caused her to doubt her place for years, even before the curse had fallen. Now she knew why he had ignored her.

She'd been nothing to him but a pawn in a deadly political game that had begun with the murder of the villagers who had agreed to raise her as their own to protect Vasilisa's heir. He'd killed her real father. He'd kidnapped her and kept her heritage hidden. He'd seduced her grieving mother.

But then there had been Soren.

He had never ignored her. They had been friends long before she'd begun to see him in a different light. Then, after her mother had discovered Vladimir's treachery and punished him with the curse, they'd been inseparable companions. Neither could have survived without the other. She was certain of it now. But, in her case, that was true even before the curse.

He'd helped her make the aviary into a hideaway. He'd helped her fill it with baubles and treasures that made her feel insulated against a world that had treated her harshly.

And then he'd fought for her.

Where did they go from here?

She'd almost thrown it all away. The emerald sword was propped in the corner near the bed, where she could reach it quickly if she needed to. The jewel in its hilt winked at her knowingly. She thought she had loved Soren enough to let him go, but she'd discovered a deeper truth—he needed her. Not just any woman. Her specifically.

Only she could help the Romanovs against further manipulations from her mother. It would take a witch to handle a witch. Madeline was still on the island. Trevor was still asleep. Lev was anything but himself.

Anna had stopped Soren from pushing Lev over the cliff, and she'd helped him get his brother back to Bronwal. And she had been able to do all that because of her *Volkhvy* blood, not in spite of it.

She had controlled her power. She hadn't hurt Lev, even when it looked like hurting him or sacrificing herself were her only options.

It was time for her to accept that the emerald sword knew exactly what it was doing when it had Called her. Soren had given her the gift of his trust. It was high time that she trusted herself.

It wasn't the sword or her *Volkhvy* abilities that alerted Anna to Soren's presence. Maybe it was science, the movement of molecules or a change in the air, but she thought it was probably because the filament that bound their hearts to each other was so well established that it tremored when he was near.

"You'll be happy to hear that I don't have to fight the alpha wolf," Soren said.

Anna rose from the pillows and faced the door. How many times had he crossed the threshold of the aviary on four paws? This time he walked in on two long, strong legs.

"Don't make macabre jokes. You sound like my mother," she scolded.

Soren stopped in the center of the room. Lush woven textiles had replaced all the old worn rugs. He glanced down at the colorful mat between the door and Anna's bed. Her heart squeezed when she realized he was fighting a habitual urge to lie down and guard her from intruders.

She left the bed and went to his side. She took his hand with one of hers and placed her other bare palm on his cheek. She'd abandoned the gloves. She didn't need help to control her power. And she didn't need to be ashamed of her abilities. When her fingers glowed, there was a reason for it. Her defenses were part of her now. She would no longer reject them.

Anna looked up into Soren's amber eyes. The firelight colored his irises a warm gold.

"You would both be surprised how quickly Elena and I would stop any fight you two thought to wage against each other," she warned. But her tone was gentle and teasing. He'd come to tell her what kind of welcome she faced at a place she'd been ordered to leave.

"I trust you, and Ivan trusts the swords. Neither of us trusts Vasilisa, but we're willing to overlook that," Soren said.

"I don't trust her, either. Sometimes *Volkhvy* love is as dangerous as human greed and hate," Anna said.

"I'm my father's son. His blood flows in my veins as Vasilisa's flows in yours," Soren said. He leaned into her palm and closed his eyes. The contact caused tingling to rise in her fingers. It wasn't self-defense. He didn't pull away. If anything, his cheek flushed in pleasure as the electricity of her touch caressed beneath his skin.

"We can reject the things they've done without rejecting ourselves or each other," Anna said. "We will do better things. We'll stand against the Dark together, and our love will stay as true and strong as it ever was."

"I'm sorry," Soren said. He reached up to take her hand from his face. He held it wrapped in both of his. "I never should have doubted you."

"You didn't doubt me. You doubted my mother. And for good reason," Anna said. "I know, because I felt the same. I didn't trust that I could be my own kind of witch. Not until I was tested. Now I know. I'll die before I dabble in Darkness. I can help bring honor back to the Light

Volkhvy. But I also know that my abilities can help in the fight against witches like Aleksandr. And I can help the Romanovs deal with Vasilisa, too."

"Lev isn't accepting help from anyone right now," Soren said.

"We need to bring Madeline and Trevor home. To Bronwal," Anna said. "Madeline will be able to reach him in a way we can't. Lev, the ruby sword and Madeline are a triumvirate that has been unfairly wrenched apart. They have to find their way back to each other."

Soren leaned down to touch his forehead to hers. His russet hair tickled her face, and the forest scent tangled in his wavy bangs filled her senses along with his nearness. He was warmth and woods and wilderness.

He was hers.

"If Ivan hadn't relented, we would have gone elsewhere. Together. You're home to me, Anna. You have been for a very long time," Soren said.

Anna gathered handfuls of his loose tunic in her hands. She looked up into his beloved face and pulled him closer. She never would have been able to budge his large Romanov frame if he hadn't wanted to move. He came willingly. Their bodies pressed with her arms trapped between. He wrapped his arms around her back, and she was completely enfolded in the tingling aura their connection created in the air around them.

Oh, there was no green glow. There was only the natural heat of a lovers' embrace. She didn't have to tap into her power to enhance what was already there.

"I'm glad to be here with you, though. I dreamed of this moment so many times," Anna confessed. Her aviary was empty compared to its cluttered glory of before, but Soren more than made up for the barren shelves. He filled the space with his presence and with the heart he was finally willing to share with her again.

"When Aleksandr sent me into the Ether alone, I finally understood that it wasn't the Ether I was afraid of. My nightmares were never about losing myself and disappearing into the dark. They were always about losing you. I feared the Ether because I always thought it would be the Ether that separated us," Soren said. "I feared the Ether would take you and I would materialize to find you gone."

"And I almost made your greatest fear come true," Anna said. Soren pressed his lips to her forehead and then trailed them down the side of her face to the curve of her jaw.

"You were going to sacrifice yourself to save me and my family, and I was going to sacrifice our connection in order to save you from my family. I was so afraid that Lev would hurt you, I didn't realize I was hurting you— and myself—far worse than he ever could," Soren said.

He finally found her mouth. He feathered his lips over hers, but then his teasing grew more serious. He paused to suckle her lower lip between his. He licked the spot he savored, and Anna gasped at the arcs of electricity that flowed from the touch of his moist tongue to all her erogenous zones. Her power flared with the flick of his tongue to join with their natural chemistry. It sparked with visible green tendrils between their lips as they parted to breathe, then as they sank back into tasting again, the green became a glow in her eyes.

In the corner, the emerald in the hilt of the sword brightened as if it approved of their reconciliation. It was a powerful weapon. It was also an enchanted matchmaker that Anna trusted with all her heart.

But not as much as she trusted the red wolf who had

always saved her. He'd been her dearest companion. As a man, he was still that, but also so much more.

"I've brought you something. Elena and Ivan have been busy, and foraging is much harder than it used to be," Soren said. "Although I have to admit having opposable thumbs is useful."

He brought one hand from behind her back and held it up for her to see. On the first knuckle of his pinkie, a heavy silver ring caught the light. In an oval setting surrounded by diamond and citrine chips, an emerald gleamed. The citrine reminded her of the gold in Soren's eyes. The diamonds reminded her of the glass they'd shattered to defeat Aleksandr.

And the emerald was their stone. It shone with a green she would always associate with making love to him in the forest. It represented their connection in more ways than one.

Anna suddenly couldn't breathe. Of all the objects she and Soren had foraged to bring to her aviary and add to her magpie collection, the ring he took from his pinkie to slide onto her left hand was the most beautiful.

"I don't know its history. The Romanovs came from royalty. Many jewels have been loved and lost in Bronwal. But I knew when I found it this one was meant for you. Will you be my wife, Anna?" Soren asked.

Anna could only nod in reply. Her words of acceptance were lodged in a throat closed by emotion.

But she laughed when Soren leaned down to scoop her into his arms. Her weight was nothing to him, but his broad chest and strong back were everything to her. As was the large heart she could feel beating against her cheek. The aviary had been her hideaway. She'd retreated here from her isolation before and after the curse had fallen on Bronwal.

But she'd never been alone.

It was fitting that they spend their first night back at Bronwal in the aviary together. It was perfect that he'd proposed to her in a shelter they had shared through so many dark years.

"I love my new sister-in-law. Elena has to be the one who had the aviary restored," Soren said as he placed Anna on the soft coverlet. Her body sank into the softness, and she appreciated it even more when Soren's big body settled on hers. She liked the contrast between the soft bed under her and the hard man on top of her. He used his powerful arms to keep from crushing her, but she didn't even want the buffer of an infinitesimal amount of space between them.

Anna reached to wrap her arms around Soren's neck and her legs around his waist. It was his turn to laugh as she pulled his full weight against her. She couldn't help it. She admired the vintage ring on her finger as her hand gripped his shoulder. She was going to be a Romanov. She had been an outsider looking in long before she knew she was a *Volkhvy* princess. She couldn't help a feeling of triumph to know the orphan girl had grown up to marry the russet-haired prince.

"Elena must have seen how important it was to me. She helped me carry a trunk up the stairs once and…" Anna paused. She brushed her fingers thoughtfully over the hand-sewn tunic Soren wore. It was familiar. "She must have known they were your clothes I'd saved for you. This is one of your old shirts."

"The trunk was in my old bedroom when we got here. I washed and changed," Soren said. "She saved your hat, too. The hat that used to be mine."

Soren reached around and pulled a crushed handful of homespun material from the back pocket of his jeans. As it came free and unfolded, Anna recognized the hat she'd worn for years while Soren had been in his wolf form. She'd saved it for Soren, but when he had rejected her at the Gathering, she had left it at Bronwal when she'd left to go to her mother's island.

Hot moisture filled her eyes, and her throat tightened. Soren gently placed the hat on her head. As always, it was too big. Its brim shadowed her face. But Soren rearranged it so she could see and he could see her.

"It's your hat," Anna said.

"Consider it a gift. Not as shiny as an emerald, but wearing it for several centuries should give it sentimental value," Soren said.

For a second, she felt like Bell again, but she wasn't the same sad waif she'd been for so long. She was Bell with a happier ending than she'd ever thought she'd have. She'd waited to see Soren's face. She'd had his heart all along. Now she had the man in her arms.

"I never gave up. Not really. Not even when I went away," Anna promised.

Soren pressed another kiss to her lips. This one was soft and exploratory, as if he was kissing his longtime love for the first time.

"You came back. You found me and helped me to face my fears," Soren said.

Their bodies settled together more intimately than they'd been positioned before. Anna's breath caught when she felt Soren's hot and heavy erection nestled in the juncture of her thighs. She moved against him, undulating her hips in invitation.

"We survived. Together," Anna said.

And then Soren responded to her movements by deepening their kiss and following her hips' rhythm with thrusts of his own.

This time, when they pulled off their clothes, there was no white wolf to fear. Anna explored all the scars she could find on Soren's body with lingering kisses and licks until he finally flipped her back onto the bed. He settled on top of her again, and when she wrapped her arms and legs around him, there was nothing in the way of the connection they'd always had.

"I'll never let you go," Soren murmured into her neck as a green glow rose around their twined bodies. "Even when you were on the island, you were still with me. Every waking moment, and all through every night. I promise."

"I know," Anna said. When pleasure arced through her, enhanced by their connection and the pulse of energy her climax released, Soren cried out at the same time. His body stiffened, and this time he filled her with his heat.

Anna held him. In that moment they claimed a deeper connection than they'd had before.

There were still challenges to face at Bronwal, but they were home.

Anna was sleeping. Soren appreciated the flush of repletion on her beautiful nude skin before he covered her with a quilt. For once, he didn't fight sleep because of nightmares. He was simply too happy to close his eyes.

The sun was about to set.

He walked quietly outside and sat on the wall. He ran his hands over the stone and thought he detected the imprint of a wolf's paw beside him. The light had already gone a golden orange. The edges of the mountains were already on fire. The valleys had already disappeared into shadows.

He would have to be stone himself not to feel a sudden rush of adrenaline. His heart pounded in his chest. His breath came quick. He wasn't going anywhere, but he would always remember what it had been like.

He placed his hand on the paw-print impression the red wolf had left in the stone wall over hundreds of years of this vigil. He hadn't failed after all. He hadn't disappeared. He hadn't lost Anna to the Ether.

In part because his witch had been determined not to lose herself.

"I thought I might find you here," Anna said.

Her hands settled on his shoulders, and she squeezed. She molded her warm curves against his broad back.

"Do you remember? All those times you held my scruff and didn't let me go?" Soren asked.

"Yes. And I remember all the times we rematerialized together. How relieved I was to see you again," Anna said. She spoke into his ear, and her breath was an intimate tickle that caused his mouth to curve into a half smile. "Come back to bed. The sun will rise again tomorrow. We're not going anywhere tonight."

Soren stood, but he didn't turn to head back inside. Not yet. Anna pressed against his back and wrapped her arms around his waist. He accepted the comfort of her presence... and the seduction.

He reached to press his hands over hers where they pressed against his stomach.

For a dazzling moment they were bathed in the brightest, warmest hues, and then the sun went down. Darkness fell. They were left in the shadows, but their combined body heat negated the chill.

Anna's hug loosened, and Soren turned around. He captured one of her hands in his. Their fingers twined together.

"I'll never let you go," Soren said.

It was a truth she'd always known.

They'd been devoured by the cold nothingness of the Ether time and time again, but they had always found each other when they'd materialized once more. Their connection had never truly been broken and it never would be.

The warrior had won the massive heart of her red wolf a long time ago.

* * * * *

Catch up with the first book in the
Legendary Warriors miniseries,
Elena and Ivan's story, in
Legendary Shifter,
available now from Harlequin Nocturne.

And look out for Lev and Madeline's story,
Legendary Beast,
coming in October 2018!